FOSTERED MINDS

Ryan Gary Joel

Contempo Publishing

Contempo Publishing

652 Hogans Rd North Tumbulgum NSW 2490.
www.contempopublishing.com

ISBN (Paperback):   978-1-7637371-8-1
ISBN (eBook):   978-1-7637371-9-8

Cover design and illustration by Rubi Creations Digital.
Internal design by Contempo Publishing.

Printed and distributed internationally by Ingram Spark.

First published in 2026 by Contempo Publishing.

For Jo, Addison and Evan.

CHAPTER 1

NOW - September 2019
Adelaide, South Australia

Alex had woken up disoriented in unfamiliar places before. Often, even. The grogginess, the memory gaps and the heavy limbs were a familiar sensation to him. But he couldn't explain the heartache or the rough hands tightening around his arms. He was drifting in and out of consciousness as he was dragged through a maze-like house of horrors. His eyelids fluttered. Taking stock of his surroundings proved difficult. Bible verses printed on dirty walls and steel doors blurred in his periphery.

A radio crackled in the background: 'As you can see behind me, police have cordoned off all possible exits at the Adelaide Central Markets this evening. We're still waiting for confirmation from SAPOL, but multiple sources have reported fatalities. If you have just tuned in, there has been a stabbing at the Adelaide Markets. The number of offenders is unknown. Just days after the arson attack at the Festival Theatre—'

There were two men on either side of him. Their faces featureless in Alex's delirium.

'Does he need medical?' The man asked to his left.

'Nah, the doc checked him out on arrival. Psychiatric incident confirmed. We keep him isolated until we're told more.' This from the man to his right.

Alex was hit with a wave of nausea. He was dragged past a series of framed photographs. The figures in the pictures were

1

hazy. He thought he saw a face with protruding ears. The image stuck with him for a moment. Then it slipped away.

'Where …' Alex cleared his burning throat. 'Where am I?'

'Prison.'

Alex started feeling cold and dizzy. He fought to remain conscious. The air was thick and still.

'The date … what's the date? Is it still August?' Alex asked. His tongue felt dry and leathery across the top of his mouth.

'Save your energy mate, you're not the first to play the amnesia card. Gets you nowhere.'

Alex's energy was draining. It took every ounce of strength to talk. His eyes were narrow slits; his vision saw nothing more than foggy shapes and lines.

'Not amnesia. Something else.' He croaked.

Then the voices came. They were distraught, the words unclear. He picked out the little girl's first. Her high-pitched cries were on an infinite loop. The robotic ramblings rose over the top, driving Alex towards a migraine. Between the cognitive cacophony he could hear heavy breathing. The lack of words from this being unsettled him. The physical changes came next. They were out of sequence. He could feel the muscular spasms before he blacked out. His body began to betray him as muscles tightened and relaxed, altering his posture.

'What's he doing?'

'Not sure.''

Alex whispered something to himself repeatedly. The guards strained to hear. 'My name is Alex. My name is Alex. My name is Alex. My name is … *Lewis.*'

Fuck.

CHAPTER 2

THEN - July 2004

Alex sat in the dark waiting for his life to change. The main lights were turned off in the waiting room, with only the emergency downlights illuminating a skinny teenager with a slack, rounded posture. Alex sat on the chair furthest from the mirror that hung on the wall between doctors' offices. The mirror made his hands clammy. He felt cold. He avoided looking up at his reflection. He could hear incoherent voices, as if he was listening in to multiple conversations on a radio with poor connection. But the room was empty. Alex took a breath, trying to calm himself. The door nearest him opened and a single voice erupted, causing Alex to jump.

'Alex?' asked a middle-aged psychiatrist as he stepped out of the office. 'I'm Martin, it's nice to meet you. Please, come in.'

Alex stood up too quickly and got dizzy. He caught his balance against the wall and accidentally glimpsed himself in the mirror. Just a 14-year-old boy with a bad haircut. Something about his reflection didn't feel right to him. He became nauseous. He watched himself fall backwards. A moment later he was being offered Martin's hand. Alex focused on the psychiatrist's physical features while the voices still hammered away inside his head. Martin had piercing blue eyes, short hair, and ears that winged out. He wore black chinos and a short-sleeved, blue checkered shirt. Alex became self-conscious with his second-hand tracksuit pants and oversized T-shirt that made him look under-developed.

'Are you alright?' Martin asked.

'Yeah, I'm fine. I promise I'm not, like, drunk or anything.' Alex gave himself a moment to try and block out the noise in his head before he followed Martin into his office.

The office seemed unusually bare. Photos had been peeled off from the walls and qualifications were not on display. The desk was cleared except for some paper and pens.

'I'm still bringing everything over from my old office, hence the lack of … everything. My hectic hours have limited my opportunity to decorate,' Martin explained. 'We have chairs though.'

Alex pulled out a manila folder from his backpack.

'That's cool. I'm not staying.' Alex started. 'I've colour-coded the file for the various diagnoses and medication I've been prescribed. I also have my past session notes.'

Alex dropped the folder on the desk and slowly turned around to leave.

'Where are you going?'

'Home. I'm sorry, I really can't stay. Just wanted to give this to you. Let me know if you can help.'

Martin sat back and steepled his fingers. 'In the last five years you've seen six therapists, and all of them have given you a different diagnosis. Post-traumatic stress disorder, schizoaffective disorder, schizophrenia, delusional disorder, amnesia, attention deficit hyperactivity disorder, etc. You're frustrated because none of these labels fit you. Well, they are not supposed to. You're clearly a very organised young man. God knows how you got your session notes. Probably the same way you forged your guardian's signature on the intake forms. That's why you have to go I take it? Nobody knows you're here and you don't want to get caught. Usually, it's the other way around.

Can't say I've ever had a teenage boy come here of his own volition. I couldn't interest you in a biscuit before you go?'

Alex considered this. *Well, he's not lazy, that's a start.* As he sat down and helped himself to a biscuit, something about the room made him feel unsettled, but he couldn't put his finger on it.

'Did you find any of your previous sessions helpful at all?' asked Martin.

'Not really.'

'Why?'

'They prescribed me medication and spent the rest of the hour talking about getting back on the horse. If nothing changed, they upped the medication and then talked more about the horse.'

'The list of medications you're on now is extensive.'

'No shit. A 14-year-old shouldn't need a Webster Pack to keep track of his medications.'

Martin cracked a small smile and his eyebrows rose. 'This all sounds exhausting. Why are you trying yet another therapist if you've had no luck?'

Alex didn't need to think about this. 'I want the noise to stop. I don't know what else to do.'

'The voices.' It wasn't a question.

'Yes. I'm not stupid. I know logically I shouldn't hear them. But I do.'

'How often do you hear them?'

'All the time. Sometimes it's worse, depends on where I am. At the moment it's pretty bad.'

'What do the voices say?'

'I dunno.'

Martin's eyebrows inched higher again and a smirk creased his lips.

'It's all jumbled,' Alex mumbled, breaking eye contact, preferring to stare at the ground.

Martin's expression annoyed him. 'I really should go.'

'And I shouldn't be seeing you without a guardian's permission. Yet here we remain. Can the voices hurt you?'

'No.'

'Then how can they be painful?'

'I—I don't know, maybe I'm scared to listen.'

'This is a safe place, Alex. We are next door to the Greenwich Psychiatric Hospital. You are not the only one in this building that hears voices. And you chose to come here.'

Alex was unsure. 'I just wanted to know if you could help.'

Martin continued, 'These are my terms. You listen to the voices properly, right now, or you can find another doctor to give you further analogies on horse riding.'

Alex closed his eyes. The screaming and hissing got louder and louder. He forced himself *not* to shut it out. The echo came back. A gruff voice whispered into his ear. Alex still couldn't pick out the words. It began to repeat, each time the voice sounding closer. Finally, he picked up two words, and it sent chills up his spine.

Kill him.

Alex is 5-years-old, and he is standing in the kitchen staring at his mother. She takes a blueberry muffin out of the oven as slowly as possible, knowing her little boy was waiting eagerly.

'Would you like a warm one?'

Alex smiles, and nods as fast as his head would allow. As he takes one, a car pulls up the drive, the sound of the V8 engine causing immediate alarm. He darts out of the kitchen into his room and under his bed. He doesn't notice his grip on the muffin as it crushes between his fingers.

His mother's voice: 'You borrowed what? How much?'

Indistinguishable response from his father.

'They will come for you!'

His father's words continued to slur; Alex couldn't pick up what he said.

'That's crazy!'

The sound of dishes smashing on the tiled floor.

'When?' she shouts.

A dark silhouette of a man busts through the bedroom door. He reaches for Alex ...

Alex's surroundings change as sudden as the click of a kaleidoscope. He was in the back seat of an unfamiliar car as the sun began to rise. His stomach lurched as the car stopped. A big dirty hand reaches for him.

'Fuck! Fucker bit me!' curses a hulking man with a dome-shaped head.

Laughter, words are spoken in a language Alex can't understand.

'Shut the fuck up! I'll tear this fuckin' kid apart!'

Alex is pulled out by his feet ...

Alex returned to full awareness as he gradually brought his mind and body back to the psychiatrist's office. He was lying on the leather sofa with no memory of how he got there.

'What just happened?' Alex asked.

'Hypnosis. An early memory,' Martin clarified.

Martin heard someone else in the outpatient ward. The sound of a mop and bucket. Martin opened his office door just a crack to inspect the source of the sound. He seemed satisfied and locked the door.

'What is your earliest memory, Alex?'.

'My earliest? I don't know. Getting lemonade from my mum. My foster mum. I lived with a couple until I was 6 or 7. We lived opposite a park. She would take me there after my nap.'

'And then?'

Alex racked his brains, but it was hard to think back with the violent acoustics playing in his head. 'Moved into the boys' home a few years later. I had trials with other foster families, but they never lasted long. I'll be in state care until I age out.'

'But you want to change that?'

'I don't care about that shit. I'm not looking for a family.'

'We need to contact someone, let them know where you are.'

'Forget it.'

'How did you get here?'

Alex took two buses and walked 5 kilometres. 'I took a bus,' he answered.

Martin packed up and headed out of the room. 'Come on Alex, I'm taking you home.'

The bus was empty. Alex sat in the back next to Martin, answering multiple choice questionnaires with a lead pencil. The roads were quiet in Adelaide, and the bus had a smooth run as it passed through green traffic lights on its journey back to the northern suburbs.

'You really shouldn't be travelling all this way on your own, especially at this time of night. I'll organise something closer next session,' Martin said.

Alex agreed to see him again regardless of where he had to travel.

'I've got some homework for you,' Martin continued. 'First, get me signed consent from your home, and an emergency contact. That's non-negotiable. Second, I want you to write a list for me of everything that you fear.'

'Why?'

'It will help you unlock more memories.'

'What would that achieve though?'

Martin turned to him. 'It will help us both understand exactly what you are.'

CHAPTER 3

NOW

Aggressiveness, impulsiveness and disobedience were dangerous traits in prison, and his alter, Lewis, possessed them all in abundance.

'Okay, Alex. You've declined a phone call. Declined meeting with a counsellor. You made no verbal responses to your state-appointed lawyer. This is the end of the line. Poor behaviour results in swift punishment, do you understand?'

Lewis recognised the signs of losing a large block of time: the hunger, the headache, the unrecognisable taste in his mouth, the stinging of the skin. With Lewis in control, he looked taller, his posture changed. His shoulders appeared broader, his chest lifted, his head retracted further back, more in line with a neutral spine. He had a permanent snarl on his face and his eyes were narrowed, as if he had trouble seeing fine details.

'Alex?' A guard checked.

He sized up two guards on either side of him.

'Don't ever call me Alex. Fuckface.'

'Call us what you want, but you get violent, you go back to solitary. Got it?'

Lewis chuckled. 'You think I care about fucking solitary?'

The guards nodded to each other as they pushed him out of the claustrophobic dungeon and made him walk down a hallway. Lewis was turned sharply left passing several offices. He could see his reflection in the glass walls, reminding him of his choices since his incarceration. His head had been shaved and he had dark rings around his eyes that made him look older than his 29 years. His cheeks were black and swollen, his lip had been cut, and a small gash had been stitched up on his forehead.

They stopped at the gate. Lewis remained still as a guard punched in a door code and pushed him through to C block. Men reached for him behind thick bars, threatening him, begging the guards to bring him a little closer. Most prisoners were dressed in a blue tracksuit and watched him with interest.

'New meat. New meat. New meat.' Prisoners chanted, banging against the bars.

Lewis gave everyone the finger as he walked past. 'Fuck you. And fuck you. And fuck you too. Fuck your mother.'

'I wouldn't try and piss everyone off unless you have a death wish, kid,' the guard next to him muttered.

'I'm not a fucking kid.'

'In here you are.'

The guard opened one of the cell doors.

'New roommate for you, Mike.' The guard introduced.

Lewis watched a large, barrel-chested man step into the light. He thought his size was impressive for a man that looked to be in his sixties, with poor oral hygiene and a bloodshot eye.

'I can see that. Had a rough start by the looks.' His cell mate grinned, exposing several missing teeth.

'You look like you've had a rough fucking life.' Lewis spat.

'Good luck.' One of the guards muttered, pushing Lewis towards Mike and locking the door.

Lewis looked up; Mike was even bigger up close. Lewis's eyeline reached Mike's armpit stains. He could smell the days-old sweat.

'Wanna knock some of my teeth out, big fella? Looks like you could use some.'

Mike sighed. 'Hate the young and dumb ones.' He moved back to his bed.

'Who the fuck are you calling dumb?'

Mike raised a hand. 'Save your energy. You want to get the shit beaten out of you? That's fine, but do it somewhere else.' Mike sat back on the bed, causing the bedframe to creak under his weight.

Lewis sighed and pressed his forehead against the cold bars. He started chewing his nails as he scanned the biblical verses with messages of redemption printed on the walls between the first and second storey.

'What's with the fucking bible stuff?' Lewis asked.

Mike shrugged. 'Apparently the director is connected to the church and a few private schools. I did a talk at one o' the fancy schools for their behavioural program. Earnt me-self some extra TV time. Got some better meals too.'

The cell block stretched out as far as he could see. A network of steel and concrete. The upper level was connected by metal catwalks and staircases, crisscrossing like an industrial web. Each cell confined two prisoners; most of them laying in their beds, some prayed, others stared back at him – menace in their eyes.

The fluorescent lighting cast a harsh, cold glow, illuminating the biblical verses that looked freshly skinned against the white walls. Uniformed guards patrolled the hallways. Lewis heard grunting and sniffing.

'Back against the wall, kid.' Mike recommended.

'Would everyone stop calling me fucking—'

The door swung open and two fierce dogs forced their way into the cell.

'Jesus fucking Christ!' Lewis leapt back and pinned himself against the wall next to Mike.

The black Dobermans pulled at the taut chains held by two prison guards.

'What's going on?' Lewis yelled.

The guards pointed at the bed and the dogs sniffed under the mattress. Lewis remained still as the dogs inspected every inch of the cell. It didn't take long before their attention diverted back to him.

'Don't look them in the eye.' Mike whispered.

Lewis forced his eyes shut as he felt the nose of one sniffing his ankles.

'Please …' Lewis pleaded. 'I don't do well with dogs.'

Liar, Liar, the annoying little voice whispered in his head.

The guards laughed at his own unease. The smell of wet dog repulsed him.

The dogs were pulled out of the cell and ordered to inspect the cell next door. Lewis let out a breath and collapsed to the floor. He watched the guard's patrols while he tried to calm down. He noticed a young guard slip away from his patrol circuit and unlock the cell door across from him.

'Kitchen duty, Watson, let's go. Where's Trent?' The guard asked from across the cell block.

'Medical.' Watson, a dark-skinned prisoner with lean, sinewy muscles stepped out of his cell.

'I'll take his spot!' Lewis yelled, raising his arm between the bars of the cell.

The prisoner's eyes bulged. He held back a retort and bit his tongue. 'Yeah. He'll do.'

The guard said something into his walkie-talkie. There was a muffled response and another guard appeared and released Lewis. The two prisoners were escorted side by side.

'I know you,' muttered Watson.

Six weeks earlier Lewis hid in the dark when he heard the men break in. He'd placed aluminium sliding window locks across all the window ledges except for the laundry. As he anticipated, he heard the window pop open, and men clamber in from outside. Down the hallway residents of the under-budgeted aged care home were in their beds, too afraid to sleep after three break-ins across the last month. Lewis held his phone by his side, the camera app and flash open and ready.

Three gangly men walked into the hallway. Two of them carried knives.

'Hey, fuck-faces.' Lewis called out.

They all turned towards him in surprise. He took a quick picture. Lewis could tell straight away it was a clear shot with the signage for Seaview Aged Care Centre in the background. The intruders were lean and muscular in the photo, and the three of them had looks that could kill.

Lewis ran. He was faster than he looked and had lost them soon after he hurdled a neighbouring fence. He could still hear them berate each other outside the centre.

'What if that guy calls the cops? Let's just go.'

Lewis followed them back to their car. His own vehicle was parked up the street. It was midnight and the roads along the Yorke Peninsula suburb were deathly quiet. He followed them some distance away, unsure for certain if they noticed him.

They stopped at a caravan park 2 kilometres north of the centre. Lewis spied their caravan while he found a park. He rushed out of the car and knocked on their caravan door. Watson opened the door, one arm behind his back.

'How the, —you're dead meat.'

Lewis raised his phone, displaying their picture at Seaview.

'I push this button, and this picture gets sent to my partner who's sitting at the Ardrossan police station right now. Only reason I'm here and not there busting your arses is because I'm more interested in retrieving some items.' Lewis cleared his throat. 'Muriel wants her jade necklace back. Warren wants his service medals and a written apology, I told him not to hold his breath on the apology; I figured you wouldn't have the literacy skills. Andrea wants her diamond rings. Now there's no point running. My partner confirmed your licence plate on my way over here, Todd. You're on parole. This photo would send you straight back. Give me the items and I delete the photo.'

Lewis picked up several voices behind Todd.

'Get the shit!' Todd barked.

The guards left Todd and Lewis to mop the kitchen floor. Todd was shaking in anger.

'You missed a spot.' Lewis muttered.

'You …' Todd's face contorted in rage.

'I forgot to ask, how did Muriel's necklace look on you?'

Todd charged at Lewis and drove him back into the wall. He pressed the mop stick against Lewis's throat.

Alex: *Why are you doing this, Lewis?*

Lewis: *Can't you tell, Alex? You're the biggest coward of them all. I don't want this anymore. I don't want the control. You can rot in here instead.*

'Oh, I've seen that look before. You want to die in here.' Todd's breath stank. 'I'm not fucking stupid. I'm not going to kill you. But I'm going to make your life hell.'

Another voice crept into Lewis' mind: *That's survival, Lewis. Dissociative identity disorder has protectors. When an alter is created, at least one is a protector, someone stronger than the host. That's supposed to be you.*

Lewis reached for Todd's eyes and stuck his thumbs into the sockets. Todd recoiled. Lewis tackled him and both bodies slammed into the industrial fridge. It knocked the wind out of Todd. Lewis used the advantage and pinned Todd to the ground with his legs.

'Make it count, fucker. I've got my boys in here and there's only one of you.' Todd spat in his face.

Lewis wiped off the phlegm. 'Don't be so sure.'

CHAPTER 4

THEN - August 2004

Finding himself at places he never remembered travelling to terrified Alex throughout his childhood. He couldn't remember how he got to the Elizabeth Shopping Centre food court. Amongst the sea of customers, he spotted Martin waving him over to a table for two.

'How are you feeling today?' Martin asked.

Alex looked around. There were five full tables around them, but no one was paying any attention to him or his therapist. He took a seat.

'Good. A little like… hazy I guess.'

'You don't remember getting here, do you?'

Alex blushed and shook his head.

'I saw that look of bewilderment on your face. Do you remember setting up this meeting with me?'

Alex shook his head.

'You have run out of funding, my boy. You burned through your mental health care plan. The state had a small subsidy allocated to you, all of it wasted on horse riding analogies. I'm offering to take you on pro bono. But we can't do it from my office, you understand?'

Alex nodded groggily.

'We really need to get you off all that medication,' Martin said under his breath.

'No worries, I'll stop taking it tonight,'

'No, we need to wean you off it gradually. Did you do your homework?'

Alex couldn't remember a list but found himself retrieving a small piece of paper from his pocket. He recognised his handwriting.

- Medium to large dogs
- Clothing stores
- Water
- The dentist
- Knives
- Needles

Martin examined the list and then scrunched it up.

'Thank you for trusting me with this. Why dogs?' Martin asked.

'I dunno.'

'Water?'

'I can't swim.'

'The dentist?'

'Can you blame me?'

'Clothing stores?'

Alex shuddered. 'I don't like the changing rooms.'

'Knives?'

Alex shrugged.

'Can you hear voices now?' Martin asked.

Alex nodded. *Punch him in the throat and get out of there.*

'Are they still violent?' Martin asked.

He nodded.

'Great, get that negative voice to buy me a bottle of Coke. A glass bottle, none of this plastic rubbish.'

Alex looked at Martin curiously. Then, after no response, went to the counter and bought a bottle of Coke with the last of his money.

'Thanks, Alex.' Martin chugged down the Coke and passed him the empty glass bottle. 'Now break the bottle and cut yourself.'

'Ah ... what?'

Martin knocked the bottle off the table. It shattered to the floor. Everyone nearby turned. He apologised profusely to the cleaner, who helped him pick up the pieces of glass. When everyone lost interest in the broken glass, and the cleaner left to wipe down other tables, Martin placed a piece of broken glass into Alex's hands and spoke slowly, 'Cut yourself now.'

'No.' Alex shook his head.

'So, the negative voices spiralling in your head can carry your body all the way over to the register, purchase a bottle of Coke with the limited income I'm sure you have, and then waltz all the way back to give it to me. But they can't cut your wrist?'

Alex shook his head, his expression still aghast.

'Seems to me like you don't need to get rid of the negative voices, they just saved your life. You just need to give them something productive to do.'

'What do you mean "productive"?'

'You need to start listening, and once you take that information, you need to process it critically and decide on the most appropriate action, like you just did then. But it takes training to do this well.'

'What type of training?'

Martin gave the list back to Alex and tapped one of the lines of writing.

'It seems we can tackle one of these on your list right now.'

They walked through the shopping centre and Alex felt more uncomfortable the closer they got to a men's store. Casual and formal wear filled the shelves and signs on every table advertised two-for-one deals. There were two sales assistants. One worked the register while the other helped a couple in their late thirties.

Martin stopped at the front of the store. 'It doesn't have to be you that goes in there. The aggressive voices you hear in your head. Are they scared, or confident?'

'Confident, I guess.'

'Then pretend to be confident. Be the voice. Your task is simple: you don't have to buy anything; just try something on, then put it back on the rack, and leave.'

Alex tried to calm his breathing as he stepped into the semi-expensive men's store. A pimply-faced, spiky-haired shop assistant stepped forward as soon as Alex crossed the line into the premises.

'Hi, mate, what's the occasion?' the shop assistant asked.

'Just working with my therapist, thank you,' Alex replied, brushing past him, ignoring the shop assistant's confused look.

He grabbed a shirt without even looking at it and headed to the change rooms. *You can do this,* he said to himself. He was surrounded by mirrors in the change room. For a moment Alex thought he saw other faces staring back at him, all with the same hazel eyes. He couldn't be sure what he saw. But the voices were horrendous. He tried to focus. He concentrated hard. A dull ache throbbed at the centre of his head. He could feel the beginning of a migraine. His heart started to race. It got difficult to breathe. The room got stuffy. Alex collapsed in the change room. The half-priced shirt landed on the floor.

He rocked back and forth, mumbling loud enough for others to hear. When the shop assistants came over to him, he picked himself up, embarrassed, and shuffled out of the shop flat-footed, his feet smacking against the floor with every shuffle. He kept his eyes on the ground at all times, and his body swayed like he was on a ship during a heavy storm. Martin cocked his head to the side as they left the store and put a hand on the teenager's shoulder, which caused instant repulsion as though he had just developed a sensory disorder. Martin didn't flinch at the change in behaviour.

'Your name?' Martin asked.

'Tony. Tony doesn't like to be touched. Not on the shoulder or the head or the feet. Nowhere really. Not sure what's worse, probably the head. I wouldn't be able to see.'

'I was just talking with Alex,' Martin said.

Tony whined and rolled back onto his heels, then to the balls of his feet, thinking.

'Friend. Are you a friend? Tony doesn't have any friends. Tony knows he's difficult, quite a nuisance. But it's not just Tony's fault. Tony doesn't deserve all the blame.'

'No, you don't. You're dissociative.'

'Big words. Tony likes big words. Especially ones starting with D. Disaffiliation, dissolution, dissociation – not many know the last one.'

'Do you know what it means, Tony?'

Tony walked with a penguin-like shuffle. Martin followed, recognising just the amount of personal space Tony needed.

'Tony likes science. Studies everything. Learned chemistry. Knows it like the back of his hand. Is that what they say? I think that's what they say. I don't know why. I never look at the back of my hand. Not really. Dissociation. Splitting of molecules.'

'Splitting, yes.'

A support co-ordinator came out of an EB Games store shepherding two men with Down Syndrome. He nodded at Martin and Tony, as if he was acknowledging a similar path. Martin smiled back politely.

'Do you know what it means for a person, Tony?'

Tony whined again. 'Bad things. It means very bad things.'

Martin snapped a look at Tony. Tony could feel his eyes on him, knowing Martin was searching for Alex but unable to find him. Posture, voice, even the energy was different. He wasn't Alex.

'Yes, I think you're right.' Martin agreed.

'People usually run. Run, run, run when they meet Tony. Or others. You don't. Tony wonders why. Tony wonders if you have seen this before?'

'Yes. I have seen a case like this recently. Multiple personalities. Not something any of Alex's other doctors had noted. They didn't make him face his fears though. Fear can bring out alters. But you … you're a very different alter than I've seen before. You have your own set of challenges, don't you Tony?'

Tony started humming to the music as they walked past a Sanity store.

'Scary things aren't very nice. That was a scary store. Should never have gone there. Lots of better shops to go to. Like book shops.'

'What made that shop scary, Tony?'

Tony shrugged awkwardly, his body already swaying forward. It looked like something invisible had lifted him from his shoulders at an angle. 'Don't like the staff, too pushy. Tony always finds them pushy. Always asking unnecessary questions. They don't need to know about Tony's day, don't need to know what he's doing on weekends. And the cotton. And the polyester. Can get very itchy on Tony's poor skin. But the itchy clothes didn't wake Tony. It was something else. It was—'

'Mirrors,' interrupted Martin. 'Alex was afraid of the mirrors.'

CHAPTER 5

NOW

'Put this shirt on.'

Alex's shoulders rolled forward as he took control. A guard was holding out a prison polo in front of him. He took it instinctively. He realised his own shirt had been torn. His back was stiff and his nails were jagged, familiar signs that Lewis had been in the driver's seat for a long stretch of time. *A scuffle, no doubt*. Alex swapped shirts while he took in his surroundings. He was in a kitchen, but bowls and crockery lay across the floor and a mop dowel had been snapped in two. There was a dent in the fridge door. Knives chained to the kitchen benchtop dangled precariously from the edge.

'Take him to dental.'

Alex was roughly escorted to a white-washed room with a single dentist chair sitting in the centre of the brightly lit space. Alex's heart started to race. He had overcome his anxiety of the dentist chair over the last 15 years, but he still had a nervous tremor as he sat down and opened his mouth as wide as his jaw would allow. An elderly man in a face mask scooted over in an office chair to examine Alex with his mouth mirror and suction device. Alex's breathing rate increased.

'Gums are healthy,' The dentist remarked. 'Minimal plaque build-up. He takes care of himself, that much is evident. Unusual for … someone like this. We have one mobile tooth, a Grade 1, most likely the result of a brawl. We can monitor this. I can give him a needle for the pain.'

Alex tried to object, but strong hands pressed him firmly into the chair and the dentist wasted no time retrieving a needle.

'Be still, please.'

As the needle went into his gums, his thoughts drifted to the fear list that he wrote in his teenage years. The dentist, knives and needles. A piece of paper that would have broken down and crumbled to nothing after years of exposure. Alex couldn't understand how those fears were coming back to him now. He felt like he was being tested. But he wasn't 14-years-old anymore. That scrap of paper no longer held the same amount of terror. He wasn't going to break, he affirmed himself. *How could you break something already broken?*

CHAPTER 6

THEN - August 2004

Alex woke in his bed at the boys' group home without any memory of how he got there. His stomach grumbled and he wondered if he had skipped meals. His room was neat and tidy. The blinds were pulled down permanently because Alex was opposed to letting any trickle of light into his space. It took him some time before he noticed the man sitting on a chair in the corner of the room. It made him jump.

Martin just smiled back.

'How did you get in here?' Alex asked, recovering from the shock.

'Your group home parent let me in.'

Alex's cheeks flushed red. 'I'm sorry, I couldn't do it.'

'You did, Alex, you tried. That's all I asked of you. If you feel my methods are too intense, or if I have overstepped, I apologise. I could refer you to someone else. Your care plan will renew in January. I can refer you to another psychiatrist in town who will re-assess your medication and consolidate everything appropriately. The system let you down, but he won't. That's option one.'

'What's option two?'

'You persevere with me. It will involve you doing things far worse than purchasing a shirt. But you will need to stop feeling ashamed when you lose time. It is just part of the process.'

'I don't want to see any more doctors. I'm sick of starting all over again.' Alex asked.

'I understand.'

Alex no longer wanted to be in bed, so he sat up and realised too late he didn't have a shirt on. Martin gaped in horror. Alex was covered in burn marks and scars, from his chest all the way down to his pyjama pants.

'Good god, Alex. What happened to you?'

***

Alex stumbled in the freezing cold hallway of an animal shelter. The barking was everlasting. Teeth, saliva and claws were all Alex could see as he followed Martin down a corridor of unwanted dogs.

'I'm sorry,' the 20-something shelter volunteer said. 'They don't usually act like this.'

'It's fine, I must have that effect on them.' Alex forced a smile.

A Rhodesian ridgeback was chained at the end of the corridor in its own cage. The volunteer looked around nervously, but other customers were coming through, so she left Martin and Alex alone. The chain was taut as the ridgeback's muscular shoulders throbbed and twitched against the tension.

'I'm not going in there,' Alex said.

Martin stepped into the cage. There was a foot's distance between the entrance and the dog.

'He can't hurt you, Alex,' Martin assured. 'He's scared too. He doesn't have a home. He may have been abused. Sound familiar?'

'Do you think we could maybe find a smaller dog? Surely, we could find a Chihuahua that's been abused.'

'Don't feed on your fear, Alex.'

Alex slowly stepped into the cage. The hound's eyes were yellowed, and his teeth appeared sharper the closer Alex got.

The dog sat for just a moment. Martin moved away and the dog rushed for them. Alex fell back against the wall …

Alex is 6-years-old and sitting inside the cage, snuggled up to a little girl not much older than him. The pair are shaking. Her hair is braided in two parts. Alex strokes them every now and then.

'Why won't Mummy come?' she whimpers.

'Don't think anyone wants us,' Alex whispers. 'I shouldn't've had the muffin. I thought my new mummy made them for me.'

Their clothes are filthy. They both cry softly. Six large dogs snap at the cages, rooting the children to the wall with fear. A torch shines on Alex's grubby face as a group of men examine him from the other side of the cage.

Alex is blinded by light. Rough hands pinch his jaw. Another figure is writing notes. One of the dogs is close enough for saliva to land on Alex's bare foot.

Alex hears muttering come from the tall man doing the writing. He's wearing over-sized, thick-framed glasses and carries a clipboard.

'Don't need to scare the boy, what's done is done. Strict protocol. Very, very strict. Mustn't tamper with the project.' The man continues to mutter as he stares at the ground, unable to provide eye contact to those around him.

Another pair of rough hand grabs Alex's foot and pulls him out of the cage …

But it was Martin that pulled him out.

'Where did you go?' Martin asked.

'I—I was with other kids. There were dogs. Men were examining us for something. Like they were window shopping, I—'

'It's alright, Alex, you did well. Very well.'

'Hey, mate, so how old are you?'

It took Alex a moment to get his bearings. He was sitting in front of a young man no more than 19. Acne still pockmarked his face, and his arms were thick and veiny. There was banging and clattering behind him. He turned to see a busy kitchen full of young staff at McDonalds. The boy in front of him had a badge with 'Manager' printed on it next to the Golden Arches logo. Memories came back to Alex in fragments. Martin had organised a job interview.

'Hey, mate, can you hear me?' the manager asked.

Shouting and laughing in the background.

'I'm 14.' Alex answered.

'And why did you apply to work with us?'

'My therapist thought it would be a good idea.'

The manager looked confused. Alex cleared his throat.

Be confident, Martin had reminded him, *rationalise your thoughts before you speak.*

'Just joking. I, ah, do a lot of the cooking at home, and I thought this would be a good opportunity to develop my culinary skillset.'

'Funny guy, huh? How do you go at school?'

'Quite regularly now.'

Idiot.

The manager was distracted, his gaze crossing to a group of girls at the front of the store. After less than 3 minutes, Alex was able to leave through the back, as the kitchens were getting busier, and he didn't want to get in the way. They would keep his resume on file and give him a call if anything came up. *Yeah, right.*

As he made his way to the carpark, Alex heard a whine from one of the dumpster bins. He followed the sound and found a dishevelled-looking cat stuck between two rubbish bags. He reached for it and the cat swiped at him. The claws drew thin red lines across Alex's arm.

'Ow!'

Kill it. Kill the cat. Put it out of its misery.

After some struggle, Alex retrieved the cat and held it tight as it thrashed and scratched on the walk home. When Alex made it to the boys' home it had just started to rain, and Martin was waiting for him on the front porch.

'How did it go?' Martin asked. 'What have you got there?'

'It scratched me.'

The voices did not stop. *Did Martin say something?* He couldn't tell who was saying what.

'The voices are getting louder?' Martin asked.

Alex nodded.

'We need to do something.'

Martin took a pocketknife out of his pocket and weighed it in his hand. Alex felt as though time slowed down when he passed it to him. He was suddenly aware of his heartbeat.

'You know what you need to do,' Martin said slowly.

'Listen to the voices,' Alex said, almost hypnotically. 'Give them something productive to do.'

The cat tried to claw its way out of Alex's arms as he brought it inside the home.

Martin stepped inside a few minutes later and found him in the small kitchen.

'I don't understand,' Martin said, looking confused at what he now saw.

The pocketknife was still flipped open, but it had not been used. Martin's eyes ran over the cat gratefully drinking a saucer of milk while sitting on the boy's lap.

'I used that negative voice, like you said. Can we take it to the shelter now?' Alex asked.

Alex was walking back to Greenwich Psychiatric Hospital. He couldn't recall what day it was. It was easier to find the outpatient clinic during the day, so he followed the signs to the reception area. Nurses were rushing around checking on patients and family and friends were signing in and out. The gardens were in full bloom, even in the warmer weather.

Alex made his way to reception, and this time there was a receptionist working at the front desk. Her chair was lifted higher to make up for her short stature. He was about to introduce himself when she put a finger up. She was on a call, and he hadn't noticed the earpiece headset until now. He waited a long two minutes while she rescheduled another patient before she turned to him with a fake smile.

'Hi, how can I help?' she asked.

'I think I'm here to see Martin.'

She looked confused.

'I'm not sure if I've got the right time. My name is Alex?'

'Sorry, who are you here for?'

'Martin.'

The receptionist's expression was vague.

'The psychiatrist,' Alex added.

'Umm …'

'I had an appointment with him here a few weeks ago. Has he moved?'

'Sorry, love, we've had the same three practitioners here for years, and none of them are named Martin. Perhaps you have the wrong clinic. Can I call someone?'

'No, no, there must be a mistake, I'll show you.'

A knot tightened in his stomach. He rushed past the waiting room where he first met Martin.

He spotted Martin's office immediately. But printed on the door on a glass panel was:

DR RICHARDS

'No, that's not right.'

Alex opened the door. The receptionist tried to stop him but he pushed through. The office that was once bare now had pictures and credentials hung up on the wall. Two annoyed strangers looked up at the intrusion. A doctor he had never seen before sat with a patient. The doctor got up and looked at the receptionist.

'Cassie, is everything okay?' Dr Richards asked.

Alex ran out of the room and out of the clinic. He kept running and didn't stop until he made it back to the boys' home. He sat at the front gate, rocking back and forth.

'This is okay. This isn't okay. This is okay. I'm okay.'

He thought for a moment he might cry, but he didn't. He was too confused to summon emotion. 'What is happening?' he whispered to himself.

'You're getting better. You're starting to pick out the voices,' Martin said, announcing his presence.

Alex didn't dare look at him. 'You don't work there. But we were there … You—' Realisation dawned on Alex. 'You were never there.'

He looked up at Martin for a split second, who smiled back at him by the front door.

'I've always been with you,' Martin reassured.

Alex thought back to every moment. The clinic was empty when they met. He couldn't recall Martin speaking to anyone except him. For the first time in a long time, Alex finally cried. Martin didn't move; he just smiled.

'This can't be. I can't be this bad,' Alex cried out.

'Of course not. You're thinking more rationally. More than ever before.'

'No. No, no, no.'

Alex kept crying. Martin just stood there, watching. Alex finally looked at him again.

'Why didn't I know you were just in my head?'

'Oh, you knew Alex, deep down you knew. It was all so noisy in there. You needed a soft voice in the dark, so you created one.'

Alex was quiet and still for a long moment. He kept looking down. When he next checked, Martin hadn't moved.

'Will I always see you?' Alex asked. *You have no control. You will always see him.* He started hitting himself in the head, trying to stop the noise.

'Alex, stop it!' Martin yelled. 'No, you won't always see me. You're a smart lad. For a broken boy you are … genuine. In fact, I think this is the last you will see of me. Goodbye, Alex.'

'No wait!' Alex pleaded. 'I don't know what to do!'

'Perhaps one last piece of advice? Stay out of the darkness. You can thrive in the bright world out there. Don't let those negative voices stop you from living. Life's too short.'

Martin walked off into the distance. Alex squinted at the sun in his eyes. When he looked back there was no trace of the one man who listened. He was truly alone.

CHAPTER 7

NOW

Alex wasn't a stranger to the consequences of his alters' actions. He was thrown back into the pitch-black cell of solitary confinement, his mouth still numb from the dental assessment. A tin of food was tossed down by his feet. At closer inspection it reminded him of cat food. His stomach ached so he forced it down. He knew he needed his strength if he was ever going to unravel what had happened to him. His headache started to ease.

'Jesus, Alex, what the hell have you got yourself into?' Alex asked himself.

'I told you to stay away from the darkness,' a voice replied.

Alex sat upright. He was not alone. The voice chilled him to the bone. He slowly turned. A dark figure sat on the chair, tapping his knuckles against the table. As his eyes adjusted to the darkness, Alex could make out the winged ears. *It can't be.* He rubbed his eyes, but the figure would not go away.

'No, no, no. Leave me alone!' Alex yelled.

'You've heard voices all your life. Why are you so afraid of mine?'

Martin leaned forward; Alex could see his eyebrows raised. His face was more wrinkled than last time, but the piercing dark blue eyes had not changed; he could almost see the blue irises in the dark. Alex's head began to throb.

'If you're here, it means I have truly lost it,' Alex said hoarsely.

'What did you expect, chasing serial killers?' Martin asked.

'Killer. I've caught one – that was enough.'

'*No!* You took down the Archangel of Death when you were 23-years-old. That's not normal, Alex. You should have been looking for a real job, started dating. Not you. You fed your urge again and again until you were chasing the very worst. A PI? Really? Now look where you are.'

'Just leave!' Alex said through gritted teeth. 'Every good thing I've done has been without you.'

Martin laughed. 'Leave? I've been with you more than you know, Alex. You just haven't had the strength to open your eyes. It's only now that you've hit rock bottom, that you need me again.'

'Why do I need you?' Alex asked.

He could see a smile form on Martin's lips. 'I'm going to set you free.'

Alex's heart began to race. Everything he fought so hard to overcome was unravelling in front of him. He never saw a physical body with his alters. It never made him feel crazy when he connected with them. But Martin was different. Martin's presence made him feel like a madman. Alex staggered back from the 15-year illusion.

'What is it about me that you fear and hate so much?' Martin asked.

'I know what you were doing. What you wanted me to become. I've thought about it. You wanted me to kill the cat.'

Martin's laugh carried over the music drumming from behind the door. Alex began to shiver.

'I did not care about a cat.' Martin rose from his chair. Alex pressed himself against the door, inching further away from him. 'I wanted to free you from your reluctance.'

'No. You are the worst of me. That's why I never let you out. That's why I will never, ever see you again.'

Alex pulled himself off the floor and faced Martin, nose to nose. Martin grinned. '*Never* let me out? You have much to learn in here, boy. When you learn what you are, not even this prison can hold you.'

'What do you mean?' Alex asked, his eyes wandering in the dark.

'Your fractured psyche is your weakness. Look at what they are doing to you in here.'

'I'm losing time. I've had control for so long, but now I can't even …' Alex looked down at his hands. They were trembling.

'You can't do anything if you keep losing time,' Martin said simply.

Alex nodded. He was right. He needed to fight this. The music got louder. Alex dropped to the floor and started doing push-ups.

'What are you doing?'

Push-ups, mountain climbers, dips, burpees. Alex repeated every bodyweight exercise he could think of.

After, Alex brushed the sweat off his face as he pushed himself against the wall next to Martin. He heard the big dogs eagerly sniffing the door to his cell. More barking. Then the dogs were pulled away from the door.

'Do you know why I'm here?' panted Alex.

'Of course.' Martin placed a hand on Alex's shoulder. 'You're a murderer.'

CHAPTER 8

THEN - September 2004

Alex became a criminal at the age of 15. He stood before 36 Ayling Avenue on a chilly evening in September. He could see his teenage frame reflected in the glass window. The red brick home immediately brought back memories of sipping lemonade out the front with the first of his failed foster mothers. He couldn't remember how he got there, but he knew why. After realising he broke into Greenwich, he discovered he had a talent for breaking and entering. Since then, he had broken into various businesses around town, stealing anything he could stuff into his pockets or backpack. Money was rarely kept on premises, but laptops, food and books were up for the taking.

He was no master thief; he targeted bowling clubs, small offices, and abandoned houses. Nothing with any alarms or serious security. Several library books had taught him how to pick a basic lock, but he often preferred to climb around and find windows he could jimmy open.

Alex watched the house from the adjacent park. The streetlights were dim, and he sat close enough to a tree to go unnoticed by local traffic. There was a light on in the kitchen. It was just on 9 pm, and he assumed his ex-foster mother was doing the dishes. There was still only one car. Alex wondered if the man he once feared was away.

Alex didn't take any chances. He waited another hour, watching for any activity from the neighbours. By then the only light came from a TV four houses down. He double-checked the road before he sprinted across it and jumped over the side gate of the house. He landed quietly on the other side. He could smell damp soil from the recently watered veggie garden running along the side of the fence with a homemade wooden retaining wall keeping the garden intact.

The house looked dilapidated. Nails stuck out from the broken verandah, which had caved in and slanted precariously to one side. The gutters had come loose and seemed to be hanging onto the roof by a thread. Even in the dark, everywhere Alex turned he saw erosion. Except for the veggie garden. It was immaculate and thriving. He found some strawberries hanging in a pot and picked some. Alex's heart rate began to slow down. *He must have left years ago.*

The woman of the house still tended to her garden, but everything else was in ruin. The fences were high, and Alex couldn't be seen by any neighbours, making his job easier. He found the bathroom window with nothing but a flyscreen blocking out the elements. He got out his knife, not remembering how he had come by it, and started sawing away at the screen designed more for air flow and preventing bugs, and less for keeping out teenage thieves.

The cutting was louder than he would have liked, but he worked slowly and after a few minutes he climbed into the bathroom. It looked less familiar than he expected. *Perhaps it was just too dark*, he thought, but the room held no memories for him.

He could hear snoring from the bedroom and relaxed a little more. He went room by room, searching for anything of value. But there was no fancy silverware, no hidden stash of money. The 50-inch TV looked valuable, but Alex knew he could do nothing with it.

The hallway looked somewhat familiar. He tried the master bedroom. He turned the door handle slowly and then pushed it open quickly to avoid it squeaking. The snoring continued. He took his shoes off before entering the room. He was glad he did when he stepped onto floating floorboards. He moved to the bedside chest of drawers near the sleeping woman and slightly opened a drawer. His forearm was skinny, and he fumbled around blindly to avoid opening the drawer further. He found a necklace and stuffed it in his bag.

Then he heard crunching gravel. Car headlights illuminated the walk-in robe, and he saw several high-vis tradie tops hung up. In a panic, he saw a mobile phone on charge and grabbed it. Moving quickly, he dashed to the next bedroom just as the front door opened.

The bathroom was on the other side of the hallway, three rooms down. Lights came on and he heard a groan and keys hitting a table. Alex's heart raced. He could smell smoke and alcohol as footsteps became louder. He quickly moved to the wardrobe and shut himself in, breathing heavily. He waited for several minutes. Tuning his senses to the footsteps, Alex created a mental map of the house.

He could not remember his ex-foster father well; the only emotion that he could remember was fear. He couldn't help but wonder if Martin would be proud of him for this. Facing fears. Alex waited for the footsteps to reach the master bedroom so he could sneak out slowly and quietly.

'Shit,' Alex said under his breath. He realised he'd left his shoes by the main bedroom door.

He exited the wardrobe as silently as possible, hearing belching and scratching. *His name was Ian*, Alex suddenly remembered. He heard the fridge door open but didn't dare leave the spare bedroom. But he was running out of time. The light was still off in the hallway, but as soon as Ian switched it on,

Alex's shoes would be found. He decided it wasn't worth it and headed for the window, but it wouldn't budge. The bedroom window was locked. The crunching stopped and Ian made his way to the hallway.

Alex couldn't remember what Ian looked like, but he could imagine a big, rugged man reaching for the light at this very moment. Alex grabbed the phone, found Ian on the contact list, and sent a quick text: *I smelt gas from outside, could you check? X.*

A beep. The footsteps paused.

'For fuck's sake,' swore Ian.

Footsteps moved to the front of the house and Alex heard the door open. He rushed through the hallway, pulled on his shoes, and stepped lightly back into the bathroom before pulling himself back outside. He landed quietly and then noticed something large fixed to the wall next to him. The gas system. Hairs pricked up on the back of his neck. He turned around and saw a shovel swing towards his head.

Alex dodged the blow, but the second sweep of the shovel winded him and knocked him to the ground. Ian flicked the carport light on and Alex saw him clearly. Ian was tall and wide, overweight but strong. His facial hair was thick and unkempt, but his head was balding. His eyes looked bloodshot and Alex could smell alcohol.

'How dare you break in, you fucking snake!'

Ian swung hard and hit Alex in the back of the legs. The teenager held out his hands in defence, but it was no use. He was tiny in comparison. Slinging the backpack off, he threw it at Ian's feet.

'I'm sorry, I'm sorry, please! You can have it back!'

Ian stepped over the bag. 'I'm going to fuck you up and then I'm going to call the cops!' Ian spat as he swung the shovel.

'I'm Alex. It's me. I'm Alex!' he screamed in despair.

Ian hesitated. He lowered the shovel and looked closely at the trembling boy.

'What did you say?' Ian asked groggily.

'I'm Alex. I used to live with you. I'm 15 now.' Alex panted. 'She used to make me blueberry muffins. I don't remember much but I remember that.'

Ian lifted Alex's shirt up with the tip of his shovel and saw the burn marks.

'Jesus. You're supposed to be dead.'

'What do you mean?' Alex asked, shivering.

Ian stepped back and looked back at the house. 'You need to leave,' Ian hissed, now trying to be quiet.

'What?'

'Go! Now. Never come back. Or I'll bury you here.'

Ian's chest began to rise, his eyes wide. For a moment, Alex thought Ian was showing fear. But not of him. Alex gingerly picked himself off the ground, but he could barely put any weight on his left leg. Ian turned the light out and pushed another button. The automatic roller door came alive and rolled up, exposing the carport to freedom. Alex limped towards it and hesitated.

'I don't remember. Where did I go after … here?'

'To Hell, kid.' Ian's eyes began to moisten. 'I sent you to Hell. Now get the fuck out of here and never come back.'

Ian hit the button again. Alex stepped away as the roller door closed him off to his only childhood memories. His ribs began to sting. He limped away, fear still gripping him.

CHAPTER 9

NOW

Alex had a sinking feeling that things were going to get worse. A crack of light momentarily blinded Alex as the door swung open. A guard entered and examined him with a flashlight.

'It's the quiet one, best to transfer him back to C block now.'

'Think he's faking all this?' Another guard by the door asked.

'Deserves a goddamn Oscar if he is.'

'Uncanny, isn't it? He looks shorter again. Smaller even.'

Alex cleared his throat before he asked, 'What's happening?'

'Move. Now!'

The muscle-bound guard stowed his flashlight and pulled Alex out of the cell, leading him down the hallway.

'I need to make a phone call,' Alex pleaded.

The other guard pushed him hard in the lower back, causing him to stagger forward.

'Later.'

He stepped into C block. He caught the musty odour immediately. It was warmer than solitary, with close to 50 bodies caged in together. He spotted a black-eyed prisoner running his finger across his throat, eyes locked on Alex.

'I've been here before, haven't I?' Alex asked.

'Yep' The guard to his left avoided eye contact.

'Am I safe here?' Alex asked.

'Safe enough.'

'How long am I here for?'

'No more questions. Move.'

Alex was directed to a dark cell. He saw a hulking shadow in the background. His heart pounded in his chest as the electronic lock flashed green.

'Dead meat, Lewis! Dead meat!' An unrecognisable voice shouted behind him.

More prisoners continued the chant until the banging of a baton against steel bars silenced them.

Alex: *What have you done, Lewis? Lewis? Lewis!*

A guard muttered under his breath: 'Advice for you, kid. Whether this is an act or you have a real problem, let's try and cut out the Lewis schtick, hey? It will make life easier for the both of us.'

Alex was thrown into a cell larger than where he had come from, but with barely enough space to fit him and the giant of a man sitting on the bunk bed. The man's arms were raised. Morrison locked the cell and broke into a jog, heading somewhere else. Alex's new cellmate relaxed his arms and broke out into an ugly grin. Several teeth were missing from the bottom row. The man looked to be in his sixties, but he maintained an impressive size. An abusive foster father from a lifetime ago no longer seemed as big, Alex thought.

'You're back,' his cellmate declared.

'I am?'

'Oh, jeez, another personality, hey? What's wrong with this one?'

'How long have I been here?' Alex asked with more urgency.

'A week? Look, Tony and I had an understanding. He could have the bottom bunk as long as he kept his claws off my fuckin' pillow.'

'You'll have no problems with me.'

His cellmate suddenly looked very serious. 'Question for you first,' he started. 'What does Alexander the Great and Winnie the Pooh have in common?'

Alex shrugged.

'They both have the same middle name,' he revealed with a grin.

'Good one.'

'See that's great, I've told you that joke three times, and it's impressed you every time. Tony knew it though.'

'What's your name?' Alex asked.

'It's still Mike. You been following the news? There's been some attack in Adelaide.'

'I'm not following the story,' Alex said flatly. 'Wait. I think I heard something about the markets.'

'Hmmm, I thought it was the Adelaide show. Who knows? News reports are always delayed here.'

'Where is *here*? Exactly?'

'You …' Mike shook his head. 'If I hadn't met Tony, Julie and Lewis, I would slap you silly. You really don't know where you are?'

'Last I remember, I wasn't in prison. You can understand my confusion.'

'You're in Harslett Prison. Biggest prison in South Australia. Maximum security. Every time I asked what you did, you changed into someone else like some twisted party trick.'

Alex remembered Martin's words: 'you're a murderer'. *Not possible.*

The alarms stopped suddenly. A recorded voice: 'It is Tuesday, the 7th of October. We give thanks to God on this new day. We are blessed with light showers and—'

Prisoners groaned in unison as the feminine voice broke out across what sounded like hundreds of speaker systems throughout the cell block. There was something hellish about the smooth tones of the voice. Lights flickered on, temporarily blinding the prisoners. A biblical verse emitted from the speakers next, loud enough that not even the groans and threats of his neighbours could drown out the recording. 'Ephesians 4:32 … Be kind to one another, and merciful, forgiving one another, even as God for Christ's sake forgave you.'

Mike belched, then as he shuffled, the bed frame wobbled and buckled under his weight. Alex took no chances and slipped out of bed.

'So, what are you in here for, Mike?'

Mike belched again and gestured animatedly. 'Is this where we share our personal thoughts and give each other foot massages?'

Alex ignored him and gripped the bars of his cell.

'Will we still be let out? Lunch? Exercise?'

'Why the hell would you want to do that?' Mike grimaced. 'Since your Julie charade, the Stinkers try to corner you any chance they get.'

'Stinkers?'

'The second personality. You came in here acting like a little girl. Julie, right? I've seen weird acts before, but that took the cake. The Stinkers have their eye on you. Or her? Fuck I'm confused.'

Alex: *Julie?*

No response. It unsettled him. Then a flashback came on suddenly.

Julie believed herself to be reasonably tall for her age, with short blonde hair and puffy cheeks. Her innocence did not take full stock of her situation. Locked up in a maximum-security prison was beyond her understanding. It was like a strange excursion to her. She was used to waking in 'funny places' and enjoyed following instructions.

42

Julie fit in better with the staff. They acknowledged the severity of the mental illness when she first came to and asked where to find 'the ladies' so she could 'do a quick wee'. Her walk — more of a waddle, with quick bursts of speed when she got excited — caused various bumps when she wasn't looking where she was going. And her voice: feminine, high-pitched, with exaggerated facial expressions, made her a target for a particular group. She was shepherded away from other prisoners during the day.

The Stinkers scared her. They looked at her differently than everyone else. It was a look of hunger. Always watching. Always waiting.

She sang to herself in the toilet cubicle. The bathroom was empty. A guard had already inspected each cubicle before standing outside. Security was aware of how Julie's unusual presence attracted some groups, and isolating private acts was preferred. But Julie heard chatter outside. Then the heavy bathroom door opened with a bang. She heard multiple footsteps.

'Julieeeeee ... Oh, Julie ... It's play time. Come on, Julie.'

Julie jumped when the cubicle door next to her got kicked open. She muffled a cry and slid underneath the dividing walls to the other end of the bathroom. Another door kicked open.

'Lewis. Lewis.' Julie called out silently.

She didn't get a response. Julie's heart hammered in her chest, and she accidentally soaked her underpants.

Another door. Two left. The next door smashed open and Julie screamed. She hid. As far into the darkness as she could. Her door was busted open. Three skinheads grinned when they found her. But her posture changed. Her normally shrunken spine elongated and her body began to sway. Her voice changed to a whine. Tony had taken over. The skinheads looked at each other and shrugged before they grabbed him. His voice was louder than Julie's. He shrieked and screamed, and before they could do anything two guards ran in.

Alex shook his head. This was no place for any of them.

'Then you've got the Watson gang, who've taken a liking to beating the crap out of you. Well, not you exactly,' Mike added.

'I'm guessing Lewis?'

Mike nodded. 'He's a real piece of work.'

'Yeah. I'm surprised he hasn't pissed everyone off.'

Mike shrugged. 'Pretty well-rounded effort.'

'Okay, so I need to stay clear of two groups.'

'Three. The guards hate Tony.'

'Of course. How do we make a phone call?'

'Easy, just ask a guard when you're around lots of people. Stick with large groups, the more people you're with, the safer you are. More guards, you see. Been a long time since anything serious has gone down in front of a guard. Petty shit they don't always care about. But any major stuff done in front of a guard ends poorly. This is a privately run prison. They can afford to do the job properly. Just don't find yourself alone in here. It's going to run out eventually.'

'What is?'

'Your luck.'

CHAPTER 10

THEN - September 2004

Alex knew his arrest was inevitable. He didn't challenge authorities when he moved from a boys' group home to a detention centre. Like the pimples that had started to develop across his forehead, getting in trouble was a part of growing up. Part of him knew then he would one day end up somewhere worse. He stared out the window and spotted a short, old man with thick white hair, light-blue eyes, and a small pot belly arrive at the detention centre. The old man walked past the large 100-year-old building with a spring in his step, as though he heard the war had just been won. He whistled to himself as he noticed the extensions to the building. Alex remembered Crighton Juvenile Detention Centre was once a residential homestead, but the property was now owned by the state, and his room was in one of the poorly constructed extensions. The walls were paper thin, and he always heard more than he wanted to. Alex watched the old man doublecheck some details in a little black notebook before making his way to reception.

Curious, Alex crept out of his room, ignoring the shouts from the other boys fighting in the hallway. He pressed himself to the wall and spied on the old man as he arrived.

A tall, attractive woman with long red hair greeted the old man. She dressed well, with her social worker credentials displayed on a badge. Alex found her beautiful, but conservative. He assumed she was in her thirties.

'Hello, sweetheart!' The old man chortled. 'Lovely to see you again.'

'Back again?'

'I'll always come back for you.' The old man winked. 'So, he was brought in two nights ago?'

'Yes. He broke into a pawn shop and tried to steal some electronics. Police were notified by a silent alarm and caught up with him on his way out.'

Alex's heart pounded. This was about him.

'And his living circumstances before now?'

'He had been in a boys' home for most of his life, with several failed foster homes along the way.'

The old man followed the social worker toward his room. Alex ran back before he was spotted eavesdropping. The other boys took no notice of him; most were too caught up brawling or ogling the social worker.

Alex could still hear the old man's booming voice when he reached his room.

'Back in my day, boys treated a woman with a lot more respect. What's he been like since he arrived?'

'Quiet, when he doesn't have an episode. He's been rather polite, really. Doesn't engage much with the other teens.'

Alex made it back to his bunk bed when the social worker and the old man knocked and stepped into his room. He watched the old man survey the room. The interior was similar to his small space in the boys' home. Dark. Minimal possessions. Cold.

'Love what you've done with the place.' The old man winked.

The social worker motioned the old man to a chair and excused herself.

'Who are you?' Alex asked.

'Just an old fart. You can call me Graham. Did you want anything? I passed a vending machine on the way in. Otherwise, there was a nice café down the road if you wanted something more substantial?'

Alex shook his head. 'Why are you here?

'How old do you think I am?' Graham asked.

'I don't know. Seventy?'

'Hah! You and I will get along well. I'm five days into my 85th year.'

Alex took a good look at the old man who hadn't wiped the smile off his face since he arrived. He had big ears, a pockmarked face, kind blue eyes, and a posture that appeared shrunken after a long battle with gravity.

Graham kicked off his shoes and put his feet up on Alex's bed. 'You're welcome to do the same, lad. No women here to tell us off!'

'Shouldn't you be in a nursing home or something?' Alex asked.

'I couldn't do that, kiddo, no way. Full of bloody old people. I'd be bored shitless!' Graham cracked up in a fit of laughter.

'Why are you here?' Alex repeated.

'I heard you've been having some trouble. The centre here called me … have before. My partner and I have done respite care for some time now. They thought maybe I could teach you something.'

Alex smirked. 'You? Teach me? Teach me what?'

Graham's eyes narrowed. 'Trust.'

'I don't trust anyone.' Alex sighed, reaching for a book.

'And I don't trust you either. You'd probably nick off with my wireless when I'm not looking.' Graham's grin faded. 'But you deserve the opportunity to trust someone. Really trust. It breaks my heart that nobody's ever given you that. I want to try. You can have my full attention. You can have my home. I'll

never ask for anything back. I just want to give you a chance.
What have you got to lose?'

'You don't understand. You wouldn't be able to handle me,'
Alex said quietly.

'I got through bloody World War II! What's a 15-year-old
boy got on that?'

Alex's shoulders slumped forward, his feet now dangling
from the edge of the bed. He curled his hair around his finger
and started to cry.

'Are you alright, kiddo?'

Julie looked around in confusion. Graham didn't understand.
The energy of the teenager in front of him was different. Julie
tried to control the sobs, but her little voice let out a wail.

'Hey now, what's the matter, kiddo?' Graham asked.

'I'm always waking up in funny places. I thought I would be
gone from here now, but I'm not. It's full of stinky boys.'

The little voice unsettled Graham for a moment. 'I don't
blame you—it is rather stinky.'

'Who are you? Are you taking me to an old people's home?'

Graham watched Julie swing her legs from the bed, even
though her feet could have reached the floor easily.

'I'm a little confused. I thought *my* memory was shocking.
My name ...' Graham collected his thoughts. 'What is your
name?'

'My name's Julie, I'm 6-years-old and I don't like it here.
And I like chocolate.'

Graham watched closely. 'It must be scary and confusing
waking up in funny places.'

Julie shrugged. 'Yeah, but I have my imaginary friends to
keep me company. Do you want to play a game?'

'Ah! Now I'll never say no to a game. How about a game of
cards? Must be something in this depressing dungeon.'

Graham pushed himself up and placed a hand on Julie's shoulder as he inspected the room. Something made him stop. Julie's body lifted higher. He turned. Something had changed again. The boy in front of him looked livid. Dangerous. The boy's tone of voice was suddenly dark, low and flat.

Lewis snarled. 'Fuck off!'

Graham's hand trembled. Lewis could see perspiration run down the back of Graham's neck. Graham withdrew from the room and closed the door. Lewis's posture was broader than Alex's, his walk more confident as he moved to the door and pressed his ear to it.

'Shall I deny the respite care?' The social worker asked.

'You make sure you get that boy's bags packed. I want him with me before the end of the week.' Lewis heard Graham take a breath. 'Thanks, sweetheart.'

***

Alex woke to the sound of an alarm in a room he couldn't recognise. It was 6 am. He could see the ocean from his window. He had never seen the ocean before. A thick bed of seaweed ran across the shoreline. The dark blue ocean continued as far as he could see.

He had a queen-size bed to himself that felt more comfortable than anything he had ever slept on. He ripped the sheets off the mattress and thought it looked brand new. The bedside tables, the lamp, the radio, even the sheets, looked like they had only been used for the first time. Alex had lost time again. But he remembered meeting the old man. *Did he buy all this for me?* Alex took in the wallpaper of his bedroom; a bright green psychedelic design that looked like snakes twisting, turning and splitting, morphing from one body into multiple.

'Come on, lad, put some clothes on!' Graham called out.

Alex forced himself out of bed and got dressed. Graham knocked on the door and entered, wearing a white singlet and matching blue headband and wristbands.

'Forgetting something, lad?' he asked.

'Umm …'

Graham pointed to the bed. Alex had to remake it twice before Graham was satisfied.

'We have some rules here, kiddo. We get up at 6 am, seven days a week. You'll thank me later. Each of those mornings, we make the bed.'

'Why?'

'Habits. You're going to start making good ones. Plus, it's a tick in the box with the ladies. Not that you will find many your age here, I'm afraid.'

Alex got ready and took in his surroundings as he followed Graham's voice out the door. The interior of the house was outdated, with wood panelling covering the walls. Dado rails held small ceramic figurines of dogs and birds. Alex stopped at the wall adjoining his bedroom with Graham's master bedroom. It was covered with photos of Graham shaking hands with a young man. Alex counted 20 photos, each of them with a different boy in their late teens. They all looked healthy. Happy even, he thought. Alex didn't keep Graham waiting any longer. He followed him down to the beach. It was crisp at this time of morning. Alex noticed the ocean sparkling beneath the rising sun. He followed Graham down to the shore. Although the old man was power walking - his arms were swinging with ferocity - Alex only had to walk casually to keep up with him.

The beach was completely empty. The sand wasn't as fine as the pictures Alex had seen of tropical islands, but with no one else around, he felt freer than ever before. He breathed in the fresh, salty air. They moved away from the sand and followed a path that travelled towards the jetty and town centre of Ardrossan.

'Welcome to Tiddy Widdy! This is usually the part where you open up and tell me all your darkest secrets so I can help,' Graham declared between puffs.

'I'm not sure how you can help,' Alex muttered.

'Me neither,' Graham admitted. 'Come on, kid, what have you got to lose by telling your story to an 85-year-old man?'

'I hear voices.'

'Hah! We all hear voices, young man. I've had a nagging one that keeps popping up for the last seven years. Tell me something I haven't heard before, I dare you.'

Part of Alex wanted to prove to Graham that he was different. More troubled than anyone he had ever met. But deep down that wasn't something he really wanted. He'd always wanted to be normal.

'I was seeing a therapist for weeks. Martin. He got me to face my fears and tried to get me a job.'

'I have a fear of the damn bingo nights at the RSL. Bore me to bloody tears. You won't see me facing that fear. Point is we all get them from time to time.'

'He was an hallucination.'

Graham chuckled. Alex's face went red. Two ladies in their early sixties walked past them at a brisk pace.

'Hi, Graham!' they chortled in unison.

'Morning, ladies!' Graham cheered.

Alex waited for the women to be out of earshot before he continued. 'I knew I was crazy, but I didn't think I was that bad.'

'Why do you think you saw Martin in the first place?'

'I think I was seeing Martin to work out what my dark urges meant.' Alex thought about it as he spoke, 'I think part of me wants to be really, really bad.'

'Like a thief?' Graham asked, raising an eyebrow.

Alex shrugged. 'I think more like a psychopath.'

Graham looked Alex in the eye. Then without a word, he continued his power walk. Alex needed to break into a run to catch up.

'The voices want you to hurt people?' Graham asked.

'Yes.'

'When do you hear them?'

'All the time. Now. Some days are worse than others.'

Graham stopped again. He shielded his eyes from the rising sun with his hand as he looked over to the jetty.

'I'm going to make a deal with you, boy. If I can't silence those voices in your head right here, right now, I'll do all your chores for as long as you're here. Deal?'

Alex sniggered. 'Sure.'

'Okay, so I want you to run to that jetty and back to me. Whatever you do, don't stop. When you see my arm swing down, I want you to sprint to the finish.' Spittle ran down his mouth.

'Why?'

'Just indulge an old man.'

Alex started jogging; he couldn't remember the last time he ran for no reason. He could just make out the jetty from where they were. *That's a fucking long way,* he thought. His ribs started to burn after the first few strides. The voices started to curse Graham as the stitch intensified. His legs were burning; he pumped his arms, and his heavy legs seemed to follow. Alex warmed up quickly. His heart thumped faster and harder, and his stitch worsened. He was about to give up when he realised that he was near the jetty. He pushed himself that little bit further and tapped one of the weathered wooden boards holding up the early morning crabbers. On his way back he slowed down and tried to control his breathing. Instead, he just hyperventilated. His breathing caused him to panic. He couldn't find Graham but finally picked out the small old man with his arm raised. When he was 50 metres away, Graham swung his arm down with ferocity.

'NOW!' Graham yelled.

What the hell.

Alex ignored everything and pumped his arms as fast as he could. Everything burned as he sprinted towards the old man. He rushed past him, staggered, and fell to the sand, heaving deep breaths.

'Well?' Graham asked.

'What?' Alex gasped for breath.

'Any voices?'

Alex stopped and listened. Silence. *Holy shit.*

'Ahoy, there!'

'Oh bugger, here's that nagging voice,' Graham muttered, but with a smile.

Alex and Graham had made it back to the house, both panting. A woman watched them from Graham's front deck. Alex guessed she was in her seventies, unless she shared Graham's youthful secret. She had a fit, lean frame with sun-kissed skin. Her hair was short and dyed in an array of gold and silver.

Graham made the introductions. 'Alex, this is Yolanda. You can call her Yoddi. My old lady. Yoddi, this is Alex.'

She smiled at Alex and pouted at Graham. 'I'm 15 years your junior, mister. I'm sure you have a better way to introduce me with that extensive vocabulary of yours.'

'Apologies. Alex, I want you to meet the love of my life.' Graham placed a hand on the small of Alex's back as he guided him up the driveway towards the ramp that led up to Yolanda. 'She's been in my life for quite some time. You'll notice how smooth she is, even if she does go out in the sun a bit too often.

In good shape, I'm sure you would agree, kiddo.' Graham kept walking towards the carport. Yoddi rolled her eyes. 'She's quiet for her age—a rarity in women, let me tell you. She's a beauty alright.'

Alex followed Graham into the carport. Graham looked back at Yoddi, who gave him a look. He chuckled to himself. Alex suddenly realised he was talking about the car. Sitting inside was a Toyota Crown Super Saloon.

'I bought her in 1966.'

It had a classic, boxy shape with a long hood and chrome grille. The side of the car had a chrome trim. Alex didn't know anything about cars, but his initial thought was that it looked timeless. Graham caressed the bonnet of the car.

'You can drive?' Alex asked incredulously.

'Excuse me?'

'Are you allowed to drive at your age?'

'How do you think you got here? I've never stopped driving since I was your age, and I've never needed any bloody glasses. Any other stupid questions from you?'

Yoddi slipped an arm over Graham's shoulder and gave him a kiss.

'The boy has a point. Maybe it will be safer getting you one of those gophers? I think you would look quite endearing.' Yoddi winked at Alex. 'Hello, young man. It's wonderful to meet you. Welcome to Tiddy Widdy. If you ever get tired of this one's jokes, let me know, and I'll take you fishing on my boat. Have you ever fished?'

Another voice went off in Alex's head, softer than before. Alex shook his head.

'Let me get him settled, woman. Come on, I'll make us a cup of tea. I'll show you where the towels are, Alex. You did well back there, but you stink.'

Alex ran the shower but pressed his ear to the door and listened hard.

Yolanda's voice: 'It's my name on the paperwork too, Graham. We normally make these decisions together.'

Graham: 'Thought I would surprise you. You know you're even more stunning in the morning. Did I ever tell you that?'

'Thank you, sweetheart. But … I've read his file. This is a very ill boy. You're an 85-year-old man. I don't want to see you get hurt. And I don't want to see the boy get hurt either.'

'You're right. You're always right. It's too much just for me. If only I knew some other beautiful woman with adolescent respite experience that could give me a hand.'

A sigh.

'And here I was thinking my name was on the paperwork just because you aged out of the foster program. Why this boy, Graham?'

'Every boy we ever took on had something. They just needed to get their shit together before they realised it. This kid has nothing, Yoddi.'

'So, let's say we work our magic and the kid becomes as independent as he's going to get. What then? He's got to face the world again at some point.'

'Kid's got heart, Yoddi, I know it. If he's got that and nothing else, he can make it work. Now where's my cup of tea. I thought you women could multi-task?'

'I'm just taking this seriously, Graham. We've seen what happens to kids that don't get the right support. They end up dead, or in prison.'

CHAPTER 11

NOW

Alex couldn't ignore his reality any longer. He couldn't let Graham down after everything. But he couldn't understand why Graham hadn't reached out to him. It made Alex's chest feel tight. An electronic beep sounded. Every gate on his row opened, and prisoners began to shuffle single file out into the hall. Harslett Prison was known for its tight corridors, dark corners and small rooms, which heightened prisoners' sense of claustrophobia. There was no standardisation of cells. Everywhere looked different, yet the same. Even without the medication, the cells brought on a state of delirium for anyone that moved about. New prisoners often got lost on their way to the mess hall. Routines changed daily. Staff changed hourly. And among all the confusion, Alex felt a foreboding sense of déjà vu. It reminded him of his younger days when he had less control. He wondered if anything had really changed.

Alex joined the queue which followed the arrows marked on the walls for **MESS HALL.** His eyes darted from one table to the next, looking out for any dangerous groups Mike had warned him about. The tables already began to fill with prisoners greedily digging into their trayful of food. Some tables seemed to have more food on trays than others, which Alex considered a sign of the socioeconomic status at play. He assumed the private prison supplied more food and comforts to those who could afford it.

Each prisoner gave their name and were presented with a designated tray. There were no choices here, everything was pre-selected.

'Blakemore, Al—'

'Yes, yes. We know who you are. Fucking loon!' the kitchen hand spat.

A heavy tray of food was placed in front of Alex: two pieces of toast, a bowl of porridge, a banana, a plastic tub of orange juice and a small muffin. Alex assumed he had given the kitchen staff trouble over the last two weeks with some mistaken identities, so he wasted no time thanking them and looking for a seat.

On his way to a table, Alex took a double-take at a phone in a hallway just off the centre of the room. He rushed to it. A guard stopped him. Alex begged him to use the phone. The guard looked off into the distance, got approval from somewhere, and let him pass.

The phone was bulky, but he picked up the headset and heard a dial tone. He punched in a number on a reverse charge and listened to a recorded message: 'You've reached Graham, I'm not at the phone right now. I'm either working, playing golf, taking a leak, or talking to a beautiful young lady. Leave a message.'

Alex tried the home phone next, and then Yoddi's number. Each call went to voicemail. Another prisoner was waiting for the phone, and he was pushed way.

He started feeling nauseous. He wondered what awful thing he had done to make the most forgiving people in his life abandon him.

A medley of religious tunes including *Amazing Grace, A Mighty Fortress is Our God, What a Friend We Have in Jesus* and *It Is Well with My Soul* echoed in repeat across the 3,000-square-metre courtyard of Harslett Prison.

Alex followed Mike outside and took in the sparse, dry land. Whatever funds that were pumped into Harslett, there was clearly nothing in the budget for the recreational courtyard. The asphalt had long since cracked on the basketball court. The ring on one end of the court was held lopsided by a single screw. The weights area contained one rusty bench with even rustier weight plates lying in the dirt. The prisoners kept mostly to park-style benches where they smoked and played cards. Three inmates not much older than Alex ran along an oval-shaped track in the centre of the courtyard.

Mike walked over to the weights bench and started loading up a barbell.

'You're gonna wanna join me here, kid.' Mike urged. 'Blending in is your number one priority right now.'

Alex knew he needed exercise to clear his head. He followed Mike to the bench press.

'Tunes really get you pumped, don't they?' Mike commented as he shuffled himself under the bar.

'Is this all they play?' Alex asked as he spotted Mike. He already knew the answer. Whether the owners were deeply religious, or they used it as a form of torture for the prisoners, it didn't really matter. All that mattered to him was Graham. He had to reach Graham.

Alex worked through sets with Mike and matched him pound for pound. It showed how old the weights were, as everything was still measured in pounds. All the while, Alex kept his eyes open for trouble.

'Did Lewis say anything to you? I know this must be weird for you. I have a condition. I usually have more control,' Alex explained.

'What's the condition?'

'Dissociative identity disorder. I went through a trauma when I was kid and I … developed what people know as multiple personalities. I really don't know why I'm here.'

Mike's expression was gloomy. 'I'm sorry, I can't help you. Lewis swore a lot when we first met, but after a while he got real quiet. Depressed like.'

'Depressed?'

A raspy voice sneered, then hissed, 'Lewis.'

Three dark-skinned prisoners walked over to him. They were skinny, but their dark eyes frightened him. They were huddled in close together, concealing anything that might be in their hands. Alex assumed this must be the Watson gang. Something about them looked familiar.

He scanned the courtyard for the nearest guard and found one observing them on the watchtower directly above the courtyard's entrance. He held a sighted rifle.

'Lewis …' the ringleader hissed again.

The two other Watsons were also searching the area for the nearest guards. The one that spoke had bad teeth and less hair than Mike. His eyes were slightly yellowed. His singlet showed off sinewy muscles on his lean frame.

'We have unfinished business.'

'I'm not Lewis. Hell, I look nothing like the guy,' Alex started. 'Look, it doesn't matter. Weights are yours.'

He left with Mike.

'Wait!'

The voice stopped Alex in his tracks. He turned around. The prisoner kicked the bar.

'Put it back on the rack,' he ordered.

'Look, I don't have time for this. Whatever Lewis did I apologise. Whatever he did couldn't be worth all of us getting into more trouble, surely?'

'The kid's not well,' Mike added. 'Can't remember shit.'

'Couldn't be worth ...' Todd, the lead Watson, shook his head in disbelief. 'How the fuck do you think we ended up here?'

'Fuck him up, Todd,' sniggered one of the others.

Todd clenched his fists and stared down at Alex with a threatening look.

'I got nothin' to lose,' Todd menaced, flexing his muscles, 'I'm not buying this amnesia shit. Last time you got lucky.'

Alex jumped out of the way as a 5 lb weight plate flew past his face. A whistle blew just as all the Watsons charged at Alex. Between the punches and bites, Alex saw Mike pull one man off him. More whistles blew and the guards were pulling everyone away from each other.

Alex spat out blood.

Alex: *Really, Lewis? Nothing? Not going to help clean your own mess?*

Lewis: *It's a fucking mess that can't be cleaned, Alex.*

CHAPTER 12

THEN – September 2004

Alex started to see the beauty of Tiddy Widdy Beach. He heard the drumming against the roof first and opened his bedroom window. His nostrils took in the fresh scent of rain mixed with the salty aroma of the ocean. Mist and rain blended into a grey veil that covered the shore. He could make out a lone seagull huddling against the wind on the deserted beach. Small streams of water trailed past the wind-battered shrubs towards the dark sea. It was a peaceful sight, but he was disappointed that he couldn't run along the coastline this morning.

Alex stretched his adolescent body and found Graham in the kitchen wrapping up a conversation on a mobile phone. Alex recognised the model, a Nokia 6680; he'd stolen several in the past few months. Graham put a little black book up on the kitchen shelf.

'What's that?' asked Alex.

'It's my new mobile phone, do you like it? I surprise everyone with my knack for technology.'

'No, the book.' Alex pointed.

'That's my little black book. You know what a little black book is, don't you? It's got all my lady friends' numbers, so I don't get mixed up.' Graham clapped Alex on the back.

'I thought Yoddi was your lady friend.'

'She's my favourite.' Graham winked.

'You must have a lot of lady friends. You know your mobile can do that too? It can store phone numbers.'

'What a bloody stupid idea. I guess you've figured you're not running out in this bloody weather this morning. Are you ready for a drive?'

Graham drove for 10 minutes (*quite well too*, Alex thought) before they reached an abandoned shopping centre. The shops had closed long ago, and the lease signage had eroded from years of sunlight. Alex followed Graham to the end building, which was easily the largest. All the signs had been removed, so he had no idea what he was stepping into when Graham pushed open an unlocked door.

The giant room looked like it hadn't been accessed for years. It appeared mostly untouched in that time, except for old bed sheets that had been hung up on the walls. To the left of the room, Alex saw what looked like medieval torture machines with metallic arms twisting in all sorts of directions. *If you added mirrors, this place would be terrifying*. The machines had collected dust over the years but still looked dangerous. The room smelt musty and foul. Alex jumped at the sound of a *thud* and turned to find that Graham had dropped a large coil of rope into a corner.

'Graham? What is this place?'

'Somewhere that can help.'

Alex looked nervously around the room. He counted at least 12 torture devices, all of which must have been designed to break every bone in the body. Alex forced himself not to be afraid of this dark, dusty dungeon.

'Well at least there's no mirr—'

Graham yanked at one of the bed sheets and exposed a mirror that covered the entire wall. Alex's heart leapt and he steadied himself. He turned away from it, but a magnetic presence drew him towards it. He could handle one mirror. Then he realised what must be behind all 20 bed sheets that covered the entire room.

'What is this place?' Alex repeated.

Graham flicked a button on the stereo, and it started playing '70s music.

'This was a gym,' Graham explained over the music as he started dancing. 'The social worker said you covered up your mirrors. We will do the opposite. We will expose one at a time.'

'Why?'

'When you're as handsome as me, kiddo, you need to admire yourself at any opportunity. Truth is, I don't think hiding from your reflection is doing any good. You will have to trust me. Are you ready to begin?'

Graham directed Alex to skipping first, which left him with lashings on his shins. The torture devices came next, which he learnt were strength machines designed to target a specific muscle group. He felt more co-ordinated with these. When the voices got too much, the music got louder.

'I'm thinking of playing this song on my 100th birthday. What do you reckon?' Graham asked as he started dancing like John Travolta.

Stayin Alive by the Bee Gees filled the room.

'I don't like loud music!' Alex yelled out.

'Yeah, quiet music really gets my blood pumping too. That was sarcasm,' Graham called back.

Alex heard nothing except the rhythmic beat of the song. It gave him a headache, but he continued the session, hoping it would make the time go quicker.

'This can help.' Graham said when they finished. 'But you have to apply two principles. Number one, it's got to get your ticker going. If you're not breathing heavy, you won't get the benefit. Today you passed that one.'

'And the second?' Alex puffed.

Graham smiled. 'You actually have to find a way to enjoy it.'

When they got back home, Yolanda had left several large parcels for Alex on the kitchen table, which were full of various textbooks for distance education. He flipped through them and started to feel on edge, despite the endorphins racing through his body.

'I'm finishing school here?' Alex asked.

Yoddi was putting the groceries away, while Graham sipped some prune juice.

Yoddi looked at Alex and smiled. 'Your school is three hours away. I think you will find this much more preferable.'

'How much longer do I have to stay here?' Alex asked.

Yoddi shot Graham a look.

'Until we can find permanent care for you. A permanent foster family. Could take months. Could take longer,' Graham replied.

'Months!?' Alex slammed his fists onto the table. 'I'm not staying here for months! I never agreed to that. There's nothing here! We're in the middle of nowhere!'

'I think that may have been the point …' Graham muttered.

'And you will probably cark it before then anyway.'

Yoddi appeared nonplussed. She took a seat and listened to the banter.

'Excuse me?' Graham rose from his seat.

'I can't live here. I was fine where I was. I could do what I wanted.'

'That might have been the problem,' Graham interjected.

Alex stormed out of the house and grabbed the car keys by the door. Graham tried to stop him, but Alex was far too quick. He ran out of the house and jumped into Graham's car. Alex had no plan, and he had never driven a car before. Graham's car was old, but he figured out how to reverse, ignoring Graham's calls. The car moved faster than he thought, and he sped out of the driveway, over the road, and hit a rubbish bin on the edge of the dirt path that led to the beach. He switched from reverse to drive and hit the accelerator, but the car just hummed. He looked back and saw the bin had damaged the back of the car. He didn't know anything about cars, but he assumed this one was expensive. Graham, purple-faced, was storming over towards him with that same power walk. Alex switched the 'gear-thing' and tried to accelerate, but nothing happened.

Graham made his way to the car and got in the passenger seat. He was puffing and tried to slow down his breathing as he reached for his seat belt.

'Pull this lever here and push a little harder on the accelerator,' Graham instructed.

Alex did as he was told and drove over a small ditch.

'Now the indicators are on the right side. You're going to push down on that one to signal that you're turning right.'

'What are you doing?' Alex asked.

'Might as well teach you how to drive, kiddo.'

Alex spotted an echidna crossing the road. He kicked against the other pedal while Graham directed him to the handbrake, and they screeched to a halt. They watched the spiky mammalian cross the road to seek out an ant's nest.

A small sedan behind them beeped and overtook them, blasting their horn the whole way across.

'Ignore them. They're just neighbours. They're probably thinking I got stuck into the sherry.'

'Why am I here?' Alex asked, hands still shaking.

'Take a look at where you are, kiddo. The middle of nowhere, like you said.'

Alex took in the sight of the Tiddy Widdy Beach: long stretches of dirt road, native shrubs blocking most of the view of the shore, retirees tucked inside their homes, the dark sea off in the distance.

'As you said, stuck with an old fart that could fall from the perch at any minute. You've been abandoned. Have been your whole life. Parents, authorities, imaginary friends! But I won't. I'll feed ya, I'll clothe ya, I'll teach ya.'

'Why are you doing this?'

'I have experience.'

'In what?'

'Everything. I'm reaching 90-bloody-years-old. Shouldn't drive. Shouldn't live independently. Shouldn't help people. Shouldn't have coffee with beautiful women. But I prove all those naysayers wrong when I get up every morning. Sorry to say, kiddo, but social workers, the authorities, don't expect much from you either. Wanna prove 'em wrong together?'

CHAPTER 13

NOW

I have to prove them wrong. Alex's heart rate was still elevated when he was carried back into solitary confinement. Martin sat in the dark corner of the cell, a look of expectation on his face.

'This isn't doing you any good, Alex. Your stress is causing frequent flashbacks, yes? Perhaps the time has come to listen?'

Alex could still feel the positive hormonal effects of the high intensity session in the yard.

'I don't think so.'

'So, what's your answer? More push-ups?'

'We need to find out what's going on. Why I am here.' Alex muttered.

'*We?*'

'Yeah, *we.*'

Alex: *Lewis, whatever's going on with you, put it aside. We need you to keep us alive.*

Alex removed a key hidden beneath his sleeve that he'd pickpocketed outside from one of the guards. He pushed his ear to the door, placed the key in the lock, and closed his eyes. His body started to sway from side to side, and his head nodded back and forth. His change in posture made him taller as his chest lifted. Alex was gone. A different being presented himself. Tony hummed away. A moment later he unlocked the door with the key and shuffled out. Then he stopped suddenly by the door.

Tony: *Feeling much safer in there ... Not sure why I have to get out into the light. Rather be in the dark with the phantom. But no, always has to be Tony because Tony can count four, three, two, one.*

Tony shuffled through the door as a CCTV camera in the corner of the hallway swivelled to the left. He made it to a steel door with a keypad.

Alex: *Dammit. I never saw a number.*

Tony: *Roku, san, ku, hachi.*

Alex punched in 7398.

Alex: *Jesus, Tony, have you been learning Japanese? And where did you get the code?*

Tony waited another moment. Cameras moved from side to side. When he found his moment, he opened the door and shuffled around the corner towards a row of offices. He saw various guards and prison staff through the glass walls.

Tony: *Tony watches, not very tricky to watch. Guards cover their hands. One guard, George, his hand moves direction when he presses his numbers, one-two-three, four-five-six, seven-eight-nine, star-zero-hash. Anyone could figure out the rows and columns even in another language. I would pick Japanese because I like the anime.*

Lewis: *Fucking wonderful but we're in plain sight; any chance of moving the fuck along?*

Tony: *No, thank you.*

Alex: *What do you mean?*

Tony: *If we go any further Tony gets caught. Tony doesn't want to get caught. Tony would rather go back. Only way forward is to stay low, below desk height. Air vent grate at the end of the hallway. Based on length from left to right acromion process, Tony would not fit through. Also, Tony hears people coming.*

Julie: *I can fit. Shove.*

Tony fell forward … and landed softly. Tony was gone. Julie grinned as she crawled forward on her hands and knees, moving easily. The hallways were narrow, half that of a shopping aisle, forcing single file for adults. When Julie reached the crawlspace, she looked both ways before she pulled at a grate.

Alex: *Can you do this, Julie?*

Julie: *You bet!*

Julie struggled, her face red with effort. Gradually the grate slipped off and she landed on her bottom. She laughed at herself and crawled through the tight space. Getting stuck halfway, Julie had to slither inch by inch until she made it to an office space full of desks, computers and printers. There were two prisoners in this computer room. Their ankles were cuffed to steel chairs.

Julie: *Can we use these computers?*

Alex: *No, we need access to the system. Computers that the guards use, Julie.*

Julie continued crawling, following the power cables of the PCs that led to a power point on the wall. She anxiously glanced at the back of the prisoners' heads as they remained fixated on their screens.

'Holy shit!' one of them shouted. 'Are you seeing this shit? News story is up.'

'That shit's always several weeks behind. No point even watching,' the other replied.

'I think you might want to look at this. It's the Adelaide Show. Serious shit went down.'

Julie: *Ooh, I would love the show. I've never been.*

Alex: *Julie, focus.*

Julie peeked at the computer screen and craned her neck to see over the prisoner's shaved head. The prisoner increased the volume. Julie saw the Royal Adelaide Show on the computer screen with a bird's-eye view of the showgrounds. Ferris wheels, rollercoasters and sideshow alley attractions lit up a scene of chaos in an assortment of colour. A stampede of thousands of people had bottle-necked at the main entrance as police cordoned off other exits, the frightened crowd spilling out onto Goodwood Road and stopping traffic. The backdrop showed flashing lights and plastic litter caught in the wind.

The reporter declared over the noise of the sirens: 'We can confirm that seven people were shot and killed by an unseen sniper at the Royal Adelaide Show this evening. In a bizarre connection, SAPOL tents were overwhelmed before the shooting when pictures of dead bodies were found in Yellow Brick Road showbags.'

Lewis: *Sounds hard core.*

Julie: *What's a SAPOL?*

Alex: *South Australian police. We really don't have time for this. Julie, please.*

Julie pulled the power cords out. Prisoners behind her started swearing at their machines.

Julie: *It's okay, they won't see me, I'm only little.*

Lewis: *Is anyone going to tell this crazy fucker? Anyone?*

Alex: *She's got us this far.*

Tony: *Tony got you approximately 45 metres; the child has moved 11 metres.*

Alex: *You need to move, Julie, someone will come.*

Julie moved back to the crawlspace as two guards came in from the other side of the room and escorted the frustrated prisoners outside. When she heard the door close, she crawled to the other side of the room.

Tony: *Stop!*

Julie halted on all fours by the door.

Julie: *He'll see my bum!*

Tony: *Wait!*

Julie: *Okay, Tony.*

She knew somewhere out there cameras were shifting position. Julie's heart raced.

Tony: *Now!*

Julie crawled out of the room, staying low and turning the first corner out of fear of being caught. She nearly collided with four prisoners walking in a line. The one in front wore glasses and looked at her in confusion. Julie was overwhelmed with fear. A vein started to pulse along her forehead. She clenched her knuckles as her body changed, slowly rising to full height. Lewis had taken control. He appeared almost barrel chested, head lifted high, deeply breathing, a permanent snarl on his face … and something else. He appeared as though he was managing chronic pain, his jaw continued to clench and his eyes were watery. He stared down at the four men. They reeked of cigarettes.

Lewis hissed, 'Fuck you. What ya lookin' at?'

The man in front held Lewis's gaze for a moment before his shoulders relaxed. 'Nothin', man, we're just headin' to the workshop, not lookin' for any trouble.'

'Mmmpff.' Lewis groaned. 'I've lost my way … where's the nearest security office?'

The man at the back of the queue pointed to another left turn with his thumb. Lewis nodded and followed his direction, shoulders swaying in an exaggeration of his masculinity. The area didn't appear to be restricted but Lewis followed Tony's advice and stayed out of the line of sight of all the cameras as he followed the claustrophobic hallways. He heard crashing and crying. The source of the noise came from a bathroom. He stepped quietly and peered into the bathroom to see a prisoner barely out of his teens sobbing as a red-headed guard beat him. The boy was skinny and his whole body heaved during each cry as the guard attacked the young prisoner mercilessly with a baton.

Alex: *We take him down without him seeing us.*

Lewis: *Fuck that.*

Lewis maintained control and stuck to the path. An office door was slightly ajar and he could hear a TV playing. He peeked in and saw four security guards glued to the screen.

There was a reporter in front of the Festival Theatre. The news ticker read: *Five victims in serious condition rushed to RAH during a school choir concert.*

Reporter: 'Reports coming in suggest the victims were burnt in their seats, the seats themselves rigged with flammable—'

Lewis: *Adelaide's really fucked at the moment.*

Alex: *Multiple attacks at such public events? They must be connected.*

Lewis: *Not our fucking problem though, is it?*

Alex: *I've never seen anything like it.*

Lewis made it to the security room. He could see two guards working on computers behind tinted glass. Another door with a keypad appeared to be the only entry/exit.

Lewis: *No way into that. I say we go back before we're even more fucked.*

Alex: *There has to be a way.*

Lewis: *There's no way, Alex. We're in over our fucking heads. This is our life now.*

Alex: *What are you talking about?*

Lewis went silent. Alex regained control. He could hear others coming. If he didn't move now, he would be caught on camera when he was supposed to be in his cell. There was another door to his left. There was no sign of what was behind it. He turned the handle and relief washed over him when he found it unlocked and abandoned. The room was empty except for a table, two chairs and a phone. The footsteps were coming closer. Alex refrained from closing the door. He watched through the crack in the door frame as two more guards headed to the security room. One of them punched some numbers on the keypad and they entered the room. Alex struggled to see anything, but he could hear their conversation.

'Anthony? How long has the missus got left?'

'Couple weeks.'

'Hah! You thought Afghan was rough, let's see you after two weeks of sleep deprivation. Fuck … Don't miss those days. You catch the game last night?'

Alex noticed a pile of newspapers in the corner of the room. The Advertiser was three weeks old, but the headline caught his attention: *Four murdered at Adelaide Airport.* Alex was drawn to the article. He flicked to the main story.

Four bodies were found in the men's toilets at Adelaide Airport on the first of September. Police found knives at the scene. Investigators reported they were made from nitinol. Experts explain this is a unique blend of nickel and titanium with a low magnetic permeability and conductivity, resulting in an undetectable response from the metal detectors.

Alex moved away from the newspaper as the guards completed their shift change. Alex picked up the end of their conversation.

'Nah, police are saying it's a serial killer. My money was on a terror attack, but I'm kinda glad it's just a nutcase, you know?'

'Yeah, but a shooting, a burning, and a stabbing. Very different MOs. Not something we would expect in Adelaide, that's for sure. Are they going to start cancelling events?'

Alex closed the door before the other guards walked past. He tried phoning Graham again but only got the same voicemail. He tried Yoddi's number again, but the call wouldn't go through.

Tony: *Not enough data.*

Alex: *There was enough. Just let me think.*

Alex took advantage of the quiet. He had enough, he was sure of it. First name: Anthony. Served in Afghanistan. Wife is expecting. *It would take some luck.* Alex decided on his plan and picked up the phone. He dialled Telstra's directory assistance and requested a connection to Harslett Prison. A list of options came up for various departments of the prison. Alex opted for administration and dialled the number.

A young female voice answered, 'Hello, Sheree speaking.'

Alex cleared his throat. 'Hi Sheree, this is Jackson from DCS payroll. I have an electronic payment pending but the staff member forgot to put his last name in so we can't identify his staff number. Can you provide me with the last name for an Anthony – role description is corrections officer?'

'Ah … One moment … We have three Anthonys.'

'No problem, give me one at a time and I'll see which employee's pay hasn't been processed.'

'Anthony Shrike.'

'Date of birth? I need to confirm against the DCS database.'

'11th of June, '63.

'His payment's already gone through.'

'Ahhmm…Anthony Bark, 9th of April '66.'

'Not him, last one?'

'OK. Anthony Livingstone, 8th of May, 1988?'

'Yeah, that's the one. Thanks, Sheree.'

Alex hung up. There was only one date of birth that matched the appearance of the guard that walked past him moments ago. Anthony was too young to be born in the sixties.

Alex dialled another number.

'Department of Veterans Affairs, this is Stephen,' a formal voice answered.

'Hi, Stephen, this is Andrew from City Medical Centre. We've just had a new patient this morning and I'm trying to register his intake form into our system, but his handwriting is shocking. He's written a DVA number here so I thought you might be able to give me a contact number so I can confirm his details.'

'Ahmmm. Where did you say you were calling from?'

'City Medical Centre. Calling for Dr London. Did you need his provider number?'

'Yes, please.'

'5273622X'

Alex had used this number for many calls over the last three years. The provider number was legitimate and easily located on a Medicare invoice.

'And the address this provider number is linked to?'

'1/80 Grote Street, Adelaide.'

Alex heard tapping of keys on the other end.

'Okay, what was the veteran's file number?'

'Yeah, so that's very hard to read. I've got some of the other girls to help me here. We can make out SSM but the rest is illegible. His name is Anthony Livingstone.'

A sigh, then more tapping. 'And his date of birth?'

'8 May 1988.'

'Okay.' Stephen cleared his throat. 'You gave a South Australian file number and there is only one match in SA with the details you provided. You just needed his contact number?'

'Yes, please, and an emergency contact if you have it in case we can't get through.'

Alex received Anthony's phone number, as well as a number for his wife, Cheryl. He called Cheryl. She picked up on the second ring.

'Hello, Cheryl speaking?' a young voice replied.

'Hi, Mrs Livingstone? It's Spencer from Defence Health. I won't keep you. Your husband's filled out a form for private health cover for your future child, but he hasn't listed which hospital you're planning on having the baby?'

'Bloody Anthony,' a tired voice replied. 'Ashford Hospital.'

'No problem. And your obstetrician?'

'Dr Hunt.'

'No problem. Thanks, Mrs Livingstone. All the best to you.'

Alex hung up and took a breath. He redialled Harslett Prison and opted for reception. He was put on hold for a minute. He started to get anxious. He thought he could still hear the sounds of the teenage prisoner getting beaten in the nearby bathroom. And the Adelaide attacks made him uneasy. But he couldn't understand the sense of dread that came with it. Finally, the call was answered.

'Hi, this is Jack calling from Dr Hunt's office.' Alex continued, 'I'm trying to reach Anthony Livingstone. His wife, Cheryl, had a scan today and she's been sent directly to Ashford Hospital for an emergency C-section. I've been told to call the husband immediately. Are you able to pass a message on?'

The receptionist made assurances she would, and Alex quickly hung up. He moved back to the door, leant against the wall and closed his eyes. He took a deep breath in and out.

Lewis: *Well? What the fuck happens now?*

They heard a door open nearby, so Alex discreetly pulled his door slightly open and watched as Anthony and the other guard ran out of the security office together.

'Not allowed to be off on their own.' Alex smiled to himself as he walked to the security office and stared at the panel.

Alex: *What do you think, Tony?*

Tony: *Did I have a magnifying glass? No, poor Tony gets nothing except expectation. Too far away. Tony doesn't want glasses but not a lot he could do. Saw parts, 400 possible combinations. We don't have that sort of time. Multiple errors would result in conflict.*

Alex jumped when a man placed a hand on his back. Martin. Alex thought he looked older than what he remembered under the light of the fluorescent globes. There were more lines around his eyes and lips. His forehead more wrinkled than before. It made him wonder if his alters had ever aged. No, Julie had been a little girl for a very long time. If they hadn't, why had Martin? An awful thought occurred. *What if Martin was more developed? What if Martin had taken over? Could he be an alter as well? Or is he just an hallucination - Something more powerful than the rest?*

Martin smiled. 'This is all very impressive, Alex, but what's it all for? You can only do so much like this.'

Fear rose up in Alex's gut, but he forced himself not to flee. He needed to know what had happened. He needed to understand why he was here.

'I need to know what's happened. I shouldn't be seeing you. I shouldn't have lost time like this. I've been better for so long,' Alex said through gritted teeth.

'Then let me help you. You have been here for weeks, Alex. Deep down you know the code. You just need me to unlock your potential.' Martin raised his arms in the air and preached to an imaginary audience. 'In Him we have redemption through His blood, the forgiveness of our sins, in accordance with the riches of God's grace.'

Tony reminded Alex he had seconds before he needed to turn back.

'Book 49, 1:7,' Martin added.

Alex punched in 4917. A green light flashed above the keypad and the door unlocked.

'We will chat soon, Alex.' Martin waved.

Alex entered the security office and closed the door behind him. Tony assured him he had avoided the cameras. The room was the size of a broom closet, filled with monitors, hard drives and server racks with blinking blue and green lights. The room was quiet except for the whirring of the server units. Alex found an open laptop still logged in on the desk. A tab was left open with another news article: *Individual has released sensitive information relating to all four attacks. The public have called him The Showstopper.*

Lewis: *Fucking lame name. We don't have a lot of time.*

Alex: *Agreed.*

He sat down and searched through a database until he eventually found his name.

Tony: *This is maximum security. Felt very easy to Tony. Too easy. Something's not right.*

Alex ignored him and double-clicked. His mugshot came up. It wasn't his expression. Somehow, he knew this face was Lewis. And Lewis was upset in a way Alex had never known.

Julie: *You're in demand?*

Alex: *Remand. I haven't gone to trial yet. Maybe I haven't lost as much time as I thought. Let's see ...*

He clicked on file details just as the door opened. Four guards rushed in.

'Fucking Tony again!' one of them spat.

Alex was too slow as a baton swung and hit him in the upper back, knocking him off his chair. The four guards squeezed into the tiny room and pounded him with their feet and clubs. Alex retreated into darkness. The darkness was familiar to him. It was his safe place. He never got hurt in his safe place. The pain was reserved for someone else.

CHAPTER 14

THEN - September 2004

Julie's vision was blurry from salty tears. All she could see was gravel and blood … and Graham panting hard beside her.

'Yoddi!' Graham called out. 'Yoddi!'

Yoddi came storming up from the house, horror-stricken.

'What happened?' hollered Yolanda. 'Get off the bloody road, Graham. What if a car comes?'

'Yes, well I would like to do that, dear, but I'm a little stuck. Meet Julie …'

Julie was crying harder. She wrapped herself around Graham's leg and sniffled back more tears. Graham couldn't move against the weight of the teenager, who was hidden behind another identity.

'I see.' Yoddi crouched down and met Julie's gaze. 'Hello, Julie.'

'Mmmhmm.'

'Do you have a sore knee, Julie?'

Julie nodded and pointed at her right knee, which could be seen through a hole in her pants. It had lost some skin and had started to bleed.

'I can make it better if you would like to come inside? I think there's some ice blocks in the freezer?'

Julie soon forgot about her knee as she licked an ice block while watching one of Yolanda's VHS tapes on TV, a fresh band-aid on her knee. Yoddi finished packing the first aid kit away while Graham splashed water on his face.

'What caused him to, you know, change?' Yoddi asked.

'It came out of nowhere. We were watching a cargo ship from the jetty when something inside him just switched off. I thought he was in a trance. And then suddenly, that little voice.'

'Are you prepared for this? It's not just Alex you're looking after here,' warned Yoddi.

'*We're* looking after. Don't forget I made you sign those papers too. Apparently, you're the responsible one now. Social workers obviously haven't seen you with a bottle.' Graham laughed.

Julie saw Yoddi give him a whack on his bottom. Julie thought they looked tired. Graham saw her watching and gingerly knelt beside her.

'Hey, kiddo, how's the knee?'

'Okay.'

'Alex, can you come back to us, kiddo? Are you in there?' he asked softly.

'This show is boooring.' Julie complained.

Graham cracked a toothy grin. 'Now, Julie, we can't have you watching Yoddi's 'Bold and the Beautiful' repeats. What do ya like to watch, kiddo? Barbie? My little pony?'

'Batman.'

'Batman?' Graham asked incredulously.

'It makes sense. Alex has spent most of his life in a boy's home. I don't think programs for little girls would have got too many votes on a shared TV.' Yoddi reasoned.

'Na-na-na-na-na-na-na Batman!' Julie chirped.

'Batman.' Graham nodded. 'Be back soon. Julie, you're in charge.'

Graham took the car keys and left. Yolanda sat next to Julie and started knitting.

'What are you doing?'

'I'm knitting. I could make you something if you like?'

'No, that's okay. I don't think I will be here that long.'

'Why do you say that?'

'I'm never anywhere very long.'

Julie jumped in fright, waking herself from a nap, when Graham came in through the back door. She heard groaning and creaking floorboards coming from the bedroom. Graham swore.

'Swear jar!' Julie called out. 'I know that's a naughty word.'

'Graham? Is everything okay?' Yoddi called out.

'Just dandy. You girls want to come and have a look?'

Julie followed Yoddi into his bedroom. Graham had set up a trundle bed underneath Julie's single bed and was tucking in a licenced Batman quilt.

'From the op shop. I remembered seeing it the other day.' Graham shrugged.

'Is this for me?' Julie's eyes widened with glee.

Graham scratched his head. 'Hmmm … I'm not sure. It does look mighty comfy. Maybe I should test it first—'

Julie dived onto the bed and rubbed her face against Batman's mask printed on the pillowcase. She laid back and spread out her limbs. Batman's cape flowed underneath her.

'What do you say, Julie?' Yoddi tested.

'Thank you,' Julie said shyly.

She started playing make-believe on the bed, holding imaginary action figures with all the sound effects of a great battle. Yolanda and Graham moved back to the door and watched.

'You're not going to give up on him, are you?' Yoddi asked rhetorically.

'Why would I? Not much else going on at the moment. Haven't had a case in a while.'

'You've had offers.'

'True. But this kid … Aren't you a little curious?'

'About?'

Graham tilted his head in Julie's direction. They could see his burns and scars where his shirt had lifted. Julie picked her nose.

Graham flinched. 'About what in the Jesus happened to this kid?'

CHAPTER 15

NOW

Alex stirred, feeling drowsy and sore in the damp solitary cell. He had scrapes and bruises across his arms. A draft blew in from the bottom of the door. He didn't want to cover it as it provided the only crack of light. He thought he liked the darkness at home, with his blackout blinds and door sweeps. But this was something else. The room was a black hole that made him feel small and inert. He felt a presence behind him.

A familiar voice spoke. 'You're losing touch in here. This place is rotting your mind.'

'I kinda got that when I started hallucinating a therapist again. Bit of a giveaway.' Alex shot a quick glance at Martin's position.

'Perhaps you should return to your therapy?' Martin asked, pulling out a note pad and pen.

'With you?' Alex scoffed.

'How do you expect to be whole in this place if you still dissociate yourself from your past?'

'I have overcome my past, no thanks to you. You pretended you could help me, then abandoned me. I understand my alters but I don't understand you. I only feel crazy when I'm around you. I remember enough about my past now, I'm ready to move on.'

'Oh?' Martin smirked. 'So, you acknowledge what happened to you?'

'I was orphaned, sent to a foster home, then went to some bad place that left me broken. I get it.'

'Of course. Of course.' Martin paced back and forth, 'And the ones responsible for the *bad place*, did you find them?'

'We found out enough. I moved on.'

'Moving on and suppressing memories are two very different things.'

'I'm not suppressing anything,' Alex snapped.

Martin folded his arms. 'Can you recall the faces of those who hurt you?'

Alex paced across the small room. Faces. He couldn't get faces out of his head. Past and present was becoming a blur. *Or is there a connection? Something about this place ...*

Six-year-old Alex refused to move in his cage after the girl, his only companion, was taken by the strange men. Rain soaked the child to his bones.

'This fucker needs to be moved tonight,' the man with the domed head spat. 'Deliver him to this address. Do not fuck this up.'

The big man looked down at the boy, who tried to make himself smaller when eyes were on him. He squawked and squealed when a pair of thick hairy hands pulled him out of the cage. Something hard hit him in the head as the big man reached for him.

He awoke in a car. The same man was driving. Rain pelted down at the car; the windscreen wipers were the only sound, apart from the boy's anxious moans. The man looked at the boy in the rear vision mirror. The man shook his head and drove faster.

Eventually the car stopped. Alex tried to make himself smaller. The man pulled him out of the car and into the rain. Alex bit him, but it had no effect. He was too tired to do anything else. The man threw him onto the grass in front of a tall building. Alex could see the hulking man's face clearly below the streetlamp. He was balding, with several teeth missing.

'Good luck, kid.'

The man drove off, leaving Alex in the rain in front of Lutheran Foster Care ...

Alex brought himself back to the present but now couldn't get the man's face out of his head.

'*Mike*,' Alex said to himself, his eyes wide with the realisation.

'Mike, Mike, Mike. And he's all chummy with you,' Martin whispered. Alex could almost feel his breath on the back of his neck. 'You'll need to do something about that.'

When Alex was brought back to his cell, Mike was brushing his teeth. Alex watched Mike gargle and spit before wiping his mouth on a stained towel.

Mike turned and grinned. 'One would think you enjoy solitary more than my company.'

Mike noticed Alex's eyes narrow, his fists clenched. 'What are you in here for, Mike?'

'Tax evasion. You?'

'Do you know who I am?' Alex asked, his voice low.

'Oh god, another one. Look, before we do the introductions, I've got a joke for you.'

Alex lifted off his prison shirt, ignoring the cold.

'Oh jeez, this one's a stripper, I have an even better joke for you ...'

Mike's smile faded when he saw Alex's old burns and scars stretching across his torso.

'You were part of it. When I was little. You pulled me from the cage.'

Mike's mouth opened and closed several times, but no words came out. He dropped down on a chair but didn't take his eyes off Alex.

'Do you know who I am?' Alex repeated.

Mike nodded. 'You survived. The Maninga child.' A long pause. 'So, what happens now?'

Alex didn't know.

'You're a fractured soul, aren't you, kid? The odds of us meeting here, are … well, as low as you surviving in the first place. I didn't have the stomach for what they did. I got you out, I don't know what you remember. But that was one of the last things I ever did with them.'

Alex screamed and charged at Mike. His cellmate was almost twice his weight, but it didn't stop Alex from pushing him into the wall, his hands tight around his neck.

'LOOK AT WHAT YOU DID!' Alex yelled in a voice not his own. 'LOOK AT WHAT YOU DID TO ME!'

Neighbouring prisoners complained about the noise. Others egged him on. Alex wasn't listening. He kept squeezing. His eyes were hot with tears. Mike choked against the grip but did not fight back.

'Sorry, kid,' Mike managed. 'Go on. Get it out of your system.'

'You don't get to be sorry. You have no idea the pain you all caused. Pain you still cause. You have no idea.' Alex released his grip. 'But I'm too tired to fight.'

'Just tell me what I can do to help you,' Mike offered, patting himself down.

'I am very confused.' Alex fought back the urge to hit the wall. 'I don't know why I'm here, how long I'm here for … my brain isn't working … And I can't reach Graham.'

'I—ah … get on well with a guard on D block. He can look up some information for you. No harm in that yeah?'

There were very few people Alex trusted. But somewhere in the confusion he had a thought that he couldn't dismiss. He would be dead already if it wasn't for the felon in front of him.

CHAPTER 16

THEN - September 2004

Alex's teenage reflection stared back at him from 20 different mirrors. He expected the sensation to be like stepping into a mirror funhouse, where his distorted image would trigger new voices in his head. But it wasn't. It was just him. Alex. In control. He was back at the Ardrossan gym, but the wall mirrors in the gym were now uncovered. He found himself slamming down the battle ropes as fast as he could, heart rate elevated, voices discreet. The old musty smell was replaced with the deodorant Graham forced Alex to use every day. A timer rang, signalling Alex to drop the ropes and move onto pull-ups. Another timer went off and Alex dropped to the floor, breathing heavily. Seventies disco music played in the background.

'Do you think I will start seeing him again?'

'Who?' Graham asked.

'Martin.'

'If you do, we can put him in touch with Yoddi. He will have a field day.' Graham chuckled to himself as he pulled the battle ropes into the corner of the room.

'Graham.' Alex paused. 'Do you think I could be a psychopath? Dogs were freaked out by me when I went to a shelter, and I read—'

Graham turned to the boy. 'I don't know anything about psychopaths. But I do know something – rest break's over.'

Alex, looking disheartened, walked over to the weights trolley, picked up a 20-kg kettlebell, and started performing swings the way Graham had shown him.

'Hey, Graham,' Alex asked mid-swing, 'did you have any kids?'

'Push your hips back!' Graham spat. 'No time for chit chat!'

Yoddi entered wearing a wide-brimmed hat and a white dress as though she had just been to the races. 'I brought you boys some morning tea.' She smiled, holding up a basket.

The three of them sat outside. Graham raided the basket. 'My favourite!' He chuckled in delight when he found Yoddi's homemade pumpkin scones. 'Thanks, babe.'

'Babe?' Yoddi smirked.

'You wanted me to come up with a better way to introduce you … you know, with my vocabulary and all. The kids use babe. Which suits, because you darn well are a babe too.'

Graham munched on his scone while Yolanda kept watching him with a smile on her face.

'How did you guys meet?' Alex asked.

Yoddi still smiled, but something about her expression looked sadder.

'It's alright, you can tell the kid. Might distract him from his share of the scones.'

'I cared for Graham's wife, at the end,' Yoddi said softly. 'I was a palliative care nurse. Graham's wife, Judith, had lung cancer.'

'Then she stole me away, right in front of my dying wife. Her passion for me was uncontrollable.'

'Hush, you silly man. Graham was very sweet. He never left Judith's side. He did more of the work than I did. There were always flowers by the bed. The room was stacked with photo albums, and he would relive all those special moments with her on her good days. They had an undeniable bond. When she passed, I didn't think I would see Graham again. I retired and bought a home here in Tiddy Widdy. One day I bumped into Graham at the local RSL. Then again at one of my modelling shows for the CWA. The third time we bumped into each other he asked if I wanted to try golf. I never played so thought it would be a thrill. He was a bit of a show off to be honest. But after that he invited me to dinner. We have been very close friends ever since. It took me a while to realise he bumped into me on purpose. All three times.'

Alex noticed they were both holding hands.

'Okay, Alex, it's my turn to teach you something. Graham is right, exercise will help clear your mind, but so will this.' Yoddi moved closer to him and crossed her legs. 'It's called meditation.'

***

Where am I? Alex caught glimpses of himself dancing on a sticky floor. A liquid burned down his throat. His reflection in a dirty bathroom showed something unrecognisable. Makeup was smeared across his face. He retched. More dancing. Hard bodies pressed against him. His claustrophobia heightened until rough hands pulled him outside into the freezing cold. He noticed a sign out the front of the building. The Black Dragon. His nose ran like a tap and his teeth chattered. He shivered for hours until he lost track of time altogether.

A Toyota Crown Super Saloon pulled up out of the front of the club. Graham stumbled out of the car. Everyone turned at the sight of a man in his eighties stumbling groggily towards the club entrance in a dressing gown and slippers.

'Graham?' the man with the rough hands asked.

Graham nodded.

'ID please?'

Graham passed his licence to the man. 'You alright, Alex?' Graham asked

'Shouldn't have come. Silly me,' Tony mumbled in his robotic voice.

Graham rubbed Tony's back. 'Let's get you home, my boy.'

'Hold up! The freak has damaged property which needs to be rectified.'

'What do I owe?'

'Five hundred, at least.'

'I don't have any money on me, but I can come back tomorrow and pay. You have my car registration now if I don't.'

The man seemed satisfied with that and appeared relieved when he and Tony moved away from the club. Graham helped Tony into the car. They had been driving for 10 minutes before Alex jerked awake, looking around anxiously.

'I'm sorry, I've lost time again.' Alex sulked.

'Are you hurt?' Graham asked.

Alex patted himself down but couldn't feel anything wrong. 'I don't think so.'

Graham sighed in relief. 'That's good.'

Alex took a look at the old man in the driver's seat. There were dark rings around his eyes, and he had lost weight.

'You can't keep doing this,' Alex said. 'I'm too much for you. I can see the toll it's taking.'

'My dear boy, you've read it all wrong. I'm having the time of my life.'

They were silent for a long time.

'Graham? Why am I like this? What happened to me?'

Graham patted Alex's lap. 'I had a son. A beautiful boy.' Graham smiled, 'He died when he was not much older than you.'

'How did he die?' Alex asked weakly.

'Car accident. He was driving. Sadly, he was lost to us, along with three of his mates. When he was gone … I … just struggled to let go. The car was totalled but I put it back together piece by piece. This old thing came back from trauma. Maybe you will too.'

'I'm so sorry.'

'We move on.' Graham shrugged. 'What's the point in going through life bloody miserable?'

CHAPTER 17

NOW

Tony: *Tony doesn't think we should trust anyone in here. Here for a reason. Is that what they say? Tony can be sceptical. Especially someone involved in the event.*

Alex: *Event?*

Tony: *The event that caused the dissociation. Tony can't help but wonder who would exist if Tony didn't. Would parts of all of us become one person? Would that be functional? Are other people that complex?*

Alex had waited an hour and a half for Mike's contact and he was beginning to get nervous. He avoided speaking to any other prisoners and kept his head down as he searched for Mike. The only place he hadn't checked was the shower block. He was surprised by the lack of guards on his way. He constantly checked behind him for any felons lurking in the shadows. Biblical verses were printed on the walls. Passages of salvation and forgiveness pressed against the corners of his sight. He heard whispers when he arrived at the changerooms. Discreetly, he peered in and found Mike surrounded by the Watson gang. They had cornered the big man. Mike looked pale.

Alex silently stepped back and turned around. He decided the best bet was to head back out to the courtyard. But something stopped him.

I truly am crazy, he concluded. *What could I possibly do against three of them?*

Lewis: *Two against three.*

Alex walked away.

'I'm too old for this shit,' spat Mike.

'What'choo get involved for then?' Todd spat back.

'He's my cellmate, and I don't need any trouble in this place, alright? The kid is mentally irregular, we all know that, why pummel him?' Mike reasoned.

Todd held something behind his back. Mike couldn't understand why he was hiding it. He could clearly see the reflection of a filed down toothbrush in the mirror.

'Get it over with then,' sneered Mike.

A shower started running. Lewis appeared, naked. His posture was taller, and his build appeared more muscular; his shoulders broad, chest lifted, rib cage expanded. His movements more confident.

Lewis whistled and started lathering soap over his body in the open showers opposite the change rooms.

Todd grimaced. 'Dumb fuck.'

The three prisoners pounced. Mike didn't have time to react. It was never going to be a fair fight. Todd grabbed Lewis by the arm, but his hand slipped from the soap and he took a knee to the groin. He was stunned by the sudden attack; the pain shot all the way up to his throat.

His slightly heavier-set friend reached for Lewis next, but he slipped on the wet floor. He tried swinging at Lewis on his way down, but Lewis ducked, turned the cold water off, and scolded the two attackers. Todd just stood there. Eventually he took action and lunged at Lewis, who used his momentum against him and swung him into the tiled wall. The group was slower on the second attack, each time they reached for him their hands slipped off his soaped-up naked body. Mike watched Lewis slide around as he took his time landing punches in groins and throats. When the three men were on the ground coughing and spluttering, Lewis washed off the last of the suds and turned the shower off. While naked, he straddled Todd and grabbed him by the scrotum.

'You wanted to hurt *me? Look at me.* What the fuck could you possibly do that hasn't already been done?'

Lewis forced him to look at his scars.

Todd's subordinates were out cold.

Todd laughed. 'You act like a tough guy. I can see it. You're a fake. You're not one of us. A pussy cat.'

Mike shuffled his feet, unsure what to do. He met Lewis's gaze for a moment. Then he had to turn away. He heard a mighty scream. When he turned around, Todd was sobbing on the floor while Lewis put his clothes back on and walked slowly towards Mike. He stopped a foot away from him and looked up at the old man. With a flash, Lewis pressed the sharp edge of the toothbrush against Mike's neck.

'You were with them.' Lewis sneered. 'The fuckers that gave me these.' Lewis lifted his shirt to reveal his scars.

'I was just a driver, nothing more. I moved you from one place to another—nothin' else. You were the last. I didn't have the heart for it.'

'And here we are together again. Maybe I'll just leave you with a few scars of your own.'

Mike tried to take a deep breath. 'Do what you gotta do, kid.'

'I'm no fucking kid.'

'You helped me, Lewis, so there's good in you.'

Lewis looked back at the mess of Todd. 'No, there's really not. Find a way to stay away from Alex, or you will regret it.' He dropped the shiv and walked off.

'Lewis – Alex just wants to know why he's here. He's trying to reach someone named Graham!' Mike called out.

Alex: *Lewis, what have you done?*

Lewis: *We're here forever, Alex. Graham's not coming for us.*

CHAPTER 18

THEN - October 2004

Alex couldn't remember how he got in the car with Graham, but his back was stiff as though he'd been sitting awkwardly in the car seat for hours.

'Alex?' Yolanda was sitting in the back with him.

'Where are we going?' Alex asked.

Yoddi held his hand and smiled warmly.

'We're going to introduce you to someone.' Graham smiled back in the rear vision mirror.

Alex struggled to recollect the last few hours.

'Is it your memory, Alex?' Yoddi asked.

Alex nodded. Yoddi noted the control he had over his emotions since his time with them.

'Do you understand why you're losing time?'

'Not really.' Alex sniffed.

'Have you heard of dissociative identity disorder?' Yoddi asked quietly.

'It sounds familiar. I've been given lots of different diagnoses—'

'We know. But we think this may be a large part of your life. DID requires long term treatment, which makes it difficult and expensive to study. It's not really a priority in mental health research.'

'What is it, exactly?'

'DID is a result of childhood trauma. Your brain has found a remarkable way to move on with your life. But it comes with its challenges. Lost time—'

'Voices.'

'More pronounced than voices. The voices have identities of their own.'

'Let the boy breathe,' interrupted Graham. 'This is going to be difficult to understand, Alex, but we've found someone that could help.'

Graham and Yoddi didn't say much more, despite the barrage of questions. Graham pulled into a car park. Alex read a blue and yellow sign: Sunnydale Community Assistance Village.

The building looked like an aged care centre. Windows overlooked small garden beds with various garden gnomes and ceramic animals. A group of people, young and old, were playing bocce on a patch of artificial lawn. It was a warm day in the afternoon sun but most of the players wore cardigans.

They made their way inside and Graham signed in at reception. The woman at the desk gave them each a visitor badge. Alex watched Graham attach it to the pocket on his shirt and then did the same. Yoddi took interest in the community noticeboard: 'maintenance workers wanted', 'community market next week', 'win tickets to a drag show', 'come and try embroidery'.

'You boys go ahead. I'll use the time to get some bits and pieces done.' Yolanda gave Graham a kiss and found a seat in the cafeteria. Graham walked down the hallway as if he had been here before. They heard moaning and groaning and eventually passed the source of the noise: a man with pitch-black hair rocking back and forth on his bed.

'Are we at a psychiatric hospital?' Alex whispered.

'Not exactly,' Graham said as he looked for a room number. 'This is more of a half-way house. Ah! Paula!'

A well-dressed, middle-aged woman stood in front of room number 48. She smiled when she saw Graham. 'Hello, Graham, nice to see you again. This is Alex?'

Graham clapped Alex on the back. 'I haven't filled him in yet. Was afraid I might lose him again.'

Paula seemed to understand what he meant. She looked deep into Alex's eyes. He felt like she was searching for a soul. 'Hi, Alex. My name is Paula. I work with someone very special. Now she's a little unsure about strangers, so I'm going to be in the room too.'

'I think you should speak with her, Alex,' Graham urged.

Paula opened the door to a plain room with a bed and a TV mounted in the corner. Sitting on the edge of the bed was a young woman. Alex figured she was around 20, but it was hard to tell; she could have been five years older *or* younger. Two pigtails were scrunched up in a bun on her head. Her clothes were bright. Multi-coloured socks were almost pulled up to her knees.

''Allo, Graham.' She smiled. 'Did you bring 'im this time?'

'I did, I did,' Graham said energetically. He ushered Alex inside and motioned for him to take a seat just in front of her. Graham sat on a chair next to Paula on the other side of the small room.

The girl watched Alex quizzically. He noticed thick white scars covering both of her fragile-looking forearms.

'Your name's Alex!' she said with glee. 'I'm Rochelle.'

'Hello, Rochelle. Graham, what do—'

'Rochelle has dissociative identity disorder, Alex. I thought speaking to you might be good for her.'

Alex turned back to her. He realised her eyes were red, as though she had only recently stopped crying. The smile on her face tried to hide it.

'Are you like me?' she asked hopefully.

He noticed that she wore four layers, possibly more. *She's so thin.*

'I don't know,' he said solemnly, feeling awkward with three sets of eyes on him. His face began to burn. Graham slumped in his seat.

'Are you alright, Graham?' Paula asked.

'Fine. Fine.' Graham coughed. 'It's been a long week, just feeling a little bit faint. Is there a bathroom somewhere where I could splash my face?'

Paula helped him out of the room and Alex caught a quick wink from Graham on the way past.

'Feel better soon, Graham,' Rochelle chortled.

When they left the room, her grin widened. 'He's a nice man.'

'Yeah, he is.'

'You're not what I expected,' she continued. 'You're bigger. And you have a tan. I thought you might look like me.'

Alex didn't know what to say.

'You don't talk much, do you?' she asked rhetorically. 'How many alters have ya got?'

Alters? Alex thought it was a weird term. But he knew what she meant. *The voices.*

'Ah …' Alex never thought of it like that. He supposed there were different voices. The gruff voice gave him a cold shiver down his back. The anxious voice was harder to understand. Then there was a quieter voice, someone younger. 'I think there are three,' he answered.

Rochelle tilted her head back and laughed. 'You would have a lot more than three! I have sixteen.'

'That would be really hard,' Alex said sympathetically.

Rochelle shrugged. 'Sometimes it is. Two of them are 16 and bulimic, so I'm in and out of hospital all the time. I guess you would be the same.'

'I live at the beach with Graham. He's never sent me to a hospital before.'

'Wow… Maybe-you-should-be-my-boyfriend-and-we-can-live-together,' she jumbled in excitement.

'No, thanks,' Alex said flatly.

Rochelle, a little crestfallen, scratched the scars on her forearm.

'How did you get those?' he asked.

She shrugged. 'I lose time a lot.'

'Me too. Once I woke up in a night club and Graham had to pick me up in the middle of the night in a dressing-gown.'

'Ha-ha. You're so lucky! I once woke up naked in some man's house covered in bites.'

'I broke into a psychiatric hospital without realising. Thought I was meeting a psychiatrist in the middle of the night, but it was all in my head.'

'Ha-ha!' Rochelle sniffed. 'You don't look crazy. How do you do it?'

'I've been able to reduce my medication over time. Maybe you should try it?'

'Tried that. I lost time for over two months and had to get my stomach pumped.'

'Well, I try to exercise every day. It seems to have the most benefits. And no side effects to worry about.'

'I used to too!' Rochelle shuffled forward on the bed with excitement. 'But then one of my alters just didn't stop running and they found me dehydrated on the side of the road. I was almost run over! I'm not allowed to exercise much now because that alter is addicted and takes over.'

Alex could no longer keep eye contact. He stared at her brightly coloured socks. 'I'm sorry.'

'Don't be sorry, you didn't do anything.'

'Is there some way I can help you?' Alex asked.

'You can visit me every now and then if you like? I'm always here if I'm not in hospital.'

'Always?'

'We all are. It's a cycle. Happy. Confused. Sad. Hospital. Repeat. I'm sure you're the same, just with jet skis instead of the hospital part.'

'We don't have jet skis.'

'That's a shame. What do you get to do with Graham?'

'I get to run on the beach most mornings. And Graham homeschools me. Teaches me all sorts of stuff. Even how to drive. I'm … lucky, I guess.'

'That's so coooool!'

Paula came back in, looking flustered. 'I think he's going to be fine. Everything okay in here?'

'Yip.' Rochelle nodded. 'Alex will come visit again, but there will be no sex!'

Paula shot a look at Alex. His face went red.

'I should go,' he said, excusing himself.

'Be careful, Alex!' Rochelle called out. 'Remember what I said!'

'What's that?'

'There will be more than three.'

Graham, Yolanda and Alex returned to the car and were quiet for a long time. Graham hoped Alex would speak first. Eventually he gave up. 'Well, how did it go?'

'She's not very well,' Alex said soberly.

'She's done everything she can to help herself. She's got the best care available to her. Even her NDIS funding is reasonable,' Yoddi explained.

'Then why is she struggling?'

'Because DID doesn't just go away,' Yoddi replied.

'She mentioned alters.' Alex looked down at his lap. 'When I lost time. Did you see … others?'

Graham looked at Alex carefully. 'Alex, since we've lived with each other, I've met … others. When you skinned your knee, I met a young girl … Julie. When I picked you up at the night club, I found Tony on the floor. And sometimes when you're in bed, I hear another voice. I hear—'

The name came to Alex.

'Lewis,' Alex mouthed. 'You hear Lewis. How did this happen?'

'I might have a way to find out,' Graham said guiltily. 'But it's not exactly standard practice for respite care.'

CHAPTER 19

NOW

Alex sensed a hidden danger at Harslett. It was a protective response he was becoming familiar with. But this felt worse, like a beast at slumber within its walls. Harslett Prison was eerily quiet in the evenings. Any prisoner who broke curfew was subjected to assault. The prison was known for its rules. Cells to be cleaned daily; staff addressed only when spoken to; guard to prisoner ratios upheld at all times; silence when lights are out. Even the most hardened criminals adhered to the rules eventually. Alex worried what it would take to wake the beast.

It took thunder.

Thunderstruck, by AC/DC, blasted from the speakers. Electronic gates in the cell block slid open. Running. Shouting. Alex re-took control of himself, forcing himself to recalibrate quickly after losing time again. Mike groaned. 'What's going on?' Mike asked, still half asleep.

The rock music began to incite the prisoners. Alex heard the electronic lock click on his cell. He pulled the door across. He was free. His instincts told him to be wary.

Prisoners clapped and cooed. Alarms were raised. The flashing red lights strobed across the cells once again. Doors around him opened.

'This is very, very bad,' Mike muttered.

Two prison guards bolted for the exit. A swarm of prisoners burst from their cells and charged towards them.

AC/DC's *Thunderstruck* played louder through the speakers along with the headache-inducing alarms. Prisoners and guards screamed and shouted. Toilet paper and bed sheets flew everywhere. A stampede of convicted criminals filled the hallway, following the guards towards the exit.

'What's harder to pull off than murders at the show? Or the airport?' Mike froze for a moment. Alex looked at him blankly. 'Okay, I'll tell you, boy. A maximum-security prison. Imagine the headlines.'

Alex didn't know what to think. But something was very wrong. Alex had witnessed the order and stability at Harslett. This level of chaos didn't make sense to him.

'Mike, we need to join them. *Now*.'

Mike's face was pale and he was sweating on the top bunk. 'I'm not feeling so good kid, you go.'

Alex yelled over the music, 'Mike. If this is anything like what's been happening in Adelaide, we can't afford to stay still.'

'No time for a hug and a kiss goodbye, I'm afraid.' Mike cleared his throat, 'I can't protect you anymore.'

'What?' Alex called out, struggling to hear over the music.

'They told me to keep you alive! Just … go! Go on, go!'

Alex took one last look at the hulking figure in the bed before he joined the human swarm.

He was pushed and prodded by those he slipped in front of. Up ahead he could see two prison guards ambushed by six or seven prisoners. The guards' cries could be heard above the commotion as their tormentors broke their legs and arms. Alex recognised the redhead.

Lewis: *That's fucking disgusting.*

Julie: *Swear jar! Not looking. Not looking. Not looking.*

Tony: *Cameras deactivated, gates malfunctioning, two different systems, doesn't compute.*

Alex kept his head down and followed the pack. He heard an explosion and looked behind him. A squadron of guards arrived in full riot gear. Tear gas was thrown into the growing group of inmates. Alex tried to push himself forward, away from the back of the pack.

The rising horde of prisoners pushed past the guards, who Alex assumed were dead. An older prisoner with bright orange hair bit into one of the guard's thighs like a wild animal settling for scraps. Alex avoided eye contact as he brushed past him. Torrents of water and tear gas hit the pack and Alex became disoriented. He stumbled and almost tripped over another prisoner, then forced himself against the wall to avoid becoming a victim of the violent stampede. The music continued to incite. The prisoners from the other block must also have been released – as another wave of prisoner uniforms could be seen ambushing an unfortunate team of guards wielding high-pressure hoses. Alex ducked as a riot shield flew through the air and hit the man next to him square on the chest.

Some faces Alex recognised, but he was mostly surrounded by a sea of strangers, on the winning side in a battle with rubber bullets and rock music. Some prisoners cried out in pain when a rubber bullet took them down. But the growing swarm of criminals was too enraged, and there were too many, and they pushed forward with violent malice.

Alex felt safer squished in among the vicious rioters. The sound of helicopters and cars alerted them that more men were coming. Alex thought the group had the same thought, like a hive mind … *We won't escape, but we can cause a fuck tonne of damage…*

Alex stepped over several mutilated guards. Prisoners were smashing windows in the offices as they headed towards solitary confinement, seeking anyone else left to join the fray. Alex was getting pushed forward by men behind him when he saw an open office with computers. He forced himself to break away from the fragile safety of the herd and headed for the office space.

The lights were out in the office but he found a desktop that hadn't been signed out. He quickly googled for recent arrests in Tiddy Widdy and Ardrossan. A recent news story came up. He checked again to see if he was alone before he clicked the link.

> *Graham Blakemore, a centenarian, died on the evening of his birthday under suspicious circumstances. A 29-year-old male suspect has been arrested in suspicion of Mr Blakemore's death and is currently awaiting trial at Harslett Prison. Graham Blakemore was a highly decorated serviceman and was one of the last remaining World War II veterans in South Australia. He was a police officer, provided respite services for troubled youth and ...*

A lump began to rise in Alex's throat. The words on the page became blurry. He collapsed to the ground, feeling giddy. *It can't be.* Another stampede of prisoners came in and started rustling up table legs and shards of glass as weapons before they charged ahead. Alex fought back tears. *There must be a mistake.*

Lewis: *It's true.*

Alex: *No. No!*

More prisoners jumped into the office and started breaking furniture. He rolled out of the way just as his table flipped over. Skinheads grinned when they saw Alex pick himself up off the floor.

'Julie! Hello, Julie! Hi, Julie!' they all cried out in unison.

Julie: *They said I was pretty.*

Lewis: *If you were a real girl, you would be the ugliest motherfuc—*

Alex's heart fluttered in his chest. He recognised these men. The Stinkers. He should never have lost control in this place.

Julie should never have come out. But her personality had attracted these men. The four men looked like skeletons. Their skin was deathly pale, their eyebrows waxed to a thin line of hair that could have been drawn on with a pencil, and their eyes were bloodshot, all of them showing cases of conjunctivitis. They were breathing heavily, survivors of the chaos. Alex took the opportunity to rush them while they were still recovering from the last brawl. One of the Stinkers in the back lifted something and Alex fell backwards. It was a gun. A rubber bullet hit him in the ribs, and he yelled out in pain.

The Stinkers chuckled and dragged him to the back of the room. The one that shot Alex vomited in a waste bin. The others ignored him as they watched Alex with glee and took off their pants. Alex looked around for a weapon, but there was nothing. He was winded from the rubber bullet. Moving was difficult for him. One of the Stinkers stumbled towards him, tried to regain his balance, but fell on top of him. Alex could smell the stench of blood and tear gas on his clothes. Alex's eyes bulged and he went limp with terror. Someone else vomited. The music stopped. The Stinker on top of him started convulsing. He pushed him off and saw the other three men on the ground, covered in their own blood and vomit. He looked back at the article on the screen. *Graham Blakemore ... died on the evening of his birthday.*

Lewis: *It's true. I saw the light go out of his eyes. I thought maybe it was a nightmare. It's why I didn't want the control anymore. Graham's dead.*

Guards rushed in, taking in the scene of dead bodies. They found Alex at the back of the room. They thought they were witnessing an exorcism. Four distinct voices wailed and wept in a blubbering symphony from the one body. Guards watched in disbelief as Alex's body distorted itself as his posture shifted from one alter to the next. Alex's joints began to internally rotate and he couldn't sit still. His vacant gaze was directed to the floor. He showed signs of autistic distress. His rocking became more violent, and he started hurting himself. The guards gathered themselves and rushed towards him.

Alex: *Did I kill him?*

Lewis: *I dunno. Maybe.*

Alex saw a baton come up close and everything went black.

CHAPTER 20

THEN - October 2004

Alex couldn't believe Graham had found someone from his past. He didn't believe it until it almost tore him apart. He could only see the back of the man's head as he tapped away at his laptop at one of the booths in the bar of the Stamford Plaza Hotel. Alex recognised it as a PowerBook G4. Alex played on a pinball machine in the room opposite. He wanted to sneak into the bar and take a closer look, at least to see his face, but he remembered Graham's instructions. *Stay away from the man at all costs.*

From Alex's position he could just make out an Excel spreadsheet that had both English and Chinese characters filling up various tables. Several empty packets of chips littered the glass-top table of the booth. The man ordered another bottle of expensive-looking red wine from one of the young female bartenders with a low-cut top before he continued with his calculations.

The bar was filled with sleazy customers and cocky young businessmen drinking and chatting up the female staff.

'Hey, sweetheart, how are you today?' Boomed Graham's voice.

Alex watched Graham enter the bar from outside, neither of them taking any notice of each other.

'Christ almighty, when did a bloody beer get so expensive?' Graham was easily the loudest in the bar and turned a few heads.

The man watched Graham try to chat up various staff, but they politely moved away from him as soon as they could. Eventually Graham made his way to the man at the booth.

'Hey there, mate, if you can guess my age, give or take 10 years, I'll buy you another one of those,' he challenged him.

Alex saw the man rise from his seat, then changed his mind and sat back down.

'Seventy-three?'

Graham slapped his licence on the table. Alex knew that it read: GRAHAM BLAKEMORE DOB: 8/8/1919

'You're 85-years-old? Is this fake?'

'Quick maths, my boy. You know your numbers,' Graham complimented. 'Nobody here would let me buy them a drink. You were wrong but I'll still get you another one of those for some company?'

Graham reached back into his pocket and pulled out a thick wad of $100 bills. Alex put another coin in the slot, and the next pinball was released on the *Ghostbusters* machine.

The two men shared a drink. Graham tried to keep up, but the man started ordering shots and cocktails with Graham's cash.

'We have a lot to learn from your generation. And you certainly don't look your age. What's your secret?' The man asked as he drained his cocktail.

'Well, first off, what do you do?' Graham asked.

'Researcher,' he said and stretched.

Graham waved over a waitress and ordered two more.

'Does it make you happy?' Graham asked.

'Wealthy.'

'That's not what I asked. I've met plenty of rich, miserable people. Does it fulfill you, what you do?'

A young woman with short dark hair and flowery tattoos on her arms and waist served them their drinks. She winked at Graham as she gave him another small glass of vodka. The man received full view of her cleavage as she reached over and slid another martini in front of him. He watched her go.

'Why does it matter? It's a job. It keeps this ticking away.' He tapped his forehead.

'That's good,' Graham started. 'Research is important. The knowledge provides progress to our race. What's your field?'

'Psychology.'

'Fantastic. My niece is a child psychologist. Do you get to work with children much?' Graham asked.

Their voices had gotten quiet, more slurred, but Alex could still pick up what they were saying. He lost another ball in the game as he concentrated hard on the conversation.

'I sure am proud of her. Helping people gives me more pleasure than any other vice ever could. Trust me, I've tried.' Graham chuckled.

Graham patted the man on the lap. 'Tell you what though, the bladder certainly isn't what it used to be. I could fill a bucket back in my day, now a cup of tea makes my knees wobble.'

The old man nodded as Graham excused himself. Graham stumbled on his way up and used the wall to help guide himself to the bathroom. A security guard kept an eye on him as he left.

Alex started getting worried. It had been several minutes and Graham hadn't come out. Just as Alex was about to go in and check on him, Graham stepped out of the bathroom. Although Alex was directly in his line of sight, Graham avoided eye contact and made his way back to the booth. As the same waitress placed their drinks on the table, Alex noticed Graham's sleight of hand. He placed something, he assumed the man's wallet, back on the seat from under the table.

'You have a lot of questions, old man, but you didn't answer mine. What's your secret to staying young at heart?' The man asked.

Graham downed his last drink. Alex thought he looked pale and unwell. He had never seen him drink alcohol before. He started to realise why Graham had taken so long in the bathroom.

'I don't know about any secrets, but I didn't remarry. So, I don't have the mental strain.' Graham chuckled to himself, slammed his glass down and walked away.

Graham made his way towards Alex. When he was close enough that Alex could smell vomit, Graham brushed passed him, ignoring him. Alex felt something slide into his pocket.

Alex wasted no time strolling through the Stamford Plaza Hotel, knowing exactly where the lifts were located. It wasn't long until he was on the 20th floor and made it to Room 203; a bottle of sparkling red wine sat on a serving tray in a bucket of melting ice.

Alex used the key card Graham had passed him discreetly and let himself in without delay. The room was fancy and spacious and could have quite easily suited several couples. He checked all the rooms first, anxious that someone else may have been present. But the two bedrooms and two living areas were empty. The room was largely untouched, so he assumed whoever was lodging here had not been here for long. His job was simple enough – find any electronics or paperwork and grab them. Just like he had done many times before.

The first bedroom was empty of any personal items, but the second bedroom had several suits hung up in the wardrobe. The welcome letter on the bed side table was addressed to Cheng Mah. There was a safe in the built-in wardrobe. *This is way out of my skill set*. Voices started to creep into his head like a throbbing headache, but Alex started to recognise the different voices.

Desk. Desk. Desk.

Alex: *You're Tony, aren't you?*

Alex focussed on the job at hand, but the voices got louder and louder. He blocked his ears as if he was trying to shield himself from a loud noise. He pictured Tony in his mind and let him embrace him.

A moment later, he found himself running down the stairs two at a time with a manila folder. Most of the words were in Chinese but Alex didn't care, he was just glad to get out of the room.

When Alex made it to the lobby, he started feeling anxious. Voices spoke in his head simultaneously, making them incoherent. He ran faster, attempting to silence them so he could concentrate. He banged into a man and a laptop fell to the floor. Alex slowly looked up. He made eye contact for the first time with the man he had stolen from.

Time slowed for Alex. The face looked familiar, but he couldn't place it. Hair on the back of his neck prickled. Goosebumps covered his skin. His breathing suddenly became forced. Alex tried to keep going but he was frozen to the spot.

The man, purple faced in anger, saw the paperwork in Alex's hands and his eyes went wide.

Then Alex let out an ear-piercing scream. Everyone turned. Cheng stuck his hand out and grabbed Alex by the shoulders. Alex could not control his crying. His body felt heavy. The man looked around anxiously at all the onlookers checking in and out of the hotel.

Another voice: *Christ's sake! Get your shit together or I will!*
Alex: *Lewis?*

Alex saw the Toyota Crown Super Saloon pull up out the front of the hotel in the pick-up zone. Yoddi was behind the wheel. Graham got out of the back seat and gasped when he saw Alex in the man's grasp.

The voices became louder for Alex. He had no control over them. He couldn't explain it, but he knew this man was dangerous. He knew he needed to retreat into his shell. *Give the voices something to do. They could take the pain for me.*

A car horn blasted loud enough over the screaming voices in his head. Alex turned and saw Yoddi honking the horn. Cheng tried pulling him away from the open. The fear brought a metallic taste to Alex's mouth. Something in his chest constricted.

Run!

Alex closed his eyes, and the voices took control.

'No!' He heard Graham cry out.

There was nothing Alex could do. Cheng was strong and started pulling him towards a narrow corridor.

Lewis: *Alex! You need to let me do this.*

Then, like a sprinter at the sound of a gun, Alex's expression changed. The way he held himself changed. Cheng saw it. Lewis grunted and kicked the man in the shins, sprinting back down the lobby, grabbing the broken laptop on his way. Cheng stumbled after him but Lewis was too fast. He shoved himself through the revolving door and jumped into the back seat of the car. Graham got in and slammed the door behind him. The car took off with surprising speed.

Yoddi grimaced. 'Hold on, you two!'

Yolanda manoeuvred the gears with expert precision as she treated the classic car like a high-performance vehicle on a bank heist getaway. Lewis and Graham slid back and forth in the back seat.

'Jesus Christ, woman! Will you stop showing off!' Graham roared. 'The boy's going to start thinking you're the better driver.'

Lewis watched the man curse from the back window. He gave him the finger.

Lewis: *Sucker.*

The whistle blew on the old-fashioned kettle. Yolanda poured teas while Alex and Graham sat opposite each other in awkward silence.

'What the hell did I just do?' Alex stammered. 'Am I going to get in trouble?'

Graham looked pained as Yoddi handed him his tea.

'I put you in harm's way, my boy,' Graham said shame-faced. 'A terrible idea on my behalf, and it won't happen again. I don't blame you if you want to leave. Actually, I blame Yoddi for this really.'

'Me?!'

'You're the sensible one. You should have stopped me.'

'The boy needs to know who you are, Graham.' Yoddi placed a hand on his shoulder.

'What does she mean?' Alex asked.

Graham sighed.

'Graham helps his community in a very special way,' Yoddi interjected. 'His skillset, besides talking shit, was developed during his career after service.'

'What were you?' Alex asked.

Graham sighed again and looked into Alex's eyes with a stern gaze. 'Not a lot of people know this, kiddo. But I was renowned in my time. One of the best. I was a gigolo.'

'Oh, for Christ's sake, Graham! If anyone is a gigolo here it should be me. This silly man was a detective,' Yoddi explained.

The words sobered everyone in the room.

'Whose laptop did I steal?' Alex looked over at the broken device on the table.

'Not sure yet. A suspect in a child trafficking cold case. I've been looking into your history since before we met.'

'You're still a detective?' Alex pushed.

'Well, yes and no.' Graham started to look uncomfortable. 'Retired is a strong word. I don't see why people just stop doing things at some random age. I'm a private investigator.'

'Wait. You're not joking anymore?' Alex gaped. 'How many cases have you solved?'

'You would have to look at my little black book.' Graham pointed to the book stashed in his kitchen. 'I keep all my client's details in that. Just in case.'

Yoddi smiled. 'He said it was for his girlfriends, didn't he?'

'How much money have you made doing this?' Alex asked.

'Very little. I don't work for money, never have. Sounds like a stressful way to live.'

'So, you're … trying to find out what happened to me?'

'A foolish endeavour, I know. I look into small cases for people who can't afford help or don't know how to ask for it. Cheating husbands, long-lost relatives, domestic violence, that sort of thing. Not this.'

Alex didn't know what to say. Voices came again, but they weren't as loud. He tried to focus them.

Alex: *One at a time.*

Lewis: *Tell the fuckin' old codger to get his own evidence next time.*

Julie: *I think you should say thank you.*

Tony: *Tony thinks he's a nice man. Tony's a good judge and jury of character. He's a nice character.*

'Can I see what you do?' Alex asked Graham.

Graham hated himself for what he did to Alex.

Graham shot Yoddi a forlorn look. She gave him the slightest of nods.

CHAPTER 21

NOW

Alex wanted to stay in the dark vacuum of space where he could remain detached from his fractured reality. But he was powerless to do even that. Alex regained consciousness handcuffed to a bed in the infirmary ward. His throat was sore. He recognised the beginning of a flu. He could taste blood in his mouth. The ward was empty except for Mike lying unconscious on the bed next to him. His thoughts drifted back to Graham and the grief overwhelmed him.

'Don't beat yourself up. Graham wouldn't have lived much longer anyway.' Martin's soft voice echoed across the small ward.

Alex strained against the chain securing his left wrist to the bed frame as he tried sit up. Martin sat across from him on a visitor's chair.

'What's happening to me?' Alex whined. 'How could I ever—'

'Your emotional distress is blocking your unique ability to take stock of a situation. You need to open up your mind. To remember.'

'Remember what?'

'Me, for starters.' Martin stood and started pacing back and forth. 'You need to solve the case, Alex. It's always about the case with you. You have been here for almost a month. Now tell me, who is the Showstopper?'

'What has that got to do with this—'

'Everything!' Martin's voice was raised. 'You say you don't supress your memories, but you are the alter that supresses everything.'

'No, I—'

'No? Adelaide Airport. Festival Theatre. The Royal Show. The Markets. Can you tell me where you were during the attacks?'

'Here.'

Martin dismissed him with a wave of his hand. 'No. The attacks happened before you found yourself here.'

Alex forced a laugh. 'I'm not the Showstopper. It has nothing to do with me.'

'The Showstopper was here, Alex. Do you know who was killed? Of course you do. The so-called Stinkers and the Watson gang. Poisoned. You had trouble with them, did you not? Even Mike here gave you grief once upon a time. It appears he had a smaller dose. That larger body of his must have saved him.'

'No, no, no … Get out of my head!'

'You spend most of your life waking up, Alex. You lose time *all* the time. You recognised it in yourself long ago – it's why I exist. You, Alex, are the Showstopper.'

Alex went numb. 'Shut up. Shut up. Shut up.'

'What makes this so difficult to believe?'

'Graham,' Alex mumbled. 'Graham knew I wasn't psychotic! He knew I was good. I was good with him.'

Martin put a hand on Alex's shoulder. 'My dear boy, Graham found out, so you *killed* him.'

'No!' Tears streamed down Alex's face. 'You're wrong. I'm not capable of planning any of that.' Alex slurred his words.

'I saw you escape your cell and move around this prison with no planning, no tools, just your alters. You have talent.'

'I'm not capable of murder.'

'Would you be capable of killing the ones that hurt you in your past?'

'I don't know anything about that. I don't know who they are. I would never be able to find them.'

Martin put his hands in his pockets. 'You had it all, Alex. Cheng Mah. Do you know that name? You stole his laptop once upon a time. Didn't you?'

Tony: *You dropped it, remember? Little bit clumsy, Tony thought.*

'No, I dropped it. Graham tried to use it but it was busted.'

Alex's stomach became queasy. He remembered the day he ran into Cheng. But he couldn't remember all of it. He started to doubt himself. *Did I lose time in his room?*

'You found something though, didn't you? Or perhaps an alter found something? The dark thing that lives in you kept it – *used* it – when the time came to find them. That other alter … hidden deep inside you.'

Alex started to rock back and forth, but Tony did not come out. Alex would not allow himself to lose time. Not now.

'The extravagance of the murders, the locations. Blinding authorities to what this really is. Revenge killing for your past. Lewis is not your protector, Alex, I am. I keep the details until you are ready for them.'

'No. No. No,' Alex whined. 'It's impossible. This place has fucked me up. I haven't had any control since I arrived. The riots. They weren't me. It was someone else.'

Martin laughed. 'That someone else is inside of you. That's the point. The time for denial is over. Now you can fulfil your potential, Alex. You have always been proficient at pickpocketing.'

Martin placed a small key into Alex's right hand. Alex's heart began to race. Martin began to hum. Alex shuffled over to the handcuff and fumbled with the key until he heard a *clink*. He rose off the bed and took in the room. The ward had three beds, the end one vacant. Mike was hooked up to a patient monitor, his heart rate slow and steady. Alex wasn't attached to anything except the handcuff. He assumed he was on psych watch. But there was no one watching. The office next door was empty and the security room adjacent was unmanned.

'Freedom, my boy, is knowing who you truly are. Imagine your power if you took control of all of your alters. This place was never a match for you. Now you have one final task.'

His words made Alex dizzy and exhausted. 'What task?'

Martin looked across at the bed. Alex followed his gaze. Mike's breathing was slow and steady, and Alex could see the gentle flaring of his cell mate's nostrils.

'It's time,' Martin said. He placed the toothbrush shiv from Todd Watson into Alex's hands.

Alex weighed the crude weapon in his hands. It was like holding nothing at all. Graham had raised him to become whomever he wanted to be. And in this infirmary, in this prison, Alex was understanding what that was. It revolted him.

'You expect me to kill him?' Alex grimaced at the spectre that considered himself a protector and threw the shiv to the ground.

Martin picked it up. 'I see the disgust in your face, Alex. There are two options that I see. You accept what you are and kill the insult on that bed. Or you end things yourself and kill the Showstopper.'

Alex took another look at Mike, who was beginning to stir. Alex didn't remember taking the shiv back, but it was trembling in his hands. He started to hyperventilate.

'Do it now, before he wakes.' Martin urged.

Between staggered breaths Alex put the shiv to his own throat.

It's what Graham would have wanted. Take down the killer. Kill the one who killed him. I deserve it.

The blade cut into Alex's skin. Graham's laughter came into his head. He screamed and threw it across the room.

'You see? The voices protect you, Alex.' Martin pressed his face against his. '*I* protect you. If you won't kill yourself, then accept yourself. *Kill him.*'

'No!' Alex yelled in defiance and punched Martin in the face.

Martin fell backwards.

Alex was shaken. Graham had put so much into him. And he had let him down. Sharp pain ran through his fist. He ignored it and sobbed. He had let everyone down. The control he thought he had didn't exist. Never did … *Why did that hurt so much?* He looked down at his hand; his knuckles were red and swollen. *It doesn't make sense.* Martin rose from the floor and picked up the shiv. He knew then. *My fist would only hurt … if Martin was real.*

His body turned to ice. Alex was frozen to the spot. He watched Martin lunge towards him with unsettling speed. Then the shiv drove into his own belly. He looked down at his blood-soaked hands.

'I told you to stay away from the darkness,' Martin whispered. 'But you were drawn to it. Instead of achieving anything you tried to play hero, blatantly opposing what I had done.' Martin pulled out the shiv and Alex felt cool liquid run down his legs. He slid down against the bed. Everything happened in slow motion. Martin pressed the shiv into Mike's hands, who began to wake. Martin removed a pair of bloodied transparent gloves and stuffed them into his pocket.

'You … killed all of them … and … Graham …' Alex managed.

'Help!' Martin called out, pushing an emergency button on Mike's bed.

'What's happening?' Mike blinked.

Martin moved back to Alex and held him in his arms. 'And many, many more,' Martin whispered. 'Now you've faced your fears, showed strength. I tried to break you in here, but you defied me at every turn. Now it's time to let you go.'

Alex felt faint. The double doors busted open. Security and nurses ran in. Alex ignored them. Something else caught his attention before the double doors swung shut. A framed picture outside the ward. It was a photo of Martin with a title underneath: **Martin Harslett – Director.**

'Are you alright, Mr Harslett?' asked a guard.

Tony: *His prison ... His prison ... He is the director. Owns the whole facility. He unlocked the cells. Poisoned the prisoners. Set up the music.*

Lewis: *I would never have hurt Graham, Alex.*

Alex: *I know, I know.*

Julie: *We loved him.*

Alex: *We will see him soon. I'm sorry I doubted ... all of you.*

Someone Unknown: *Rest, sweetie. I've got you.*

Darkness overcame them all.

CHAPTER 22

THEN - November 2004

Graham and Alex were welcomed into a stunning two-storey home by the concerned looking parents. Alex wasn't following the introductions. He was in awe of the opulence. The expansive hallway with chandelier lights. The indoor swimming pool. The owners, Phillip and Maria, directed them to a living area with a 14-seater modular lounge next to a wall-to-ceiling fireplace.

'We have spoken to the headmaster several times,' Phillip said.

'They clearly don't want to take responsibility!' Maria added.

'The police were useless. Just wrote a report every time and said they will look into it. They don't fucking do anything,' Phillip spat.

'They passed your information on to me.' Graham smiled.

'What is it exactly you do again?' Maria asked, as she crossed her legs.

'Oh, I'm a private investigator. Semi-retired though for 30-odd years, but the police still think of me every now and then. I assure you I'm not looking for any money out of this, and I thank you for allowing us into your home.'

The middle-aged couple looked over at Alex. He sat awkwardly in another outdoor chair.

'Your helper for the day?' Maria asked patronisingly.

'My grandson,' Graham answered. 'My eyes for the day. Now I would like to know a little more about Thomas. You said over the phone he was autistic?'

'Yes, like I said, the school used to cater for him very well, but in this last year we've noticed bruising at bath time. Whenever we ask him about it, he … becomes hard to settle,' Phillip explained.

'What is Thomas into?' Graham asked.

'Trains. He can tell you everything there is to know about trains. He knows the metro timetable off by heart and can recall every model of train in existence.'

'Trains! Lovely!' Graham noted this down. 'What does his routine look like on a typical day?'

Phillip looked at Maria, who answered, 'He's up at 5 am and watches TV. We always have to get him to turn it down, and remind him the other boys are still sleeping—'

'Could I use the bathroom?' Alex interrupted.

Phillip led Alex down another hallway and showed him where to find the guest bathroom. Phillip returned to Graham and Maria, and Alex climbed the stairs, following the sound of an episode of *National Geographic*.

Thomas looked the same age as Alex. His posture was rigid as he sat on a bean bag, less than a foot away from an old TV. The room was filled with posters of trains. Alex knocked on his open door, but Thomas did not respond. Alex sat on the floor next to him and crossed his legs, looking at Thomas, who gave no response. Thomas was deathly pale, with a wide jaw and small eyes. Alex let himself go to the voices. His posture changed, he stared at the floor and scratched his head.

'My name's Tony,' Tony began. 'Tony with a T, just like you Thomas, like the tank engine. I've watched that show.'

'Thomas the Tank Engine was from The Railway Series novels, published in 1945. I've read them all,' Thomas said, not taking his eyes off the screen.

'Animal Farm and Stuart Little, I've read.'

'Yes, they were published in 1945 too,' Thomas said, scratching his nose.

Alex walked outside and joined the others.

'Oh, here he is.' Graham clapped Alex on the back, 'Well, thank you both for your time. Do you mind if I speak with Thomas?'

'Thomas is in one of his moods today,' Maria said. 'Perhaps tomorrow?'

'No problem. Let me speak with the school, and we will reconvene tomorrow lunch time. Would that be okay? If you think of anything else in the meantime, here's my card.'

Maria took the tattered card. The printing had started to fade, and she squinted to make out the lettering. 'Blakemore Investigations?' she read aloud.

'That's me.' Graham grinned.

Graham and Alex got in the car and waved as Phillip and Maria saw them off.

'Lovely house,' Graham commented. 'You and I would be quite comfortable there I would imagine.'

'It's the mother,' Alex said bluntly.

'I'm sorry?'

'Phillip goes jogging every second night. For the last 12 months the mother has been hurting him. The boys have seen it, but they're too scared to say anything.'

'How do you know this?'

Alex shrugged. 'Thomas told me.'

'He spoke to you?' Graham took his eyes off the road and turned to Alex in surprise.

'Not exactly. Tony communicated with him.'

Graham pulled over. 'Tony did?'

Alex nodded.

'And Tony told you?'

'I can communicate with them better now.'

Graham nodded and turned back onto the highway.

***

Alex and Graham were in a small unit north of Adelaide. Two sisters greeted them when they arrived and offered them juice. The eldest sister fussed more than the younger one. The low ceilings made her above-average height stand out. She was in her early twenties but had the look of someone who had grown up too fast. Her younger sister was 9-years-old and could have been an identical twin if it wasn't for the age difference. The long mousy-brown hair, the button noses, even the freckles on their faces were almost indistinguishable.

'Thanks for inviting us, ladies.' Graham smiled as he accepted a juice from the older sister.

Alex eyed the younger sister, who looked intently at her mug of juice.

'Now what seems to be the problem?' Graham asked.

The eldest explained. 'I've been taking my sister to one of the doctors in town. A psychiatrist. He diagnosed her with Alice in Wonderland Disorder.'

'That must be very hard for you both. What does that mean, exactly, for your sister?'

'She has episodes every now and then. She complained about terrible migraines and believed her head and hands grew bigger some nights. I took her to this doctor.'

'And how did that go?' Graham asked.

'He diagnosed her, like I said, and started seeing her a lot. He didn't charge us much, was one of the only ones to bulk bill. But the episodes are getting more and more frequent. And she barely says anything anymore.'

'I gather you're very protective of your sister, so thank you for inviting us to your home. How exactly do you think I can help?'

'The police blew me off when I suggested the doctor might be … you know. I saw your card on the wall at the station and thought it would be worth a shot.'

'Definitely so. I think the best thing we can do is establish some trust with your sister. Penelope, isn't it?'

The younger sister recognised her name and looked at him for a split second before diverting her attention back to her mug. Graham wrote another name down in his black book.

'If it's alright with the both of you,' Graham continued, 'I would like to leave Alex alone with Penelope. He can be a fantastic communicator in special cases. After that I will do some digging into the doctor. No matter what we find, I will report back to you, and there will be no charge. Does that sound alright?'

Alex was left alone with the young girl. Voices began to overwhelm him. He let himself go and his legs started to swing in the chair. To Penelope, the transition appeared to be very slow, but a moment later Alex appeared younger in posture and expression. His voice became more feminine and child-like. *Julie*. They both giggled.

An hour later Graham was back in the car with Alex.

'Did she speak to you?' Graham asked

'Julie.'

'Should we pay a visit to her psychiatrist's office then?'

Julie: *The one with the collar does yucky things*.

'No,' Alex replied sadly, 'her church.'

***

Alex and Graham returned to the abandoned gym. The sheets were torn down and the mirrors revealed Alex's reflection from every angle. He closed his eyes, arms stretched out wide. He spun around the room, taking several deep breaths.

Lewis: *Why did you ever fear this?*

Tony: *Can you stop now? I'm getting dizzy. Tony's getting dizzy.*

Julie: *Can we get ice cream?*

Alex opened his eyes. His heart rate was elevated; the voices grew louder … but it did not disturb him. He walked over to the pin-loaded weight machines, remembering all the workouts he pushed himself through.

'We could construct an office space in here you know, get rid of the equipment? Are you sure about this?' Alex asked as he inspected the room.

'Yes, it's time to move on. You can't isolate yourself in Ardrossan forever. There's a big wide world out there. When you're ready, I'll help you find a place to live, somewhere closer to civilisation. But Tiddy Widdy, forever, will be your home. Of course, I'll charge you an exorbitant amount of rent.' Graham chuckled.

'As long as I can visit you and Yoddi,' Alex bargained.

'Visit? You'll be taking Yoddi with you too if I have it my way! Give me some peace and quiet.' Graham said as his phone began to vibrate. He jumped at the sound but answered quickly.

An old woman asked, 'Hello, is this Blakemore Investigations?'

Graham looked up at Alex. 'Yes. That's us,' Graham said proudly.

CHAPTER 23

NOW

Photographs of a 15-year-old boy violently beaten were examined and placed carefully on the table. A broken nose, cut lip, two black eyes, missing teeth, bloodied clothes – the brutality was evident. Martin licked his lips and shot a look at the small boy in front of him. He continued flipping through photographs: dead cat, dead puppy, and a burnt down horse stable. Martin stacked the photos on the table and sat back with his legs crossed. He admired his surroundings. He had been provided with the school counsellor's immaculate office each Friday afternoon for the last year. Various quotes printed on canvas hung from the walls:

Do unto others as you would have them do unto you. Matthew 7:12

With God, all things are possible. Matthew 19:26

Be strong and courageous. Do not be afraid; do not be discouraged, for the Lord your God will be with you wherever you go. Joshua 1:9

'That last one resonates with me, Samuel. *Do not be afraid; do not be discouraged, for the Lord your God will be with you wherever you go,*' Martin recited.

'I don't think God's with me on my journey,' Samuel mumbled.

Samuel was 14, small for his age, with dark hair that got in his eyes unless he swept it back over his ears. His posture was slack and rounded after years of schoolwork and video games.

'The Bible also says: *We have different gifts, according to the grace given to each of us.* And: *Each one should test their own actions. Then they can take pride in themselves alone, without comparing themselves to someone else.*' Martin smacked his lips. 'Did my workshops help you?'

Samuel attended a workshop with seven other students who had a history of bullying and involvement in domestic violence. Martin presented an eccentric series of role-playing scenarios around handling bullying encounters. The students, usually reserved, had engaged with the program. Convicted felons were brought into the second workshop and students were captivated by their stories both in and out of prison. At the end of the series of workshops, Martin had offered a mentoring service. Samuel had opened up to someone for the first time in those one-on-one sessions. He hadn't had any success with teachers, counsellors, psychologists, or even his own parents. Martin never dismissed Samuel's dark thoughts, instead he encouraged experimentation. The experimentation grew, which only seemed to develop Martin's interest in him further.

Samuel shrugged. 'Helped me with my anger. But the urges never really go away. I did what you said. You have the proof in your hands. And it did settle me, I guess.'

Martin sat a little straighter and Samuel flinched.

'Do I frighten you, Samuel?' A thin smile formed on Martin's lips.

'No. I dunno, maybe. I don't know what you are exactly. You're not a teacher, not a counsellor. You're not one of those prisoners either that you brought in for that show an' tell. But …'

'But?'

'But you're not … I dunno … a man of God.'

Martin titled his head back and laughed. 'I appreciate your diplomacy. I selected you, Samuel, because you are unique. You have done everything I have asked. You have been attentive and courteous. You have faced your flaws and your fears and developed strategies to overcome them. I have worked with many boys and girls like you before, and you have caught on quickly.'

'There are others?'

'You are not alone. There was a time when children had to suffer great pains before they could get to this stage. I learnt later in life that trauma wasn't a necessary ingredient. My bullying programs that your twit of a headmaster approved gives me access to finding students like yourself. This has all been for you.'

Samuel swallowed. 'I've been practising on the firing range with my dad.'

'I'm aware. I had people watching. Your aim is ready. Are you?'

'I think so.'

Martin placed a map of the school on the table and pointed to the assembly hall. 'This is where your journey begins. I will provide you with a Glock 22; it carries 15 rounds. I will have additional ammunition placed at these sites.' Martin pointed at various toilets, cleaning cupboards and classrooms. 'I will organise a rehearsal in the coming days.'

Samuel's heart started racing. All of this planning was coming to a conclusion. He had never heard of a school shooting in Australia. Not like this. But so much had happened in Adelaide over the last month.

'The other attacks in Adelaide, was it you?' Samuel asked.

Martin stared at Samuel with his piercing blue eyes. Samuel thought it was. He looked out the window and watched as teachers and students walked past, oblivious to the carnage being planned.

'What happens to me after?'

Martin ushered Samuel out of the office, hand on his shoulder, and walked out through the church. Outside were hundreds of students sitting in their groups eating lunch and scrolling on their phones. Norton College was one of the biggest schools in the southern hemisphere. There were seven campuses across the metro and districts, but the heart of the school was this senior campus in Marion. They stopped at the edge of the new recreation centre. It was closed, but builders were going in and out for last-minute tasks. Next to the emerging reception area there was a large office space for school tutoring. Samuel could read the name on the door from where they were: **HARSLETT HOUSE.** Five teenage boys ran past, narrowly avoiding a collision with the mentor and mentee.

'After … your time at this school will be over. For all intents and purposes, you will be dead. I will have your name changed, and your face changed if need be. Our achievements are not done for adoration. But you will finally know who you are.'

The headmaster, dressed in a formal black and navy robe, guided several men in suits out of the recreation centre, marking the end of the guided tour of the new facility. The headmaster noticed Martin and gave him a big wave.

'Mr Harslett. What timing. Gentlemen, some of you have met Mr Harslett before. One of the school's most generous benefactors.'

'Good afternoon, gentlemen.' Martin smiled.

'Mr Harslett has taken on a very special behavioural program,' the headmaster announced. 'His workshops have really caught on. We have noted a systemic difference in a challenging student cohort. He's done an amazing job.'

Martin exchanged further pleasantries and eventually guided Samuel back towards the church. Samuel grew more anxious after Martin's exchange with the school's leaders.

'What happens if I fail?'

Martin's grasp tightened. 'This is the end of the line for you, Samuel. I will guide you. But if you mess up, you'll find yourself in a horse stable of your own.'

Samuel had fantasised about killing for years. His interests were with famous killers, not football players. Gory horror films used to settle him at night. Listening to the horses when he lit up that barn had frightened him, he hated to admit. The horses had managed to escape. *Did I let them go?* He didn't like to think about it. The bell rang and students filed towards their classrooms.

Samuel wondered how many he would need to kill to please Martin.

***

Hands shook uncontrollably under the bathroom sink of the shabby motel room. The man scrubbed at his hands vigorously as the water washed the blood off. He looked at himself in the cracked mirror. Puffy wet eyes gave away his earlier crying. He still wore the dark blue scrubs and his surgeon's cap.

'Oh, fuck!'

The man dried his hands and started throwing items into a garbage bag. A dismantled mobile phone, debit cards and licences were tossed away. Someone knocked on the door, causing his nerves to rattle with a flush of adrenaline. He turned in horror. Even in the darkness he could make out the shadow of the winged-out ears against the blinds. His shoulders slumped. Instinctively he hurried to the door, determined not to keep him waiting.

Martin smiled when the door opened. He stepped in and looked around the room curiously. The single bedroom was neat and tidy, but the dilapidated furniture looked older than him. He opened one of the blinds to let the moonlight in. The man tried to hide his nervous tremor by sticking his hands in his pockets.

'I'm so, so, sorry,' the man blabbered.

'Shhhh …' Martin soothed. He took a seat on the bed and patted the rosy quilt cover, inviting the man to sit next to him.

The man stumbled over and sat down. 'I—I couldn't do it.'

'Tell me exactly what happened. I'm a stickler for detail.' Martin maintained eye contact.

'I got in. And I followed protocol. Everything you said. It was …' He gulped. 'There were kids, man …I—'

'Anthony, please, start from the top. You got into the hospital, that much is clear. What happened next?'

'I—ahhh … got to the lobby, said what you told me to say. Someone from admin led me to a room and asked me to fill out some forms, like you expected. I killed her and hid the body in that space. It was there just like you said. And, um, I followed your instructions to the letter. I found the dirty bombs and made my way to the wards. And I ah … saw cots. I saw babies. I-I-I couldn't go any further. I put the bombs back. And I ran. And I didn't want to let you down. So, I kept running. How did you find me?'

The man didn't realise Martin had been rubbing his back.

'I was at the hospital too, Anthony. I like to be there. I followed you to this quaint establishment,' Martin replied.

Anthony started shivering all over. Martin patted his knee. 'You learnt a valuable lesson about yourself, Anthony, which made today worthwhile.'

'Lesson? What happens to me now?'

'We learn what makes you tick. When I found you on the streets you were a confused master of mayhem. Remember when you told me how dangerous you were as you were mugging me?'

'I was stupid,' dismissed Anthony.

'You were lost, not stupid. I had never been mugged before. It was thoroughly entertaining. You know I have used a similar scenario in my workshops with the children. You had such colourful language back then. You really got my mind working. But your eyes have often been bigger than your stomach. You wanted the QEH project, so I gave you the opportunity.'

'And I fucked it! And now you have to kill me.' Anthony fidgeted.

'What do you take me for?'

'If you don't kill me now, you'll do it later. There's too much on the line, I know. But I'm younger than you.'

Anthony reached for Martin's neck with stunning speed and locked him into a choke hold. Martin slowly raised a fist.

'I'm sorry. You were everything to me, but I don't want to die,' Anthony cried.

He tightened his grip. Martin appeared nonchalant. Anthony couldn't see the lack of expression on his face. Anthony used both arms to tighten his grip further. Martin stuck a thumb up. Anthony instantly released.

'Stop! You've got a fucking sniper!'

Anthony moved away from the window. Martin coughed and wheezed.

'Why would I bring a sniper to a bed and breakfast in Salisbury?' Martin said hoarsely.

'You want me dead!'

'I'm going to get you to take a deep breath, in and out.' Martin collected himself. 'Do it with me, iiiin and ouuut. You have been through an ordeal, Anthony. If I wanted to kill you, I could have done it at the hospital. Do you think you're the first not to go through with a project? Of course you're not. I have come here to help you. And to ask you one important question.'

'What?' Anthony sniffed.

'Do you have it in you to try again?'

Anthony thought back to his time at Queen Elizabeth Hospital. He had killed a young woman just to gain access. It was awkward and messy, not like how he had been trained. He was angry at himself for that. He could kill again.

'But I can't kill kids,' Anthony announced.

'If we reset our floor plan away from the paediatrics, could you have another go?' Martin asked, stifling a yawn.

Anthony thought hard. 'I dunno, maybe.'

Martin stared at him long and hard, Anthony had never felt so vulnerable. Martin withdrew his gaze and searched for Anthony's phone in the bin bag that was tossed to the side. He reassembled the phone.

'Our minds are always clearer after sleep. When you wake, give me a call. We all have highs and lows. The main thing to remember is not to go off the deep end at either end. Think of Jessica Watson, the 16-year-old lone sailor. She just kept pushing forward at six or seven knots an hour and got there in the end.'

Anthony took back the phone and relaxed on the bed. Martin climbed down the steps of the motel and walked to the bus stop in front of the fluorescent motel vacancy sign. The cool breeze felt good on Martin's skin. Just before the bus pulled in, he raised his thumb.

Boom ... whizzz ... crack!

CHAPTER 24

THEN - November 2005

Thousands of people, young and old, gathered together in silence. Only bagpipes could be heard as four men in uniform played *The Last Post*. The Australians gathered at Centennial Park wore red poppies and bowed their heads for the minute's silence. It was Alex's first Remembrance Day event. He watched Graham, who at 86 years of age, dressed formally, and wore his eight medals with pride. He was surrounded by younger veterans. Since their arrival at the park 45 minutes ago, Graham hadn't stopped shaking hands and posing for photos. Alex couldn't imagine that he knew all of these people, but they knew him. He stayed a few paces away from the old man to remain out of the spotlight.

There was a small podium in front of a stone plinth with the words, *Their name liveth for evermore*. At the end of the song, everyone cleared a way for Graham to walk up to the podium. Alex could not detect any nerves as Graham stood in front of thousands. He winked at him, and spoke the ode:

'They shall grow not old, as we that are left grow old:
Age shall not weary them, nor the years condemn.
At the going down of the sun and in the morning
We will remember them.'

'We will remember them,' everyone chanted back.

Graham stepped down from the podium, only to be called over by the local mayor and various reporters. Yolanda smiled at Alex and put an arm around his shoulders. Alex thought she was dressed nicely with only a light touch of makeup.

'He will be going like this for a while,' Yoddi explained. 'Politicians and the media like to get some airtime with him, being one of the last.'

'Last of what?' Alex asked.

'Of the World War II veterans.'

Graham had taught Alex about history during his time at Ardrossan, but he never spoke about the war. Alex took himself back to one of his first history lessons.

'You want a real history lesson? This won't be in that school curriculum of yours. You've had a rough start, kiddo, but you're not the only one. What you call a basic necessity to me is a privilege.'

Graham and Alex were sitting in Yolanda's boat. She sat in the back angling the motor as they pushed away from Tiddy Widdy and onwards to Mac's Beach.

'Give him an example, Graham,' Yoddi called out.

'Have I ever told you about the long drop?' Graham asked.

Alex shook his head.

'When I was growing up, we didn't have toilets, we had an outhouse in the back garden. No flushing back then.'

Alex cringed. 'So, what did they do with all the...you know.'

'Men came over and picked it up once a week. We called it the night cart.'

'Hell of a gig back then.' Yoddi smiled as she dipped a hand into the sea.

'Nothing like nowadays. If we ever went back to that you would see a revolution, my boy,' Graham said gravely.

Alex could see Mac's Beach in the distance. It was deserted. Long stretches of sand and large mounds of dried-up seaweed snaked its way across the peninsula.

'So did you bathe?'

'Of course I bathed! What do you take me for? We had a tin bath. You had to carry rainwater in from outside and heat it up. You could imagine how long that took. Needless to say, the family shared the bath water back then. No choice.'

'How long did this go on for?'

Graham looked out into the distance. 'Long time. We didn't get piped water, gas and electricity until I was ten. Even then we couldn't use much. My father didn't have the money for so-called appliances.'

'Why were there so many poor people back then?'

'The devastation of World War One. The banking system between the wars didn't give credit. If you didn't have money, you didn't have much.'

'We're all in control of our own lives, Alex,' Yoddi added. 'No matter your setbacks, you have to find your purpose. Otherwise, you'll find yourself picking up someone else's shit in the middle of the night.'

A round of applause stirred Alex from his thoughts. Graham was now shaking hands with several other elderly men who weren't in the same physical condition. They must have been younger than Graham, but they were sitting on their walkers while they tried to stay out of the sun.

'He knows a lot of people,' Alex observed.

'You see those three young servicemen?' Yolanda pointed at two men dressed in formal military uniform with badges pinned to their chest. Alex noted that the one with a thick black beard had a set of wings above his medallions that signified he was air force. 'They were in the same position you are. They spent time with Graham and me as part of the respite service. Doing alright for themselves now.'

'Were they as much trouble as me?'

Yoddi pointed to the other serviceman in his formal army uniform. 'That one's Clint. He nearly burnt the house down one day. I would say that trumps trying to take off in Graham's car.'

Clint saw Yoddi and beamed. He walked over and gave her a hug. He said something to her, but Alex didn't catch it.

Tony: *Many over there...not right.*

Julie: *Gives me the willies.*

Clint's and Yoddi's voices were in the background. But Alex's attention was diverted, and he moved away from them. He watched Graham interact with some children that presented him with a poppy. He struggled to get down onto his knees but he made the effort so he could talk to them at eye level. Alex watched the kids, they're faces beaming as they showed off their poppies. His gaze followed the line of children, like finding the source of an ant's nest, until his eyes came upon a small cart decorated with poppies set up in the car park. Another middle-aged veteran gave out poppies to the children. He had a younger-looking face, except for the small moustache, but he was severely overweight. Alex locked eyes with him, and the voices returned.

Someone Unknown: ... *Delicious.*

Alex zig-zagged around the children until he made it to the poppy cart.

'Would you like one?' the poppy seller asked him.

'Sorry, what's the date today?' Alex asked.

The man looked confused for a moment, checked his watch, and then gave him the date: 'November 11.'

Lewis: *Imposter. Run, Alex, run.*

Alex could not understand exactly what was going on inside his head. It was physical too. His heart started to race, and his mouth became dry. Something felt off about the man in front of him.

Alex: *Everyone checks their watch when asked for the date, it's nothing.*

Lewis: *He's a veteran working on Remembrance Day, so he should know the fucking date.*

Julie: *Swear jar!*

'Would you like one?' the poppy seller repeated.

Alex took one and pinned it to his shirt before he walked off.

After the sausage sizzle, everyone started heading home. Graham was left farewelling everyone, but Alex kept his eye on the poppy stall. When the man packed up his cart into a van, Alex walked ahead and memorised the licence plate.

Yolanda got Graham's attention and pointed at Alex. Graham nodded in response and made his way over to him.

'Where have you been all morning?' Graham asked.

'Do you know the man that was handing out poppies?' Alex asked.

Graham thought about it. 'I think he was here last year. I didn't get a chance to speak to him. Why?'

'Nothing.'

'Nothing my ass!'

Alex watched the van take off. 'Do you remember the day we went to the church, and I got a weird feeling talking to the chaplain?'

Graham nodded.

'I had that same feeling. About him.' Alex pointed to the van as it turned the corner.

***

Alex woke coughing up water, fighting for air. It was cold and dark. He couldn't make out where he was. Remembrance Day. Man with the poppies. Darkness. He couldn't remember anything in between. He had a migraine. The ground was damp. His hands and feet were dirty.

'Hello?' he called out. He tried to stand but hit his head. His eyes re-adjusted to the darkness. He crawled on his hands and knees towards the source of light. He realised he was under a house. When he reached the end of the foundations, he found a loose wooden beam through which he must have crawled in. He did not recognise anything but heard crashing and banging from above. Adrenaline surged through his body when he noticed the poppy cart in the shed.

Alex: *For God's sake, somebody say SOMETHING. Lewis!*

Lewis: *It's not me and it's fucking hilarious.*

Tony: *Can't leave. Can't leave. Can't leave.*

Tony's voice startled Alex. He searched his pockets and found a set of car keys for the van. He knew then that Graham had found the poppy man. *Is Graham ok? How much time has passed?*

The crashing and banging continued. Alex pushed himself through the small gap under the house and sprinted to the carport. He unlocked the van doors. The van beeped. Alex turned to the house. The poppy man, dressed in a singlet and boxer shorts, turned in his direction. The man let out a wail and violently shoved the screen door open so he could get to the van. Alex wasted no time. He jumped in, started the ignition, and took off down the road. Poppy man was too large and too slow to get near the van in time.

Tony: *No. No. No. No. No.*

Alex took no notice of the speedometer as the little house got smaller in the rear vision mirror. Then he hit the brakes hard. The roads were empty, and nobody saw the van screech to a halt. He didn't mean to do that. *Why did I do that? Shit.*

It didn't feel right. The hissing in his head only settled when he looked back. Tony screamed in his head.

Blackout.

He woke again under the house as if it was Groundhog Day. Alex: *Tony? What are you doing?*

He started to tremble. He no longer had any control. He felt like a captive to his own madness. Tony had never behaved like this before. He never knew his alters had the power to do this so suddenly.

A scream came from above. Alex froze. *Somebody else is up there.*

Alex forgot about his own problems. He was slower this time as he crawled out from under the house. Alex assumed it was a transportable house, held up by thick aging pavers. The property was surrounded by trees, and no other homes could be spotted as far as the eye could see.

Alex heard further sounds, too many sounds, and figured it must have been a TV. He took a moment to carefully climb up. There was an open window out the back. *Was it a trap? Or the way out last time?* He climbed through the window and fell into a dusty laundry. As he gathered himself, he was careful not to knock over any of the chemical bottles that filled the room. He almost gagged on the fumes.

Alex heard the scream again. This time it sounded more like a whine. The laundry had no door, so he carefully stepped out. Poppy man was sitting on a couch facing the other way, mumbling to himself. The room opposite Alex looked like the bedroom. He quietly stepped into the bedroom and followed the sound of the cries while poppy man got up and paced back and forth in the lounge.

Beside the bed, which was stripped of sheets and stained beyond repair, was a large crate. Another whimper could be heard. Alex moved towards the crate. It was a puppy, no more than six-weeks-old. It was a white and tan border collie.

Tony: *Puppy dog needs a friend. Tony will be his friend, yes please.*

He noticed something on the puppy's belly. He opened the crate and the puppy instinctively moved back, it's body trembling. It peed itself as Alex reached for it. He noticed its belly had been burnt. Alex found a lighter sitting on the bedside table.

Lewis: *Just take the fucking runt and run. Now.*

Alex picked up the crate. The puppy whined. On his way out, he stepped on something. It was one of the medals poppy man wore at the park. They had been tossed across the floor. Alex picked up the medals and placed them inside the crate with the dog.

Poppy man's mumbling and pacing stopped. Alex heard his heavy legs carry him towards the bedroom. Alex quickly scanned the room for something. Anything. The room was small, with only enough width for one bedside table. A sliding door led to an ensuite. He put the crate back and hid in the shower. Poppy man belched and scratched himself as he waddled into the bedroom.

'Shut the fuck up!' he yelled at the puppy and kicked the crate.

Lewis: *Don't move, Alex. Oh, for fuck's—*

Alex lunged back into the bedroom. Poppy man was shocked for a moment and stepped back in fright. Alex sprayed a can of deodorant in front of the man's face with the ignited lighter directly in front. A ball of flame stunned the man even further and he fell over. Alex grabbed the crate and hurdled over the obese body. The house was dilapidated and dirty, but filled with various expensive electronics: sound bars, laptops, gaming consoles. The house was filled with stolen goods. A thought came to him: *If I hadn't met Graham, would I have turned out like this?*

Alex pushed open the sliding door.

'No, please don't take my puppy!' the man cried out. There was something off about his speech.

Alex hesitated. He watched the red-faced poppy man limp out of the bedroom.

'Where did you get him from?' Alex asked aloud.

'I found it. I look after him.'

Alex looked down at the puppy, who looked wet and cold from its own urine.

'I know someone that can do a better job,' Alex said. He wasted no time running out of the house.

Tony: *Puppy. Puppy. Puppy. Puppy.*

He could see the van just up the road. The man chased after him, wheezing as he ran. Alex was much faster and the distance between them grew in seconds. Alex arrived at the van and threw the crate in the front passenger seat. Graham's driving lessons were ingrained into him. Without much thought he turned on the motor and accelerated. When he finally looked back, he saw the man standing in the middle of the road, just watching and scratching himself. When Alex was further down the road, he opened the door of the crate so the puppy would not feel like a captive.

Ten minutes into the drive, the puppy stepped its two front paws out of the crate and looked up at Alex. There was a single medal around the dog's neck. Alex could not recognise the language on the war medal, but a single word stood out: Rex.

Alex smiled at him. 'Rex. Suits you'.

***

Alex woke in his bedroom, feeling ravenous. The puppy was thumping its tail against the side of the bed.

144

Graham stood at the door. 'He's been keeping his eye on you. I'm sure Tony will show Rex that not all humans are bad.' He sat down on the foot of Alex's bed and sighed. 'I'm worried about you.'

Alex noticed Graham was sporting a black eye. 'What happened to you?'

'Never mind me, I'm still as handsome as ever. Alex, if you keep losing time like this, you're going to end up in a whole lot of trouble. Exercise has worked wonders for you. But you need more than that. You need more than me.'

'I'll keep practicing meditation!'

'This isn't about the bloody meditation! It's my fault. I should never have got you involved with my cases. I shouldn't have found the man at the park.'

Alex's fists clenched. He noticed split skin on his two biggest knuckles. Realisation dawned on him, and he was too ashamed to look up at Graham.

'I'm sorry,' Alex muttered.

'What for?' Graham asked.

Alex pointed at the old man's jaw. Graham grabbed his hand and held it. They both remained quiet for a moment.

'The police took his van back. They found a boy in his garden shed. He was only 7-years- old. I was told he's going to be okay.' Graham soothed.

Hairs on the back of Alex's neck pricked up. 'I'm sorry, I should have found the boy when I was there,'

'The boy was at the service. You saved that boy's life. Alex, you have a gift. That man would still be out there now if it wasn't for you. But you almost became a victim! This isn't something you can do by yourself. Lewis should know that too.'

Lewis: *Self-righteous fucker.*

'Your alters … They worked together for this?' Graham asked him.

Alex shrugged and nodded. 'I can talk to them sometimes, mostly when I'm in control, but sometimes when I'm not. I never used to. It's only happened since I moved in with you.'

'My boy, I don't think anyone can do what you can. But for this to work *you* still need to be responsible for your actions. If not, Lewis might just get us both killed.'

CHAPTER 25

NOW

Alex's body twitched in the infirmary of Harslett Prison. The patient monitor beeped incessantly. Heart rate 150 beats per minute. The bed sheets were soaked in sweat. Nurses checked on the prisoner every 15 minutes during the nocturnal distress. They had already changed the dressing on his abdomen twice.

140 beats per minute.

A skinny, middle-aged lawyer in a crumpled suit anxiously watched from outside the infirmary. He had been told he could see his client as soon as he was awake. Alex's kicking and fist clenching had subsided.

130 beats per minute.

The lawyer watched Alex behind a glass window. An index finger started to tap. He thought he saw Alex's eyelids flicker.

120 beats per minute.

Lightning struck the entrance gates of the forsaken cemetery. The rusted gates buckled from the storm until they fell forward with a sudden groan. The bars descended into the muddy ground as though they were set in quicksand. Another flash of lightning lit up the headstones. Alex stepped over the corroded, sinking gates. His shoes squelched in the mud. Tightening his grip on his shovel, he ignored the screaming voices as he entered the cemetery. He stumbled in the dark, checking row by row until he found the gravestone.

HERE LIES GRAHAM BLAKEMORE,
LOVING FATHER,
DECORATED VETERAN,
PILLAR OF THE COMMUNITY,
1919–2019

Alex's heart hammered in his chest. Words swirled in his mind. SACRILAGE. DISGRACE. HE WOULD HATE YOU FOR THIS.

Alex took a breath and dug, tossing the rich mud over his shoulder and digging like his life depended on it. Despite the thunder roaring around him, he could still hear the sound of a child whimpering.

Julie: This is a bad idea, please Alex, you have to stop!

Alex ignored her and continued digging. The headstone was now cracked in the top left corner.

HERE LIES GRAHAM BLAKEMORE,
LOVING FATHER,
DECORATED ABUSER,
PILLAR OF THE COMMUNITY

Julie: Alex, no! You can't. Please!

Thunder boomed around the graveyard. Heavy rain soaked him to the bone.

Alex: I have to do this. I have no choice. I can't do this alone.

Alex continued to dig with urgency. Another bolt of lightning struck the headstone.

HERE LIES GRAHAM BLAKEMORE,
DISGRACED SON,
DECORATED ABUSER,

Julie: He's dead, let him rest! Let him rest! LET HIM REST!

Alex kept digging, adding to the mound of earth behind him. The grave resembled a dark wading pool as he fought against the weather. Sweat and rain encumbered him, making everything harder. But he would not give in to fatigue. A dull ache coming from his abdomen. He looked down at the stab wound. Dark, viscous blood poured into the grave. Alex continued to dig. Another bolt of lightning crackled an inch to his left. He shot up in fright.

HERE LIES GRAHAM BLAKEMORE,
DISGRACED SON,
DECORATED KILLER,
MENACE OF THE COMMUNITY

Lewis: You? Alone? I screamed, Alex. I screamed when Martin came into our lives. You ignored me! Too terrified to listen!

Alex: I've always been scared, alright? It's why I'm so fucked up.

Lewis: But you're not alone, you fucking idiot.

Alex, now caked in mud, threw away the shovel and dug with his hands. His fingernails split as he made it down to the coffin. The heavy rain rinsed the mud and blood from his hands as he fumbled for the coffin's opening.

Thunk. Thunk. Thunk. A pounding in his head.

Alex: Tony, stop that!

Tony: You stop. You stop. Please stop hurting us. You're hurting us.

Blood ran down the engraving of the headstone. Alex found a padlock locking the coffin lid in place. He crushed it with his boot and the rusted lock gave way.

Lewis: If you won't listen, then fucking look. That's not Graham's grave!

Alex turned – only to be blinded by two bright lights.

[A nurse checks Alex's pupils. The alarm goes off on the patient monitor]

When the light subsided, Alex rubbed his eyes until he could make out the tombstone. It read:

HERE LIES RANDALL,
DISGRACED SON,
DECORATED KILLER,
MENACE OF THE COMMUNITY.

Alex pushed the heavy lid of the coffin over. A gaunt, pale figure rested inside. His hand brushed against the cheek. It was cold and leathery. But it was Alex's face. Alex, frightened now, went to pull the lid closed just as the corpse's eyelids flickered open, revealing spotted yellow eyes. The corpse reached for Alex.

Julie/Tony/Lewis: It's him ...

Alex: Who?

Julie/Tony/Lewis: The one we don't let out.

Embrace me, Alex,' the corpse said, its breath icy cold. 'I'm here now.

Randall awoke. His eyes darted around the room manically.

I have control. I finally have control.

A heavy-set nurse checked on him. 'Alex?' she said with an Irish accent.

'Mmmm ...' Randall's gaze moved to the picture of Martin.

'Who's Mickey Mouse?' he asked, pointing a bony finger at the picture. His voice was smooth and a few decibels higher than Alex's speech.

The nurse shot a look at the enlarged photograph. 'That's our director, Martin Harslett. Can you tell me your name, young lad?'

'My name? My name is Alex.' Randall lied.

The nurse got him to drink some water from a straw. 'Someone here to see you, Alex.'

The lawyer was quickly ushered in. The sight of Randall disturbed him. All those scars and burns across his torso. There was almost a pattern to some of the wounds, like tribal tattoos.

'Mr Blakemore?' He noticed his client staring at the photograph behind him intently.

The alter struggled to remember the last time he had won control. Alex had gotten so much stronger. Yet at the same time, his connection with the other alters grew as well. Randall couldn't understand it. But he was present now—always at the darkest hour.

'Blakemore.' Randall smacked his lips. 'Yes … my name is Alex Blakemore. Tell me, how are they still alive?'

'They?' the lawyer asked.

He rolled his eyes. 'How am I still alive?'

'Minor wound I was told.' The lawyer cleared his throat. 'The prison director himself witnessed the attack; self-defence has been declared. Better news still, your case has been dismissed.'

'Case?'

'Graham Blakemore's death was determined to be of natural causes, as expected for a 100-year-old man. An anonymous witness had accused you but has since come forward as

mistaken. I have organised your release immediately. You will
be transferred to Lyell McEwen hospital this afternoon.'

'Convenient … look babe, I'm sure you're good at your job
and all that, but I just wanna get outta here. No prisons, no
hospitals. I can look after my own arse.'

'Yes, I understand. Based on … experiences inside these
walls you still need to be assessed by a psychiatrist.'

Randall stared at the lawyer. His high-pitched laughter made
the lawyer jump.

'Perfect mental health here, babe. Do whatcha gotta do. Can
you do me one teeny, tiny favour? Just for little old me? None
of this Mr Blakemore formality. Granted you look good in a suit,
but that's not what I'm about. My friends call me Randall.'
Randall winked.

***

Alex was not in control, but Randall gave the performance of
his lifetime in a small courtroom as the judge confirmed the
withdrawal of charges. He attempted to speak in Alex's usual
voice, with a slightly slack posture. He used phrases like, 'Yes,
sir', 'I appreciate your understanding', 'This experience was
nothing compared to the grief of losing my father. I just need
space to process this'.

When his case was processed, he relaxed back to his
comfortable posture; with his pelvis tilted. He still stood tall and
walked with long strides while a guard escorted him towards the
prison entrance. It looked more like an entrance to a church.
There were crosses erected, bible verses painted onto the walls,
and various photos of Martin with religious figures. He got
through the discharge process as quickly as possible. He was
given a wallet, car keys and a small black book. *Another Bible?*
There was $75 dollars in the wallet. *Thank you, Jesus.*

Randall was transported via ambulance to the Lyell McEwen Hospital. The paramedics allowed him to sit up on the gurney. When they arrived, there was a hold up at the ambulance parking spot as several vans had already pulled in before them. The paramedics parked along the side of the curb and helped him inside. They admitted him into the busy hospital. He was asked to wait in a small waiting area while a bed was being made for him. Not long after the paramedics left, he slipped away as well.

Julie: *Alex, please ... not Randall!*

Alex: *I can't.*

Lewis: *Get rid of Randall, Alex! Now!*

Alex: *He's too strong.*

Lewis: *Where the hell is he taking us?*

Randall belted out *Can't Get You Out of My Head* by Kylie Minogue with two other middle-aged women at a karaoke station in a busy pub, less than a 10-minute bus ride from the hospital. His hips gyrated and he winked at several handsome men who shook their heads at Randall's theatrics. He had a microphone in his left hand and a large bottle of Everclear in his right. He took a swig when the ladies in his newfound entourage needed a breather between lyrics. He applied a glitter eyeliner he borrowed from a woman, which gave his eyelids a golden-yellow sparkle. When the song finished, he kissed the women on the cheek and took off back to the bar while guzzling his drink.

A TV on the corner of the bar broadcasted the latest Showstopper attack at Harslett Prison. The ticker tape: **MULTIPLE PRISONERS POISONED DURING RIOT AT ADELAIDE'S STATE-OF-THE-ART PRISON. SHOWSTOPPER CLAIMS RESPONSIBILITY** momentarily stopped Randall.

He took another swig of his new bottle of Everclear and walked off, tripping on his way out the door. Knees scuffed, he dusted himself off. Randall fought back the nausea and staggered across the road.

Tony: *You have consumed 1,698.75 ml of alcohol. Need to get back to Lyell now. Lyell McEwen must see Tony. Very, very sick. Poison, dehydration ... very, very bad for poor Tony.*

Drivers passing Randall shook their heads at the man stumbling along the road with a bottle in hand as he talked to himself.

Tony: *Tony knows right and wrong. Right to get back, right to help others, right to ... to grieve. My Graham is gone and Rex, we must find Rex. Rex is my mate. Can't find him if we're poisoned. Go away, Randall!*

'I can handle my liquor!' Randall screamed out loud as he reached the pedestrian crosswalk. Others moved away from him, content to wait for the next lights change.

Tony: *No. Last time alcohol was consumed was 2,810 days ago. We are not equipped. Not even you.*

He started feeling dizzy.

Randall: *I will not let you take me away, Tony!*

Tony: *Have to. Others are hurt. None more so than Tony. I miss my dad. I want my Graham back. You are not helping.*

Randall vomited on himself and collapsed in the middle of the road. Cars stopped around him. He babbled, blowing bubbles of snot and drool across the gravel road.

Eventually he passed out.

Lewis: *For the love of fucking God. Fight him, Alex.*

CHAPTER 26

THEN - November 2005

Alex never resisted Julie's emergence. He felt responsible for her in a way that he couldn't understand. Alex followed Graham in silence as they went for a walk along the beach, away from the house and further into town. The humidity was getting to him, and they prayed for a cool breeze that never came.

Alex's shadow along the seaweed-littered sand began to stoop, his feet kicked up higher in the sand, and his hips began to rotate excessively. A hand reached out and grabbed two of Graham's fingers. A little high-pitched voice spoke up.

'Hi, Pa.'

'Hello, Julie.'

There was another long silence as Julie followed Graham onto the jetty. It was abandoned except for a lone adolescent crabbing.

'Pa? Do you love me?'

Graham sighed. 'I care about you very much. But I want to see Alex grow up to be a man. I don't know how that can happen if you all lose control.'

Julie furrowed her brow in confusion, but she followed Graham to the end of the jetty where Graham sat on the top wooden plank at the edge of the jetty and let the elusive breeze cool his back.

'I don't know anything about what you have, kid. But you could be really something. And I need you, Alex, to take control of your life, because nobody else will.'

'You help us, Pa. Can we go back now?'

Julie watched a brawling pair of seagulls crash-land into the water before they took off into the sun, causing her to squint.

'Can you come out, Alex? For me? Please? I know you can control it.'

Julie squeezed her eyes and fists shut, the only response being an anxious fart. Her cheeks flushed red.

'I'm sorry, Pa, I don't know what you want me to do.'

'I think you do. But you need to do it when it matters most.'

'I wish I could do things like you, Pa …'

Graham chuckled to himself and looked up. 'There's one thing I can't do. Even after all those blood years in the Navy. I can't swim. But I do love ya, kiddo.'

Graham leaned back and flung his frail body into the ocean.

'PA!!!!'

Graham hit the surface of the freezing water. He attempted to doggy paddle, but Julie could see his arms and legs were uncoordinated. Graham's shoulders were submerged. He tried kicking harder but only sank deeper. He reached up at Julie, who was stomping and crying, snot flying out of her nose.

'Alex, please!' Graham cried.

Julie began hitting her head against the edge of the jetty, forcing something to happen. She tried climbing off the jetty, but panic gripped her every time she looked down, and she staggered back in despair. They both locked eyes. Graham's eyes began to fill with doubt. Julie could see the fear in Graham's face. Julie dropped to her knees and wailed. Graham took one last breath, and one last look at Julie, before his body slipped under.

Julie caught an image of a ship. Something from her past. She shook the image away. She could only just see Graham's scrambling body underwater. His mouth looked like it was about to burst. Julie jumped into the darkness. She withdrew.

Lewis felt a fragile wrist and pulled with all of his might. Graham coughed and spluttered. There were sounds and light, but nothing was clear beyond the much-needed coughing.

'Dumb fuck. This doesn't mean I like ya or anything.'

Graham turned to the gruff voice and recognised an expression of loathing that could only belong to Lewis. Graham had not yet regained full control of his limbs. He let Lewis pull his frail body out of the water until they could feel the sand and seaweed beneath their feet. Then Lewis pushed him, and he staggered towards the shore, collapsing onto the bank where the water was down to ankle level. Graham took several deep breaths. Lewis shook his head, disgusted at the look of the relief on Garaham's face as he looked up at the beautiful blue sky.

'Alex can't swim either, ya twat.'

'Oh …' Graham dropped his head back and erupted into a fit of sneezes. 'Thank you.'

'Alex fears water. That was a dumb move.'

'Yes,' Graham said between sneezes, 'I think you're right.'

They watched the young crabber pick up his bucket and tools, oblivious to the near-death experience on the beach. Graham turned to Lewis, who was still shaking his head.

'Lewis, Alex will never be rid of this, will he? He'll live with his conditions forever?'

Lewis met Graham's gaze and didn't respond, but the wisdom behind his eyes was enough.

Graham nodded. 'You'll look after him, Lewis? When I'm gone?'

Lewis sat on the beach and began to watch the whitecaps. Graham caught a brief nod.

Lewis refused to leave Alex that day and he didn't say another word to Graham. They spent most of the day fishing and eventually ran out of tackle.

That afternoon Lewis found himself surrounded by mirrors. He watched himself from every angle while he chewed the quick off his nail. He swiped his finger across the top of a leg-press machine, a fine film of dust caked into his fingertips. He blew it away and stepped towards a mirror pane, as if in a trance. He studied his reflection.

'Alex fears this.'

'No,' Graham whispered, 'not anymore. You don't know this place, do you?'

'Should I?'

'It's where Alex got strong. Silenced the voices. Your voice, Lewis. I knew nothing of his condition, but I thought exercise could make him whole. Get rid of you.'

'You think bringing me here will bring him back?'

'No, actually, I thought this place might help you too.'

Heavy metal music erupted from the abandoned gym. Lewis was pummelling a boxing bag with his fists. His knuckles began to split. 'I've had enough–this shit is pointless. Take me home, old man.'

'Knock? Knock?' Yoddi called out. She came in with another basket of morning tea.

'Great. If you won't take me, the service woman will.'

Yoddi, mouth agape, looked from Lewis to Graham. 'Am I missing something?'

'Lewis here has been moping for some time. I thought this might help. It's not,' Graham muttered.

Yoddi shook her head and laid down the basket. She found herself a chair and pulled out a bright purple jacket. She continued sewing a sequin pattern by hand.

'You still working on that?' Graham asked.

'I've got another show with the CWA and it has to be ready. I really wouldn't worry about this one, dear. I told you this alter was a waste of time.' Yoddi sighed.

'Excuse me? What did you say, bitch?' Lewis stormed over to her.

Yolanda placed her basket down. 'I mean no offence, Lewis. I don't know you as well as Graham. I just think you're a waste of space.' Yoddi shrugged.

Lewis clenched his fists. 'Say something else, woman. Please.'

Graham started fidgeting. Yoddi smiled. 'Oh please, you don't scare me, Lewis. I've seen seagulls look more threatening than you.'

Lewis rushed her. Yoddi swung her leg up and kicked him in the balls. Lewis's eyes bulged in shock. He crumpled forward. With quick precision, Yoddi stepped forward and punched him in the throat. He hit the ground wheezing.

'Now that's from a 72-year-old osteoporotic woman with a-' Yoddi stopped short, aware Graham was watching. '… with a predisposition for gin.'

It took Lewis some time to respond. 'That's dirty fighting!' he choked.

'That's survival, Lewis. Dissociative identity disorder has protectors. When an alter is created, at least one is a protector, someone stronger than the host. That's supposed to be you. You're loud, you're crude, you're selfish, not to mention you have a severely limited vocabulary … but you have Alex's best interests at heart. You want to keep him safe. But your actions can get him in trouble. Don't you want to know how to defend yourself?'

Lewis pulled himself up to a sitting position and stared up at Yoddi. 'Yeah, alright.'

Lewis paid attention as Yoddi demonstrated the best ways to take down a man quickly.

'Use what you have and use it immediately. Use your environment. Use your teeth. Whatever it takes.'

The two of them took turns with a variety of moves. Lewis mixed up her technical sessions with slinging kettlebells, slamming dead balls, digging deep on the rower, and finishing back on the bag. In 45 minutes, he was covered in sweat and puffing hard. An increase of endorphins, dopamine and serotonin released in his brain, making him feel light and relaxed.

'Not bad, you two.' Graham smiled.

'Same again tomorrow, Lewis?' Yoddi asked.

'Alright.'

Graham bought fishing tackle on the way home. The next night, Lewis allowed Graham and Yoddi to fish with him. They rarely caught anything, but it brought peace to all three of them. On day three of Lewis' takeover of Alex, he caught his first squid.

'I did it!' Lewis cried in delight.

Graham beamed. His light-blue eyes twinkled in the sunlight. Lewis threw the squid in the Esky, nodded to himself, and sat back down on one of the deck chairs. Graham saw his posture shift in the seat.

'Alex?' Graham asked hopefully.

'Hi, Pa! Have you finished swimming?'

CHAPTER 27

NOW

'GRAHAAAAM… GRAHAAAM…'
Graham power walked down the dark hallway in the hospital.
He wasn't connected to anything, but his vitals rang in Alex's
ears. Alex knew he was in a dream, but it still frightened him.
He was beginning to think his dreams had consequences.

Beep. Beep. Beep.
'GRAHAAAM! Come back!' Alex cried.
'No way, José! I've had enough!' Graham snapped.
Alex ran after him. Faster and faster. Pushing his arms just
like he was taught. Each time he reached the end of the hallway,
Graham managed to turn a corner.
'Graham! Please! I need you!'
'I can't help you anymore. Go find your mother instead.'
Graham called back.
Alex turned the corner and stopped. A large mirror covered
the wall. His shadow started to emerge behind him. It split in
two. Then three. Then four. And then another.
Alex: How many are there?
'How MANY?' Alex roared out loud.
More shadows started splitting, snaking their way across the
floor.
Alex: No, no, no.
Alex turned back and ran. He stopped short when he saw his
younger self, 14-years-old, sitting in a waiting chair. His

younger self fell. Martin helped him up and guided him into his office.

Alex: Stop! Don't go in there.

Alex burst through the psychiatry office. His teenage self was gone. Martin was humming to himself as he hung someone else's photos and credentials back on the wall. Martin stopped humming, sensing a presence. He began to turn his head; Alex ran back out. A hand grasped his shoulder. He broke free and stumbled out the front door. He was outside now. Hundreds of dogs barked ferociously at Martin as he guided the innocent, adolescent Alex to a cage.

Alex: They were barking at you...They had always been barking at you...

Tony jolted awake, sweat running down his neck. He found himself at the psychiatric ward at Lyell McEwen Hospital. He scratched at the IV butterfly taped to his hand. The bag to the IV drip was half-empty. He whined, high pitched like a wounded dog. Nurses continued to medicate him to settle him down after his fits.

He laid in a double room with a plastic divider separating his bed from another. He didn't move on the first day. On the second day staff pulled the divider across as a new patient was admitted next to him. With Tony in control, he paid no attention and resumed his whining.

'Oh, for Pete's sake, shut up! Or I'll come over there and give you a knuckle sandwich. And I'm tougher than I sound, mister!' a female voice shrilled.

Tony rocked back and forth on the edge of his bed. 'He wasn't supposed to go that way. Not that way. Supposed to be peaceful, not like that. Tony's dad died.' He swallowed.

'Least you had a dad!' the girl next door snapped. After a long pause she asked, 'What was his name?'

'Graham. His name was Graham. Mr Graham Blakemore. He and Rex were my two best friends. I don't know who's feeding Rex, I really need to—'

The divider was pulled open and the girl peeped across the room. She appeared gaunt, weighing under 50 kilograms. She had one pigtail growing out from the side of her head. The other pigtail had been chopped off. She wore a bright yellow shirt two sizes too big for her, which was tucked into men's shorts. Purple and yellow football socks were pulled up to her knees. Her hair was dyed pink and blue.

'Alex?' she asked timidly. 'It's me, Rochelle.'

'I don't know you. I don't know. My name is Tony. I only know Graham. Graham and Rex.'

Rochelle sat on the edge of the bed next to Tony. He stared at her shoes, avoiding eye contact. Her close proximity made him uncomfortable and he started to shuffle away from her.

'I'm sorry about Graham. He was nice to me,' she sympathised. 'It's been a while since you came to visit.'

'The boys are very busy.'

'It's okay.' Rochelle shrugged. 'I'm used to it.'

She jumped off the bed and sat on the floor. 'Eye spy with my little eye something beginning with … T!'

Tony: *This game always bores Tony.*

Julie: *Can I play?*

Tony's spine flexed and his shoulders internally rotated, making him appear smaller.

'… table?' Julie asked with her little voice.

With the youngest alter in control, Julie was having more fun than she had in a long time. That made her feel guilty, because Graham was gone now. But she found it nice having a friend that wasn't old enough to be a great-great-grandparent.

Rochelle never really saw a 29-year-old man when she looked at Julie. She had the ability to look past that. Rochelle could look past everything but the scars. She couldn't help but peek when Julie had a shower in their shared ensuite. There were scars and burn marks covering most of her body. There was a fresh wound, 2 inches wide on her belly. She could make out the stitches beneath the bandage. Rochelle felt a quietness deep in her bones where everything started to become numb. She had seen her fair share of scars from self-harm. But this was something else. She wanted to ask her friend about the scars, but another part of her didn't want to. She was afraid the relationship would be over before it truly started. But the curiosity was eating away at her, and in the end, she couldn't help it.

'Julie, who did that to you?'

'Did what?' Julie asked as she came out the shower, not realising that she was visibly drying Alex's penis in front of Rochelle.

'The scars!' Rochelle started to panic. 'Look!'

She forced Julie in front of the mirror in the bathroom and pointed at some of the deepest wounds.

'There, and there and there and there and there!' Rochelle cried.

Julie stopped breathing, and then she started breathing slow and deep. The breathing frightened Rochelle. It was enough to force her back to her bed. The breathing turned into a growl. A strong hand smacked the mirror, which made Rochelle jump. Her posture changed and she became taller and broader.

Lewis stepped out of the bathroom and took in his surroundings.

Lewis: *Jesus Christ! Why did that take so long?*

'Where the fuck are we?' he shouted.

Rochelle shivered. 'We're in the psychiatric unit at … Lyell Mac.'

'He never intended to kill us,' Lewis said aloud to himself, inspecting his new wound. 'Smug fuck. He let us go. Wants to see what happens next. Jesus … Charges against Graham must have been fucking loose at best. Bet you strings were pulled to get me into Harslett in the first place.'

Rochelle hesitated. 'I'm sorry about Graham.'

Lewis's fists continued to clench and relax. Clench and relax. A vein in his forehead became visible as it throbbed. He noticed their TV was on in the background. It was muted but he caught the headline: **SHOWSTOPPER TAKING CREDIT AT HARSLETT PRISON – NINE KILLED.**

'I know who did that.' Lewis pointed at the TV. 'And he knows I know. I'm going to get the fuck out of here before anyone comes after me.'

Lewis headed for the door.

'Why?'

Lewis pointed at the TV. 'He killed Graham, he could kill me.'

'But you can't run, you haven't got control of yourself. You need help.'

Lewis stormed over to her. 'Look, freak—'

Panic filled Rochelle's face and she began to fidget and squirm. He reached for her wrist, it felt thin and cold.

Alex: *No, Lewis!*

Lewis: *No, this is my time now. You never listened to me! I warned you about Martin when I first laid eyes on him. But you never fucking listened.*

Alex: *I didn't know what I was hearing back then. I was broken. And you scared me. I am sorry, Lewis. Let me make it up to us.*

Lewis: *Even now you can't take control. You're weak.*

Alex: *Then give me back the control.*

Lewis: *No!*

Alex: *Why not?*

Lewis: *Why the fuck do we do anything? To protect you. It's always about you.*

Alex: *I don't care about me. Graham's dead. I didn't even get to say goodbye.*

Tony: *Always lots of 'I' with Alex, never 'we'. Tony understands his place. Tony's not very important sometimes. Or is it appreciated? But Tony was part of the family. Julie too. Graham loved us for what we are.*

Julie: *And we can't bring him back.*

Lewis: *We need to get over it. He was a 100-fucking-years-old.*

Julie: *Lewis! Don't swear!*

Lewis: *I'm just saying, it was going to happen sooner or later. He had a good innings. He probably wasn't expecting to get murdered on his birthday, but—*

Alex: *Enough!*

Tony: *Shhhh ... we are not alone in here. Can't afford to wake Randall.*

Alex: *Who is Randall?*

Lewis: *Bad fucking news. And you're a fucking broken mess, Alex. You can't be behind the wheel.*

Lewis let go of Rochelle's arm.

'Now, who the fuck are you?' a firm voice asked.

Lewis looked up in surprise and saw Rochelle looking outraged. She carried herself differently. Her shoulders appeared broader, eyes wider, voice harsher. He groaned in response.

'My name is Lewis. And you are?'

'Georgia. Slip me a roofie at the club last night, didja?'

'Fuck no. I don't know who you are but—'

'Wooow,' Rochelle exaggerated. 'Didn't even get a name, ya dog.'

Lewis swore under his breath. 'Jesus Christ, we're not getting anywhere here.' Lewis enunciated: 'Can you get the fuck out of my way before I remove you.'

Rochelle closed her eyes and hummed.

'The fuck are you doing?'

Lewis watched Rochelle transform in front of him. It was quick and subtle. Her body became less tense and her expressions softened.

'So, that is fucking weir—' His eyes narrowed. 'What did you do just now?'

'Georgia didn't think you were dangerous. I'm 90 percent sure she's right. You have a *gruff voice that sounds like this*.' Rochelle imitated. 'But your eyes are still … kind. So, we swapped.'

'How?'

'I use phrases, like poetry. Smells usually work to … I dunno the word, cue? It's kinda complicated and kinda not. It triggers memories which triggers them. But it doesn't always work.'

'Show me.'

***

Lewis sat on the floor; his broad shoulders made Rochelle, sitting cross-legged, look small in comparison. He shook his head in frustration. 'This isn't fucking working. Alex did the meditation shit, not me,'

'Ay, I never said it would.'

'OK, I'm done. I don't need fucking alters. I'll figure something ou—'

'You're such a hot head. I used to think I would be in places like this forever. Wanna know what changed my mind?'

Lewis shrugged.

'You,' Rochelle looked away. 'I couldn't believe it when Graham told me he knew someone like me. And there you were! You were out there living your life with him. And a private investigator? Oh my god. I didn't even last a week working at Foodland! But you showed me that it's possible. You gave me hope.'

'Pfft. Alex didn't do anything. That was Graham. He was the investigator. I'm the strong one. Tony was the smart one. The rest are just … filler.'

Rochelle punched him in the shoulder and let out a giggle. 'Sorry, not sorry. You're forgetting the most important alter.'

'Not the fucking child.'

'Yeah! Julie would be better at this. Memories wouldn't be as scary for her.'

'No fucking way—'

'Julie, are you there? I have a fun game for us to play …'

***

Julie remembered.

The air was salty. The stench of fish. She remembered the cold. Faces from a lifetime ago flashed before her eyes. A cruel man: bald head, mean eyes, spoke vulgar words. A wise man: glasses, wrote lots of notes, spoke robotically. A little girl: Thin, shivering, helpless.

Clap. Clap. Clap.

The voices of Rochelle and a little girl could be heard throughout the ward.

'Who took the cookie from the cookie jar? Alex took the cookie from the cookie jar.'

Clap. Clap.

'Who me?' Alex sang.

'Yes, you!'

'Not me,' Alex chanted.

'Then who?'

'Tony!' Julie declared.

'Who took the cookie from the cookie jar? Tony took the cookie from the cookie jar,' Julie and Rochelle chanted.

Clap. Clap. Clap.

'Who me?'

'Yes, you!' they all shouted.

'Not me!'

'Then who?'

'Lewis!'

'Who took the cookie from the cookie jar? *Lewis* took the cookie from the cookie jar!'

Lewis: *Fuck off all of you.*

Silence.

'Anything?' Rochelle asked.

Alex took back control.

Lewis: *For the record, I'm not helping because Julie sang a fucking song, OK?*

Tony: *Tony understood. Emotional disturbance gets our wires crossed. The song acted as a prompt which triggered our responses. Julie needed to be the one. Her memories are the least flawed from post-traumatic stress. She can remember smells, faces. She doesn't understand. But she remembers.*

Julie: *Did I do something?*

'The voices are cooperating, I think.' Alex smiled. 'I think my alters came from somewhere but—'

A short knock on the door before it swung open. A psychiatrist stepped in, looking flustered.

'Alex?' he asked.

Alex turned his head slowly and nodded.

'What was all that?'

'Nothing.'

'How are you doing?'

'I'm fine. I'm ready.'

'Ready for what?'

'Whatever you need from me, Doctor. Shall we go to your office?'

Alex got up and followed the psychiatrist out the room. 'I'll be back,' Alex said to Rochelle.

'No…' Rochelle cried. 'Don't. You're stronger than me, Alex. The song proves it. Don't let me find you in this place again. Okay? Do what you gotta do.'

'I don't know what I'm supposed to do now.' Alex muttered.

Rochelle fidgeted, weighing something up in her mind. Then she pushed past the psychiatrist and embraced Alex.

Tony: *Tony does not like to be touched.*

'I had a good patch when I was 16. It was my happy year.' Rochelle whispered in his ear. 'Doctors helped me. Nice doctors. They told me I could get better if I understood my trauma. I wasn't strong enough to face it. You're strong enough, silly.'

'Strong enough for what?' Alex asked.

'To face the ones that gave you those scars.'

CHAPTER 28

THEN - November 2005

Julie had always defeated the villains single-handedly. At least in her mind. She laid on her bed reenacting a daring rescue with her Batman figure when she heard a crash and the door bang. She picked her nose while she yawned and shuffled herself out of bed, making it out like the ground was a long way down for little legs. She heard Graham's voice and tiptoed into the kitchen. A broken bottle on the floor. Julie jumped over the broken glass and followed Graham outside. She followed him all the way to the windless beach before Graham started hacking.

'Pa?' her little voice asked in the dark.

Graham turned around and saw Julie's hunched frame in the dark. Graham rubbed his eyes like a child waking from a nap. Graham had always been patient with Julie, but tonight his face was red with anger.

'I'm not your pa,' Graham mumbled.

'You look like Pa!'

Julie ran over to where he was sitting and jumped onto the sand bank next to him.

'Ooof! My fanny!'

Graham took a big swig of whiskey; the liquid burned his throat.

'What's that?'

'Here, have some,' he said, pushing the bottle into Julie's hands.

'Pa! I can't have that! That's a grown-up's drink.'

'You're almost 18-years-old, Alex. You can do what you like.'

Graham looked out into the distance.

'Pa? Why are you sad?'

'Someone I knew passed away today. Now, don't go being a smart alec, I know better than most how many bloody funerals I've been to.'

'What's a smart alec?'

'Never mind.'

Graham went to take another swig. Alex quickly took control. He straightened himself and reached for the bottle. He emptied the contents onto the shore.

'Hey, that's bloody old stuff!' Graham cried.

Alex took in his surroundings. It was the middle of the night. He could hear music from one of the houses along Tiddy Widdy Beach Road. The night had a tranquil stillness about it. The moon cast a silver glow over the undisturbed waters.

'How long have I been away?' Alex asked. 'And what's wrong with you?'

'A bus driver died.' Graham groaned as he sat down on the sand. 'Did I ever tell you about the worst day of my life?'

'During the war?' Alex asked, sitting next to him.

Graham smiled, relieved to see Alex back in control. 'I survived World War II and lived through a depression, but it was years later, when I stepped onto that school bus, that broke something in me.' Graham shot a look at Alex, who stared at the moon's reflection against the dark ocean. Ready to listen.

Graham took a deep breath. 'It was August 1979. I was still a police officer back then, despite the poor pay and corruption. I remember the bus driver waving me down in my patrol car. I— I was first on scene. I called for back-up. I can still hear the windscreen wipers in my dreams. The driver forgot to turn them off, ignition was still running and all. I don't blame him. That bus was in near immaculate condition, as one would expect from that fancy Norton College, most prestigious school in the state. I remember the vinyl seats with their thick cushioned headrests. When I stepped onto that bus … the smell … that was the worst.'

'Smell? What did you smell?' Alex asked.

'Vomit and dead children.' Graham swallowed. 'There were 20 of them. Some of the finest minds with the brightest futures ahead of them. Saddest thing I've ever seen. They all wore the Norton College dress uniform, all of it stained with blood and sick. I remember the adolescent bodies, some leaned forward in their seat, must have died vomiting. Some had made it to the driver. I remember seeing the scratch marks across his forearms. Their bloodshot eyes stood out against their pale skin. Bodily fluids started to crust around their mouths, yet their hair was neatly trimmed, their ties were meticulously knotted, and not a single shoelace was undone. They were poisoned. They would have all metabolised it at different times. It would have been terrifying, seeing what would happen as you started to feel ill.'

'They all died?' Alex asked timidly.

'All but one. A boy in the back. He was thinner than most of the others and had long hair. Sad features. I thought I saw something when my eyes rested on him. A throb. When I reached for a pulse, the boy grabbed my wrist. Scared the hell out of me. He was choking, pleading for help. By then paramedics were on scene.'

'Who did it? And why?'

Graham shrugged. 'I was at the end of my career by that point, and my detective work was left to younger lads. They found similar poison in a storage shed rented out to the bus driver. I did what I could to push for a conviction. I did some background work on the driver which helped the attorneys get him behind bars for good.'

'You couldn't do much more than that.' Alex placed a hand on Graham's back.

'I got a call from the boy not long after. Wanted to thank me. You know me, any excuse to be showered with adoration. The boy was still in hospital when I laid eyes on him again. Looked even thinner. He complained to me about the hospital food. I told him in my day all I had to eat was a small piece of bread smeared in mutton fat. We had a few jokes. He asked about the case, then the trial. Something … was off about him.'

'What?'

'To be honest, he reminded me a little of you. Sometimes when I'm looking at you, I don't always see a young lad – it's your alters, I know – but this kid … well, I didn't feel like I was talking to a kid. I did some background research on him too, couldn't come up with much … except I remembered seeing a library card on his side table in the hospital. After some digging, I got his borrowing history. Know what I found?'

Alex shrugged.

'Advanced chemistry, forensic toxicology, effects of venom. Or something of the like. But my colleagues never pursued my suspicions. There was nothing else there. But I know that boy left that library card for me to see.'

'So, what happened to the boy?'

'I tried to keep tabs on him, but he became hard to track. I spoke to the bus driver a few times after that. Admitted some of the kids were rude to the boy, teased him a bit. That driver spent the rest of his life in prison, and I don't think he was meant to be there. As Lewis would say, I think I fucked up.'

Shame overwhelmed Graham like a dark shadow.

'I have something for you,' Alex said. 'Get up. Come on now, someone once told me there's no point going through life being bloody miserable.'

Alex swung his arm over Graham and helped the old man limp back to the house. The bottle of whiskey was left in the sand.

When they got back inside, Rex gave a high-pitched bark. Graham had made a small cage enclosure in the kitchen until they figured out what to do with him.

'I didn't want you to hear that,' Graham slurred as Alex helped him inside. 'I didn't want you to know I was a bad person.'

'Bad people don't buy orphaned boys' bikes for their birthdays,' Alex replied as he sat Graham down by the kitchen table.

Graham shrugged. 'Every boy should have a bike.'

'And they don't buy presents for alters of a mentally ill teenager.'

Graham sniffed. 'Lewis needed a fishing rod. And Julie didn't have anything in the house – she needed some toys. It's just things.'

Alex rummaged through some envelopes in his room and rushed back. He threw a treat to Rex on his way past.

'Bad people don't teach you to drive when you steal their car.' Alex placed an envelope on the table.

Graham sulked. 'I didn't want to lose another boy.'

Alex showed Graham the letter he'd retrieved. 'I found this last week. My respite care is ending. I know you have extended it six times. I have to go soon.'

'I know.' Graham sniffed again. 'It's for the best.'

'Yeah,' Alex said dryly. 'An 86-year-old private investigator and a kid with multiple personalities – would never have worked.'

Graham blew his nose with a handkerchief.

'We've helped a lot of people though,' Alex surmised. 'What if there was a way to help a few more?'

Alex pushed a thick folder over to Graham.

'What is this?' Graham asked, flipping through the pages. 'Alex, what is …' He trailed off when he saw the header of a bound document: **ADOPTION PAPERS**.

'I'm not 18 yet. I don't want to replace anyone. But I like living here. With you. There's no pressure though, you don't have to—'

Graham reached up and hugged Alex tighter than ever before.

CHAPTER 29

NOW

It had been 15 years since Alex had broken into his childhood home. Fifteen years since he was caught and beaten, only to be released by his ex-foster father, Ian. The front porch light had not been replaced at 36 Ayling Avenue. The house appeared as dilapidated as he remembered. Lewis could see the kitchen light from across the road. As he approached the slippery steps from the afternoon rain, he heard the sound of dishes clattering. Ian's car was already in the driveway.

Ian Maninga snacked on a bag of potato crisps. Several chip crumbs flew out of his mouth as he spat out insults to the umpires from his seat in front of the TV. It was a close match and his temper rose after each quarter. In the last seven minutes of play he had consumed two beers and his fingers already fumbled for the last few crisps in the greasy packet.

Outside, Lewis stretched his legs and breathed in the fresh air.

Lewis: *It feels good to be outside. And fucking fantastic to be in control again.*

Ian got himself another packet of crisps during the ad break after his team scored a crucial goal to tie the game.

Lewis vaulted the fence. He never heard them until it was too late. Two German Shepherds at the other end of the backyard spun around as soon as they heard him land. Their barks were loud and vicious.

'Shut the fuck up! Shut the fuck up!' Ian bellowed, each word louder and higher pitched than the last.

Alex: *Lewis, jump back out!*

Lewis was rooted to the spot with fear. The dogs bounded for him, and even in the darkness he could see their razor-sharp teeth. Lewis retreated. The dogs went to snap but halted suddenly and sniffed the body that trespassed into their yard.

Julie: *They can smell Rex-y on me! Yes, they can.*

One of them licked Julie on the cheek with a warm but abrasive tongue. Julie giggled and blew them a kiss.

Lewis: *Upsy-daisy, you crazy fuck.*

Julie: *Upsy-daisy.*

The dogs followed Julie with interest as she searched the backyard until she found a cardboard box sticking out of the recycling bin.

Lewis: *Not that fucking box. A meter box!*

There were three minutes left of the game and Ian was on the edge of his seat, snacks and beverages ignored. 'Pick it up, ya lazy fuck! Fucking run! What? Play on? He fucking marked it! He—'

The TV flicked off. 'No. No!!!'

It took Ian a moment to realise it wasn't just the TV, but the whole house that had lost power. He pushed the curtain drapes to the side to check next door. He could still see the blue and green flashes from their TV. He swore under his breath and went out the back with a torch. He was in such a rush getting to the meter box that he never noticed someone slip in through the side door behind him.

The lights came back on as Alex was searching through the bedroom drawers for belts. He had already taken a skewer from the kitchen.

Ian was back in his chair, but he couldn't find the remote control. His agitation increased as he started searching between the cushion covers. He finally found it under the coffee table. As he got down onto his hands and knees to reach for it, something hard pressed into his lower back. His arm was pinned. He tried to push himself up with the other but didn't have the strength. By the time he overcame his shock, his hands were tied behind his back. He twisted his body around in time to see the sole of a boot.

Ian was sitting at the dining table when his vision cleared. His hands, hips and legs were tied to one of the dining chairs by his own belts.

'What the fuck?' he called out.

He saw a young man in the chair next to him, rocking back and forth.

'What the fuck?' he repeated.

'My name is Tony. Not normally my role this. Security. Numbers. Data. I deal with data. Not this. No, not me, I said, but they didn't listen. Never listen to Tony. Shouldn't have put my hand up. Not in school anymore. Shouldn't have to put your hand up, should you?'

'Who else is here?' Ian hissed.

'Several. He admits to three, but I know the truth. More like four. Too many to list. But I'm good with lists. I can write a list and check it twice if you need.'

'Whatcha want? Who are ya?'

'I already said, my name is Tony. See, nobody ever listens to Tony. Tony's read all the books. Shouldn't exist, I shouldn't. I'm an anomaly. Is that the right word? Alternative? I'm alternative. It's you, you are the cause. The reason. I am born because of you. You're like a father. Glad you weren't. Would never have fostered much. Screaming at a TV wouldn't have taught anyone anything. But a foster you were.'

'What the fuck are you talking about?'

Tony continued to rock back and forth. He watched a single ant dart for a chip crumb as he spoke. 'You made the child disappear. What do you call a magician that's lost his magic, Ian? April 2, 15 years ago. You need to remember. You had the shovel, but you weren't gardening the night he came. You remember, yes? You need to remember.'

'What …?' Ian looked closer at the young man before him. 'No … It's not? Alex?'

'No, my name is Tony. But you need to know. Need to see … need to feel what they did to Alex.'

Tony pulled off his shirt. Ian took in all the scars and burns across his body.

'Jesus …! They… You're completely … damaged, aren't ya?'

Tony watched the ant carry the crumb across the kitchen.

'You should never've come. Why are ya here?' Ian bellowed.

'Tony needs to know what happened. Needs to know why. Needs to know the story. Tony has scissors to cut you free once you've told the story. All you'll lose are a few belts. Lost weight over these years, probably could get better sizes anyway. It's important to dress to your shape, everyone always says. Is that what they say? I think that's what they say.'

Ian's anger was replaced with something else. Pity. Any thoughts of the game were long gone. 'What do you want to know?' he asked soberly.

Alex: *Thanks Tony. I'm alright.*

Alex opened his eyes wide. 'Who did you give me to when I was a boy?' Alex asked, continuing to rock back and forth to imitate Tony.

'What good is that to you? I was a gambler, alright? I lost money on footy matches and borrowed more money. I borrowed from the wrong people. I was offered a way out of debt if I gave them you. So, I did. It was the only way my wife and I were gettin' out alive.'

'Who took me?'

'Why? I don't know. I had nothing to do with them. My bookie organised it. He'd all the contacts.'

'Who is he?'

'The bookie? Not seen him in years. I ain't taken money off him since.'

'Where can I find him?'

'You don't want to. The people he knows … They're—'

Alex thumped his fist on the table. 'It never stopped you from sending me to them as a child. A *child*. Knowing full well what they would do. Do not pretend to care for my welfare. You either tell me now or I call the police, and we all sit down together.'

Ian hesitated. 'Bookie's name is Stu. Stu Whittaker. Used to find him in the Shea Oak Tavern. I don't have his number or anything anymore. I don't have anything else. It was so long ago.'

Alex grabbed the scissors and cut the belt straps, releasing Ian. He didn't move.

'What are ya gonna do?'

'I'm going to find him.'

'Look kid, it's too long ago. Even if ya did, you're just gonna get yourself killed. You're not well. How could ya possibly track anyone down?'

Alex placed a business card on the table: Blakemore Investigations.

CHAPTER 30

THEN - July 2007

Alex thought Graham looked like shit. His face was pale, and he was moving slower, his steps unsteady. Graham complained of headaches and a stiff neck during the drive. It troubled Alex.

'You sure we have the right address?' Graham asked. 'They print the road maps too damn small now.'

'Yes, I'm sure. I directed you, didn't I?'

'If you call it directing. Strain on our relationship might be more appropriate.'

Graham double-checked the name and address, bringing his little black book close to his face before he mumbled his satisfaction and knocked on the door.

The door opened and Mrs Henricksen, a weathered old woman, answered. She wasn't frail, but she carried herself in a way that is reserved for the grieving. Graham recognised the look.

'Mrs Henricksen?' Graham enquired.

'Yes.'

'My name is Graham. We spoke on the phone.'

'She killed herself, what else is there to talk about?'

'Yes, well, your daughter was the eighth suicide at that hospital over the last 10 years. That just seems like a great deal to me.'

'My nephew said I couldn't sue.'

'If we can prove negligence or malpractice was involved, that might change. Then we could sue the pants off the bastards.'

Mrs Henricksen's expression softened.

Freshly baked scones were suddenly available as they were welcomed into Mrs Henricksen's living room. Graham waited a moment until his host came back with tea.

'You think I could get some money from the hospital?' Mrs Henricksen asked.

Graham got straight to the point. 'Did Phoebe have much family, Mrs Henricksen?'

'Just me. My late husband died in a car accident. His work paid for Phoebe's care.'

'Beautiful girl. She didn't have a boyfriend?' he asked.

'She did. A serious one … He took off out of the blue right before her admission. Never said why. She never had many other friends. The depression didn't give her much of a life.'

'Was she always depressed?'

'Took a turn for the worse when her father died. And again, when that boy left.'

'Did you visit her at Greenwich?'

'Once. After that I was told no. They said it wasn't helping any.'

'How did she seem when you last saw her?'

'She was happy, almost … said she met a nice doctor that was really helping her.' Mrs Henricksen couldn't hold the tears back any longer. 'It doesn't make any sense. She was getting better. Just tell me what to say. I want the hospital to pay. They should have been watching her. I want them all to go to Hell. Couldn't even return her things to me either. Just the clothes.'

Graham pushed himself up with effort and retrieved a tissue from the hallway table for her.

'Thought you might prefer it over my handkerchief.' He smiled. 'So, your daughter's belongings are missing?'

'We lost most of our photos in a bushfire. She had a picture of her and my husband, one of the few we had left. Assholes lost it. Now I'm sorry, but I don't know how you could help. You're—'

'I know, I know ...' Graham sighed. 'I'm too roguishly handsome for a private investigator—gets too damn distracting.' He winked.

Mrs Henricksen broke into a toothy grin.

Graham examined a framed photo of Pheobe on the coffee table and handed it to Alex.

'Dunno how you think you'll get anything from them. My nephew knows a thing or two about the legal system. Never got anywhere. What can you do differently?'

'Don't worry, sweetheart,' Graham soothed. 'We have something they won't expect.'

Alex felt both sets of eyes on him.

***

Tony wore a backpack with a border collie face on it when he was admitted to Greenwich Hospital. The head nurse, Gaynor Swanson, greeted him at the ward entrance. Her physique was still athletic, but the creases people get past middle age – hardened further by years at the hospital, Tony assumed – added extra years to her face. Behind the lines she had beautiful hazel eyes.

'Lovely to meet you, Tony,' Gaynor said warmly.

'I need to do a poo.' Tony scratched his head.

'We will get you settled into your room. There's a bathroom in there.'

'When you gotta go, ya gotta go. Is that what they say? I think that's what they say. Does the room have TV? It's nearly time for my favourite program, *Big Bang Theory*.'

Tony followed Gaynor round the corner. He passed a group of visitors on their way out and bumped into one of them. She apologised and guided him carefully to his room. He had his own 40-inch TV mounted to the wall, an extra-large single bed, a two-seater lounge, and his own small ensuite fitted with a shower and toilet. Tony placed his bag on the lounge. Gaynor examined it and emptied everything onto the bed.

'They can stay in the bag. That's my bag.'

'Sorry, Tony, the hospital provides you with all the essentials. We will have to keep hold of all your personal items for now. I just need to note everything with you first. Then you need to sign a form.'

'They are very, very important.'

Gaynor picked up a small toiletries bag. There were four separate toothbrushes inside. She wouldn't have thought much of that, but the smallest brush was half the size of the others and was decorated with the *Batman* trademark symbol. There was a red toothbrush with hard bristles, which contradicted the electric toothbrush, which was soft. The final toothbrush looked cheap and had started fraying long ago.

'Tony, why do you have so many toothbrushes?' Gaynor asked.

'To brush my teeth at 6 pm and 7 am,' he replied. 'My breath won't be very fresh if I don't brush my teeth.'

'We will give you another toothbrush,' Gaynor said as she noted the contents.

She reached in the bag and found another, much smaller, toiletries bag. Inside was a brush, hair ties, and hair clips. Nurse Swanson looked up at Tony's short hair.

'And these?' she asked.

'They're not mine,' he said. 'But they should stay in the bag. I think that would be best.'

Nurse Swanson noted them. Two small fluffy toys (a bear and a rabbit) were next for inspection.

'What are their names?' Gaynor asked with a smile.

'I don't know. They're not mine, but they should probably stay in the bag.'

Gaynor went through the rest of the items and packed them away. Some of the belongings weren't as strange: paper and pencils, underwear, a packet of condoms (Lewis: 'Well, you never know in places like this'), children's cough syrup, and a framed picture of a tan-coloured border collie.

'That's Rex, my best friend. He's Tony's dog and lives with Tony. He gives me his paw when I pat him, but not the others. That's why Tony and Rex are mates.'

Gaynor was tempted to leave the photo on the floating shelf by his bed, but rules were rules.

'Sorry, Tony, you will get everything back when you leave here, I promise.'

She was about to leave when she noticed a hidden compartment in the back. She pulled it open and found a mobile phone.

'You will get your phone and the rest of your belongings back when you're discharged, Tony.'

Tony was visibly upset. He collapsed on his bed after he'd scribbled on a form and watched Gaynor walk away with all of his favourite and very important things.

'Bye, Rex,' he sulked. When she left, he went to the toilet and removed the phone he pick-pocketed from one of the visitors at reception. He had Graham's number memorised. He sent a text: *Arrived – T.*

The inpatient ward was quiet at 10 pm. One patient three rooms down called out in a kookaburra laugh.

Tony: *What's that? Scared Tony.*

Alex: *It's okay, Tony.*

He heard nurses go in and settle the patient. The hallway was dark, with only the occasional downlight illuminating a path towards the nurse's station. He could see the cameras in his periphery and hear the footsteps of the night shift going from room to room. Tony moved carefully through the hallway. He spied Gaynor in her office packing up for the evening. He had no choice but to enter another patient's room before she looked up.

Inside was a young woman in her mid-twenties, snoring. It reminded him what was at stake. Eight young women died here. Graham thought Tony could help and he wanted to help. Tony waited another minute before he pressed on. He made it to the double electronic doors that led to the outpatient ward. He pressed the green emergency exit button, and they popped open with a groan.

Tony's swaying body stabilised, and his shuffling feet took on a normal gait pattern. Alex looked at the space with wonder. *I've been here before. This is where I first saw him. Martin.* There was no staff in this section. All he could hear was a vacuum cleaner down the end. He found what he was looking for. The office that Martin led him to all those years ago. **Dr Richards** was printed on the door. Next to the door was a couple of waiting chairs and a small coffee table with magazines. He heard someone coming.

Tony: *Bathrooms, two doors to your left. Tony should go now. Don't want to get caught. Something spooky about this place.*

Alex raced to the bathroom door. Before he stepped inside, he peeked around the corner and saw a cleaner unlock Dr Richard's office. After a moment the cleaner came out with a waste bin and walked back to his trolley around the corner.

Tony: *I don't think we're that fast.*

Alex quietly moved back to the office. He tore off the front cover of a magazine and wedged it between the door and door frame. Just as he got back to the bathroom door, the cleaner returned to Dr Richard's office with the vacuum cleaner. Alex waited patiently. His thoughts drifted…

'You have done your share of breaking in, kiddo, now you're on the other side. Someone broke into this RSL last night and stole all the change in the office. A couple of hundred dollars of loose change. You need to look around, take as much information in as you can, then tell me how they broke in. Bonus points if you can tell me who's responsible.' Graham patted Alex on the back and took a seat by the bar.

It was late. The RSL was empty except for the two of them.

'Who?' Alex spat. 'How the hell am I going to figure that out? There's no way you could know who.'

'Couldn't I?' Graham smiled and helped himself to a packet of peanuts. 'My fee.'

Alex walked around the clubrooms. The bar was still well stocked with bottles of beer in the back fridge. The bar snacks that weren't getting raided by Graham remained in place on the shelves. The chairs were all stacked up on the tables. Alex examined the windows. They were all cleaned recently and in place. He checked the locks on the doors. There were no scratch marks around the keyholes. He found the manhole and a torch. He used some stacked chairs to climb up. The attic space was filthy. No footsteps. No one had been up there for a long time. He checked the kitchen next. Cupboards were full. Bathrooms were pristine and had no other entries/exits aside from the main door. The cleaning room, situated between the bathroom and an office, was bare except for a vacuum cleaner and mop. A tap was dripping in the utility sink. Alex turned it off.

'Details, Alex, collect details.'

He checked the office next. Paperwork was scattered over the table. He looked through the piles of documents. Rosters, invoices, correspondence. Something caught his eye. An invoice for a cleaning company. It stood out to him because all the other invoices used a different company. The RSL had taken on a new cleaning business recently. Alex checked the cleaning room again. He took a closer look at the vacuum and mop and ran outside.

Alex kept running, out to the carpark. Graham struggled to keep up.

'It's cold out here, kiddo. Any chance we can do the clue hunting inside?'

'It was the cleaners.'

Graham smiled. 'Why?'

'No forced entry, so someone must have had a key. I checked the member registry log, no new members over the last couple of years. So, it's either a long-serving member who suddenly decided to steal after all this time, or someone new. The cleaners are new, new enough that they wouldn't know that the CCTV camera didn't work. All the cleaning equipment is here, so they don't need to bring anything, but that vacuum cleaner needs bags.' He drew a breath. 'So, if it was me, I would put all the money in a vacuum bag then walk right out with it. There are four bins on the way out, but look—'

Alex picked up a vacuum bag caught in the shrubs. 'It got tossed out here instead – the furthest car park from the CCTV camera.'

'All deduction. How do we prove it?'

'You said it was loose change. Lots of coin, yeah? They would have to take that to the bank. There are only a couple of banks within tolerable driving distance of Ardrossan. We could get a photo of the cleaners easy enough. We have their business details – and then ask the banks. I'm right, aren't I?'

Graham shrugged and walked back towards the clubrooms. 'Cash is still in the register,' Graham barked back. 'Jimmy was rostered to work the bar last night. He forgot to put the change back in the safe. Not every case is a case. Sometimes, especially around here, it's just a misunderstanding. Come on kiddo, or I'm going to catch pneumonia. By the way, the clubrooms are pristine.

Cleaners are doing an exemplary job. Put that bag in the bin, will you?'

The vacuuming stopped, stirring Alex out of his daydream. When the cleaner moved down the hallway, Alex tried the office door; the magazine cover created enough of a wedge to stop the lock mechanism sliding all the way. Alex lifted the handle hard as he turned it. The door opened.

Dr Richard's office was filled with filing cabinets. There was only enough space for a small corner desk against the far wall. The psychiatrist was an organised man, and each of the cabinets was labelled with a letter of the alphabet. Alex found a Dictaphone on the desk and rewound it to the start. Dr Richard's voice crackled from the little device.

Dr Richards: 'Phoebe overdosed on her medication last night. The nurses checked on her the following morning, but it was too late. To me this makes no sense. Based on her progression, I was planning her discharge for next Tuesday. I've scoured through all my notes and recordings, and there was nothing in her sessions that gave me the slightest indication that she was suicidal again.'

Alex rummaged through more tapes and pressed play.

Dr Richards: 'Phoebe asked to see her mother today. She hasn't done that in weeks. She told me a demon is making her feel guilty about her abortion. She genuinely believed this, and has had no prior instance of schizophrenia or anything re—'

Alex looked through Phoebe's paperwork. Then he moved onto another name. *Sometimes a case isn't a case*, he thought to himself. *But sometimes it is*. He found the third name on his list when he noticed a yellowed folder in the back of a drawer. His file. It was the folder he brought in for Martin years ago, with a single note attached. It read:

Alex was referred to me back in August by Dr Reid. The morning of his first appointment a file was left on my office floor with Alex's medical history. Despite numerous attempts of reaching out, Alex has yet to make a session. I fear for the boy's safety and will continue to make calls.

***

Alex flicked through several documents, using the mobile phone as a light to read in the dark. He knew Graham was anxiously waiting for him at their new office they leased in the heart of Adelaide. Graham would be sitting in there, staring at the large white board with photos of the Greenwich staff pinned with magnets, waiting for the phone to ring.

Alex dialled his number. Graham answered immediately. 'Blakemore Investigations, this is Graham.'

'I've got the link,' Alex said.

'Whose phone are you calling from?' Relief in his voice.

'I know what's connecting the victims. They all had abortions.'

'Well done, kiddo. Are you alright?'

'I'm fine.'

'What have you found out about the staff?'

'There's only two that have worked here long enough. A Dr Richards and a nurse, Gaynor Swanson. I've found something else. A resume. I think this is bigger than just Greenwich,' Alex added.

'You've got to be careful now, Alex. Either we're dealing with a severe case of malpractice or—'

'It's a serial killer,' Alex finished.

CHAPTER 31

NOW

Martin was right, Alex was drawn to the darkness. Despite all the warnings, he pursued the darkest cases. Alex found himself in front of Ian's computer and began his search. There were two Stu Whittakers, three Stuart Whittakers, and one Stewart Whittaker on Facebook. Of the six candidates, three resided locally, and one profile was set to private. Two were in their early twenties. Too young. This left two possibilities (with the conscious thought that the man he was looking for didn't have social media). A Stuart Whittaker, sensible enough to keep his profile private, had a profile picture of him with a woman in AFL apparel. Collingwood supporters. There was also a Stu Whittaker who didn't have much information and had a picture of a dog for his profile picture. He clicked on the picture of the Collingwood supporters. Another woman was tagged in the picture. Caren Whittaker. The wife. Her profile was public. Alex scanned through her various uploads. He always found women posted on social media far more often than men. Every life event, every social event, every good restaurant was uploaded and shared by the helpful Caren. Several of those restaurants were within 20 kilometres of the Shea Oak Tavern. He scrolled back. It took him 15 minutes to scroll back five years' worth of photos until he found a post of Stuart and Caren holding hands in front of a house with a 'For Sale' sign. *We did it, our little piece of paradise away from the hustle and bustle of our crazy lives.*

It was a better picture of Stuart. Alex got it printed and asked Ian for confirmation. He had him. He took note of the real estate agent at Fine Realty tagged in the post and looked him up online. There was a $5,000 gift card promotion on his website for a friend or family referral. Alex called the realtor using the number at the bottom of the webpage. It was 6 pm but someone picked up within three rings.

'Jack Hyatt from Fine Realty speaking. How can I help?'

'Hi Jack, I'm not sure if you can help. My wife mentioned you have a $5,000 promotion,' gushed Alex.

'Yes, absolutely. Are you looking at putting your house on the market?'

'Well, yes, we're thinking about it. I'm not sure if you remember. You sold a house to a friend of ours, Caren Whittaker. We were hoping to move into a similar spot as we love the area.'

'Oh, yes, yes, hold on a moment.'

Alex heard furious tapping on the other line.

'Ah, yes, Caren and Stuart. You're looking at Springwood?'

Alex googled Springwood. 'Yes, that's right. They were an earlier release though, weren't they?'

'Yeah, stage two. Stage six has just come up. Could I get some details from you, and we can run through some options?'

'Certainly.' Alex looked up the stage two release. It included four streets, more than enough. 'Sorry, Jack, someone is knocking on my door. Can I call you back tomorrow morning?'

Alex scouted stage two of the Springwood release until he found the house that matched the front of the photo. He shook his head in wonder. It had taken 20 minutes to get the name and location. He wondered how Graham had managed to do this back in his day.

He parked Graham's Toyota four houses down from the matching house. The car hadn't been washed in weeks so it blended in. Two cars were parked in the driveway. Alex sat and waited. He spotted a stray cat scurrying out from underneath the gutter hole and run down the street. His mind wandered back to another stakeout.

Julie: 'This is fun.
I spy with my little eye, something that begins with C.'
Alex: Eyes on the church, Julie.
Julie: Okay, that was an easy one.
Graham looked at Julie sternly. 'Quiet, Julie.'
Graham's hand gripped the steering wheel as he watched the church across the road. They had been in the car for 3 hours and had played every car game together that had been invented. It was nearing midnight and only two cars had passed since their stakeout. They had gone back to where they started with 'I spy'.
'Can we go now, Pa?'
'You remember the deal, Julie. We have to wait and watch. And you need to pay attention.'
'Why?'
'Because this is important for him.' Graham sighed. 'I need Alex to learn how this job is done. He needs to work so he can function in society. You might remain a child, Julie, but you can't get in the way of Alex's future.'

A porch light stirred Alex out of his daydream. A man came out of the house. Alex quickly reached for his camera and took several photos of the man climbing into the SUV.

He followed the SUV as discreetly as possible. Graham had always done this job, but Alex managed it until the vehicle parked on the side of the road opposite the Shea Oak Tavern. Alex kept driving and turned around 5 minutes later to park nearby.

Alex wore a football guernsey over the top of a jumper and stuck a cap over the small amount of fuzz that was growing back on his scalp. Luckily Ian had supported the same team and had no objections to Alex borrowing some merchandise. He could hear the noise of the bar before he crossed the road. Laughter and shouting. He could smell booze by the time he hit the footpath. When he entered, he pushed through the busy crowd and ordered a beer. The taste of the alcohol made him want to gag, but he was able to blend in well enough as he found a spot where he could watch the football match on the big screen. In his periphery he scanned the crowd. Finding Stuart wasn't hard. There was a collection of people around him taking bets. He hadn't changed tricks after all this time.

He noticed Stuart's hands as they collected $50 and $100 bills from various heavy breathing patrons. Even in the dim light of the pub, Alex picked up the slight ring-finger tan on his left hand where a wedding ring should have been.

Alex followed him all evening, into the wee hours of the morning.

Stuart returned home at 11 pm. Alex waited 15 minutes before he knocked on the door. Stuart answered.

'Who is it, honey?' his wife called out.

Without saying a word, Alex raised his phone, displaying to Stuart pictures from the night before. He swiped across to showcase various images of Stuart with a woman half his age.

'Let's speak in my car,' Alex insisted.

'Just someone from work, babe. I'll be back in a minute,' Stuart called out in reply.

Stuart followed Alex's instructions and sat in the passenger seat of the Super Saloon.

'Who the fuck are you?' Stuart demanded.

'It doesn't matter,' Alex started. 'I've already connected with your wife on messenger. You're going to give me something, or I'm going to send her every picture I collected from last night.'

'You've got no idea who I am. You think blackmailing me is going to work? What's to stop me from breaking your fucking neck right now?'

Lewis: *Oh, yes, please. I love this guy.*

'Could you explain away that commotion to your wife as well?' Alex asked.

'How much do you want?' Stuart snapped.

'Not money. Information. Ian Maninga borrowed money off you once. You took a child. I need to know who you gave him to.'

'Oh, fuck this. No, fuck this,' he ranted.

Stuart reached for the door. Alex pulled him back.

'Are you a cop?' Stuart started to sweat; his face grew pale.

'No. Who did you get involved with Stuart?' Alex asked calmly.

'Ian was an idiot. An absolute fool. I had nothing to do with any of that shit. He borrowed a lot of money from some guys in town. I had nothing to do with them. I just knew someone looking for something discreet. Willing to pay top dollar. I don't know who they were.'

'Ian said you knew them,' Alex revealed. 'Perhaps I'll ask you both together.'

'No. No, just wait a minute.' Stuart breathed in deeply, collecting his thoughts. 'I *didn't* know the guys. They threatened to kill Ian. And me for introducing him. I … You're not a cop? You have to say if you are.'

'Why would I go to the trouble of getting those photos if I was a cop, Stuart?'

'Right. Well …' Stuart looked off into the distance. 'One of those guys said they were after kids. Foster kids. I knew Ian had a foster boy. I suggested it may be a way to get him off the hook. The wife wanted the kid, not him. And they were planning to send him back anyway. It wasn't a big deal.'

'And these men that took the child, they're dangerous?' Alex asked.

'Of course they're fucking dangerous! Are you stupid?'

'Then why are you still alive, Stuart?'

Stuart's face went paler.

'They needed you for something. I'm guessing you have arranged other deals with them too.' Alex suggested.

'What do you want from me, man?'

'Whatever money you made, your wife can take it from you. If she divorces you, these photos will end you financially. Would she divorce you, Stuart?'

'What the fuck do you want from me?' he repeated.

'I need to find the men that took the boy. I think you know how.' Alex didn't take his eyes off him.

'I don't. I swear. I don't. There were no names given out. Nothin'. All I did was drop the boy off.'

'Where did you take him?'

'What? I don't …' He sighed. 'They had this warehouse in Port Adelaide. Made the transfer look legitimate.'

Alex opened Google maps on his phone. 'Show me.'

Stuart pointed to a place on the east side of the port.

'Please man, don't let my wi—'

Alex didn't catch the rest as he pushed him out of the car.

Alex found a warehouse near where Stuart had pointed to on the map, but it was abandoned. *Perhaps for decades*, Alex thought, as he took in all the pigeon poo and graffiti on the external walls. The inside was worse. Walls had been knocked down, leaving nothing but a dark empty husk, to which the salty elements had laid siege over time.

Alex wondered if this was where the hunt would end. Martin knew about Mike's connection to his past. He knew what happened to Alex. Alex was certain of it. His past was a connection to Martin, somehow. But now Alex felt lost.

Lewis: *That asshole gave you a bum steer. There's nothing here! Even if they did meet, they would have just picked a random location.*

Alex: *I dunno. Stu wouldn't want us coming back to visit him again. And a child isn't your typical backalley transaction.*

Tony: *Remember. Remember. Remember.*

Alex spent his life supressing, hiding, dissociating. No more. He closed his eyes and brought himself back to the cage.

He remembered a girl being torn from his fingers and sitting in the cage wailing. There was a flicker of light as a dark hand brought a lighter towards him. The cage rocked from side to side ...

Alex set the memory aside as he walked through the abandoned warehouse. His hand swept across a dusty sign that had eroded and collapsed near the entrance. He couldn't make out the words. He sniffed the air and caught a whiff of fuel and briny seaweed mixed with the salty tang of the sea breeze. It triggered an old image of men leaving him among shipping containers with a logo printed on the side: **Rivett Shipping Company.** The cage continued to rock and all he could see was darkness. But he knew he was at sea because the waves crashed against the side of the ship, nudging the cage that broke him.

Alex picked up the old sign.

Lewis: *They had us on a fucking boat, Alex. That's why you're afraid of water.*

Alex: *And this shipping company must have known something.*

Alex's posture shifted. He shuffled over to a corner and rocked back and forth.

Tony: *Give Tony your phone.*

Tony searched through various business registries for Rivett Shipping Company until he came up with a contact name.

Alex: *That's ... Cheng Mah. Graham's suspect from a lifetime ago.*

Alex remembered his failure after he dropped Cheng's laptop. He couldn't fail again.

Tony: *I have a business address and email. I can hook him in. Can get him in a web through the big wide web but will need more than belts to extract any more data. Not my job – my job's done. You're welcome.*

Alex: *And I can't do this by myself.*

Lewis: *You're a chicken shit. I'll make him squeal.*

Alex: *It would only get us arrested or worse. We need to be more subtle.*

Julie: *When you get stuck, you ask for help, that's what Pa always told me. You get more done as a team.*

Alex: *We haven't got anyone else to ask.*

They all heard a cackle. They all ignored it. Alex remembered something Graham said in a dream.

Tony: *Make a sale, make a deal. It costs our soul but we make a deal.*

Lewis: *He's right. We meet with the devil. She will talk to us.*

CHAPTER 32

THEN - July 2007

Alex sat in the dark, unaware his life was about to change. He hid in the closet, careful not to make a sound. He had broken into another home. He found what he was looking for. The jewellery box rested in his sweaty hands. Now he waited. He heard the jingle of keys as Gaynor opened the door and stepped into her home. She walked past Alex, who held his breath, and went to the bathroom. Alex heard the running water from a tap. He could hear her move to the bedroom, which made him nervous. If she noticed anything—A knock at the door. Alex let out a breath.

Gaynor moved quickly; Alex noticed her makeup was removed on her way past. She answered the front door. Graham beamed up at her.

'I sincerely apologise for the time, madam, but this could not wait. I have something that you might want to see.'

'Who are you?' Gaynor demanded.

'My name is Graham. Proprietor of Blakemore Investigations. I've been looking into the suicides at the Greenwich Hospital psychiatric clinic. You killed them, of course, but I have something you really must see. I'm 94-years-old. I haven't carried a gun in 35 years. I'm of no threat to you.'

Gaynor's jaw dropped, and her body stood tense. She looked outside, Alex assumed she was scanning the empty street for witnesses. It was quiet and he had no problems breaking in through the laundry window earlier. She pushed the door open and waved Graham in.

'Could I have a cup of tea, please? You don't happen to have a Russian Caravan, do you?' Graham asked. 'I tried that yesterday and it was bloody beautiful.'

Gaynor appeared confused. Graham made himself at home. He pulled the coffee table closer to the lounge suite and started placing pictures and reports onto the table.

'I'll see what I can find you,' she answered lamely.

By the time he had everything laid out, she'd brought over two mugs.

'Thank you, my dear. Shall I get started?' Graham blew on the hot tea.

'Who are you again?' Gaynor sneered.

'I'm a private investigator. I do mostly rural cases, but I'm branching out to give my partner more experience. Shall I?'

'Go on. I can't wait to hear this narrative.'

'Okay, well … my investigation really picked up when I realised all of the victims, I can call them that now, had an abortion. A bloody hard thing to find out by the way—no wonder you have got away with this for so long. But eight suicides of young women with recent abortions at Greenwich, another four during your time at Memorial Hospital, another six during your residency at St Mark's … a pattern started to form. But why? I wondered if you had lost a child. I looked into your background but there was no mention of a child. I'm pretty good at this, I'll have you know." Graham winked and smiled at her, before continuing. "After working my magic, I got hold of an incident report. Your first residency was similar to Greenwich. You were working in the mental health space but dealing with some pretty rotten offenders. You were attacked by a man. It was serious.'

Gaynor's eyes reddened.

'I'm very sorry, my love, most despicable act in the world. But something came of that, didn't it? You have strong morals around the subject of abortion, and I can understand the need to carry through. But you couldn't face becoming a mother, could you?' He looked away from Gaynor. 'Did you find the trophies?'

Alex stepped out from the closet and brought in a small jewellery box. 'A hidden compartment in the bedroom – photos and trinkets of all eighteen girls. Police are on their way.'

'Tony?' Gaynor blanched, full of confusion. 'How did you—'

Graham interrupted. 'This is Alex. I have lived with him for nearly 10 years now – he is a remarkable young man.'

Gaynor snarled. 'You faked this—'

'He didn't fake anything. He has had a traumatic life but has used his sorrow to help an old man to help others.'

Gaynor smashed her coffee mug and lunged at Graham with surprising speed. Graham couldn't stop her from pulling him close and pressing the pointy end of the broken mug against his neck. Graham waved Alex back.

'I'll end this now,' Gaynor hissed.

'You tried reaching out to the boy years later.' Graham struggled, waving Alex away. 'But he was lost in the system. I found him.'

'Bullshit!' Gaynor shouted.

'Alex, take five steps back and let Gaynor review the reports on the table.'

Gaynor's curiosity got the better of her. Alex inched closer and tried to read them from behind her. The first folder had the medical reports of the baby's birth. The next statement had the hospital report of a baby on life support for 13 days. The next report had information around the infant going into state care.

Adoption forms showed a successful fostering to an Ian and Cheryl Maninga. The child was named 'Alex'.

Gaynor looked up at Alex's hazel eyes. 'Not possible.'

Alex was breathing heavily, forcing himself not to hyperventilate.

'There is a time, my lad, that I can't account for,' Graham said to Alex. 'I don't know what happened to you after you left your foster home. But this case was for you. This is where it all started. Now I know this fruit loop isn't the fairytale parent you dreamt of reconnecting with. We can keep searching–'

'No,' Alex snapped. 'I don't want to know any more.'

Gaynor couldn't take her eyes off Alex. 'You're…'

'He's perfect.' Graham swallowed. 'I will look after him for as long as I'm able. You don't need … you …' The left side of Graham's face drooped. He vomited.

'Graham!'

Police and ambulance arrived within six minutes. Alex held Graham, who muttered nonsense. Gaynor, surrounded by evidence of her murder and motherhood, stood by and watched Alex with the last few moments of her freedom.

CHAPTER 33

NOW

'Do not, under any circumstances, touch the prisoner. Do not give the prisoner anything. If you do either, you will be removed immediately. If you want to stop, press the button. If you become uncomfortable, press the button. If you are threatened, you know what to do. Any questions, Mr Blakemore?'

The red-faced guard addressing him didn't blink as Alex looked around the narrow hallway. There were seven prison guards – either behind desks, in front of monitors, or guarding doors. They all watched him with vacant expressions.

Adelaide Women's Prison had a musty smell to it when he first entered. It made him think of cheap fragrances that masked the stench of something more sinister. The prison was over 60-years-old but well maintained. He stood in a white hallway between two electronic gates. The polished floors were still damp from a recent mop.

'No questions,' Alex replied.

The guard directed him to raise his arms, and he was searched for a third time since entering the penitentiary by more state-of-the-art security systems. He could feel the stitches in his abdomen tug against his flesh as he reached up. The gate in front of him beeped and he followed the guard through a brightly lit corridor. But he couldn't withdraw. Couldn't lose control. *Not now*. The guard stopped at a door on the left and punched a number into the keypad. A green light flashed and Alex was ushered inside. The room had a single table and two chairs.

'It's not too late to change your mind,' the guard whispered.

Alex gave him a polite smile and sat down. He was handed a small remote with a red button that he could push at any time. The guard muttered something under his breath and left. The door closed with a resounding *bang*. It was warm, so he removed his grey tweed jacket and slipped it over his chair. Another door opened. He heard the jingle-jangle of the cuffs. The feet shuffled. Alex got a handle on his nerves as the two guards restrained Gaynor in the chair directly in front of him. He had expected to be separated from her by bars or a glass window, but in this private meeting area, there was nothing separating them at all.

Gaynor looked different than the last time he saw her before her arrest. She appeared younger, well rested. Her expression was vacant, as though she were looking through Alex. She didn't blink. The room was silent except for the final *clicking* of the prisoner's bonds. The guards moved away – there was another *bang* from a heavy door – signifying that they were alone.

'I expected to see you sooner.' Gaynor coughed, revealing a stretch of time since she last used her voice. 'I wondered when you would come to gloat. I saw the papers after I was caught, you know. They had a picture of your old man with that stupid grin of his, all excited to have caught a serial killer. I heard the name they gave me. Archangel of Death. What name will they give you?'

'Don't want one.'

'The names we don't want are often the ones that stick. Alex *Blakemore* … So, you took the old man's name. His own vain attempt to continue his legacy, I bet. If you haven't come to gloat, why are you here?'

'I need your help.'

Gaynor cracked a toothy grin. 'And why would I help you?'

'I get that I ruined your life. But you tried looking for me when I was very young. I was taken somewhere by people, and that's why you never found me. Things might have been different for you if you did. I have found one of those people and I need answers. You can help me, or do nothing, and help them.'

Gaynor tilted her head back and laughed. 'You are right about one thing. You ruined my life. How could I help you from in here? You're not a hotshot detective that can release me for a day to solve the mystery. You're a broken boy that was misled by an old man into reliving his heyday.'

'But it was enough to catch you.'

Gaynor weighed Alex's words carefully. 'Can I touch you?' she asked. 'Just once. I want to know what you feel like.'

Julie: *She's very, very scary.*

Tony: *Tony does not like to be touched. But she appears very malnourished. Gums are receding, could be a sign of osteoporosis. Even with Alex's abdominal wound, this woman should not be a threat.*

Lewis: *Fuck's sake, do I have to remind you all about the last time I underestimated an osteoporotic woman?*

Gaynor opened her palm. Her wrists strained against the handcuffs bolted into the table. Alex placed his left hand in hers. She closed her eyes and smiled. *Silly, silly boy.*

CHAPTER 34

THEN - July 2007

For the very first time, with all the tubes and catheters, Alex thought Graham looked old. The old man was asleep in the hospital bed, but his strained expression couldn't hide his pain. Graham's hand felt cold in his.

'Sorry Alex, did you hear me?'

Alex ignored the doctor behind him. He hadn't even noticed when he came in. All he heard was the beeping of Graham's vitals on the monitor. It sounded slow. The smell of disinfectant and toilet spray made him want to choke.

'Your father had an ischemic stroke to the left side of his brain. We believe this is due to atrial fibrillation – it's common. His heart just can't pump blood as efficiently as it used to. The area of the stroke has affected his speech, his vision, his comprehension …'

Alex's thoughts went back to Graham at the beach. *Always encouraging.*

Alex was the youngest participant and easily broke off from the crowd at the start of the Yorke Peninsula fun run. He admired the soft golden hues of the sandy dunes, which contrasted with the earthier colours of the cliffs. The sedimentary rocks along the cliffs created red and green patterns in the sunrise.

FuSwackaaaayoujaaaaAljaaaaaex!

Alex stopped. His heart hammered in his chest. No. Must go faster.

I'm here fuck-swaaaaajaaaaaa-er

The voices continued to morph and merge. His headache migrated to different areas of his brain. His legs began to buckle. He was ready to give in.

Lewis: I'm here to stay, fuck face!

Julie: Swear jar!

Alex continued running. His breathing got heavier as he moved away from the coastal wattle and banksias surrounding the park and tackled the last leg of the event in the town of Ardrossan.

Alex: Not now, I don't want to hear it.

Lewis: Like you have a choice, dumb fuck.

Julie: Swear jar!

Lewis: Shut the fuck up!

Julie: I don't like swearing, you know it's not very nice.

Tony: Eyes everywhere not very nice either. Tony doesn't like all the attention. No, no, no. What's nicer than friendly words? Anonymity.

Alex became self-conscious as he ran along the main street of Ardrossan, oblivious to the cheers of those lined up to watch the finishers.

'Keep going my boy!' Graham called out. 'You've won this race!'

Alex searched for the source of the voice and found Graham and Yoddi clapping and cheering, moving with Alex towards the finish line.

'I can't!' Alex mouthed to him.

Graham stepped over the balustrade and came over. He huddled close and whispered to Alex while all eyes were on them. 'What's wrong, kiddo?'

'I can't stop the voices,' Alex whimpered. 'Running used to control them. Now it doesn't. It's not working.'

Graham looked over to the finishing line. Alex was 20 metres away.

'Are they all as fierce as Yoddi?' Graham asked.

'I don't know. I don't think so. There's something wrong with one of them, Tony, but…I don't think he wants to hurt anyone.'

'Focus on that one kiddo, what's he saying?'

Tony: I'm no leader, not me. We all like to stay away from the citrus light. Lemon or lime. Limelight? Is that what they say? Tony wants to blend in, not working very well at the moment. If we finish it then maybe everyone will stop the staring. That would be very, very nice. Yeah, everybody should stop the staring.

'I think he wants me to finish the race,' Alex said.

'Then pump those arms, kiddo, I guarantee those tired legs will follow.'

Alex snapped out of it as hospital curtains were drawn across Graham's bed on all sides. Alex could feel a twitch as he held his hand.

'When can he go home?' Alex asked the doctor.

'He's going to require intensive rehabilitation. Is there someone else I can call? You were noted as his next of kin but is there other family we could get in contact with?' the doctor queried. 'He's going to need a lot of support.'

Alex: *He is the support.*

Graham's breathing was shallow in the bed. Alex could hear the doctor's voice reverberate around the room. A nurse came in and took some blood.

'When can he go home?' Alex asked again.

He turned to the doctor, who looked back at him with concern.

Time passed. The hospital room was dark. Alex could hear the slow beeping of the monitor and the staff shuffling around behind the curtain dividers. Alex almost drifted to sleep himself when he heard wheezing.

'Graham?'

'Wh-wh-who are you?' Graham asked weakly.

Alex grabbed Graham's hand and held it tight. 'Graham? Do you know who I am?'

'Y-you … You? Do I know you?'

'Do you remember me?'

Graham let go of his hand and pretended to draw. Alex found some paper and pen in the room and gave it to him. Graham scribbled a note and gave it to him. It read: *You are Alex. You are my ~~fav~~ best*.

Alex hugged Graham tight and sobbed into his neck.

'S-s-sorry. Sorry.'

'I love you,' Alex cried.

Graham scrubbed out the writing and wrote something else: *Did we get in the paper?*

Alex grinned. 'Not just the paper. Blakemore Investigations got on the news!'

Graham managed a smile. He gingerly lifted a hand. Alex high-fived him.

After two days of hospitalisation, Graham was sitting upright in his bed drinking an apple juice. They had transferred him to Modbury Hospital for more intense allied health treatment. Alex sat on the chair next to Graham's bed as he shuffled the deck of cards.

A young physiotherapy student introduced herself. She had dark hair with a fringe and physique that reminded Alex of Wonder Woman. She had a beautiful smile that encouraged Graham as she tested his ability to stand and walk.

'Well, if it isn't the famous detective,' she said with her beautiful smile. 'Your photo's been on the TV.'

Graham blushed. 'I'm very ang … no … very ha … happy to stay here with you. I'm going to have a birthday party this year. I'll send you an … an … invite.'

'I'd love to accept if you think I would fit in.'

'I'm not inviting any old codgers if that's what you mean. Want it to be a party, not a bloody wake!' Graham chortled.

The physio placed several puzzles on the table. 'You're going to come for a walk with me, Graham. Then you're going to make me breakfast.'

'Now you're talking!'

'He's doing remarkably well,' she said to Alex. 'We test for a lot of things before we discharge. We'll make sure he can do all of his activities of daily living. A social worker will be up at lunchtime if you will be around for that?'

'Yeah, have a break, kiddo. You're camp … bugger it! You're *cramping* my style.'

'All right. I'll give Yoddi a call with an update. She's coming up to visit tomorrow.' Alex smiled as he watched Graham shuffle off down the corridor.

Graham turned to Alex. 'Stop worrying, kiddo. Th-th-this isn't going to do me in. I-I-I know it.'

'I was really worried about you,' Alex admitted.

'S-serves you left for all the st-stress you've caused me.' Graham chuckled so much he started coughing. 'Go on, bugger off. To-to-morrow y-y-you can play nurse and wipe my bum.' He grinned.

Alex cracked a smile and left.

'Hey, k-ki-kiddo,' Graham called out.

Alex stopped by the door, 'Yeah?'

'I l-l-love you.'

'I love you too.'

CHAPTER 35

NOW

Martin Harslett was surrounded by 52,000 people. The roar of the crowd was deafening as a last-minute goal was kicked at the end of the quarter. A sea of black, white and teal against yellow and black filled the perimeter of Adelaide Oval. Martin sat in the corporate box, high above most of the spectators, where he watched the football game intently. In the box to his left sat the state premier, who was enjoying a beer with the number one ticket holders of both teams. He watched the premier tilt his head back and laugh. After the previous Showstopper attacks, the premier was praised for acting swiftly by cancelling events of any spectacle until someone was apprehended. To Martin's surprise, the football match was allowed to take place.

At the end of the half-time break, Martin's phone vibrated in his pocket. He read his text: **It's done.** Spectators began returning to their seats. Clapping and chanting erupted from the northern end of the field as the ruckmen took their positions. The umpire prepared for the bounce, and the game began again. Martin placed one earpiece in to listen to the commentary.

Commentator: *Another clearance from Johnson, who gets it to the Stallion – that is a terrible kick ... and it's touched. Play on, good handball from debutant Wilson, but jeez, he's far too slow for this league.*

Martin rose from his seat and stepped towards the pane of glass, the only barrier between him and the atmospheric stadium. His eyes were on the crowd, not the game. He watched their faces fill with confusion as a player dropped to his knees.

A replay on the big screen at the east end of Adelaide Oval replayed the legendary defensive player breaking free from a tackle and kicking the ball to the opposition before toppling forward. When he looked up, the cameras showed blood around his mouth.

Then another player from the opposition dropped. The umpires looked around in confusion. They blew their whistles. Another player at the other end of the field clutched his belly and vomited. Doctors and physios from both sides ran onto the field. The downed players started convulsing violently. Cameramen crept closer to capture the spectacle. For the first time that evening there was silence within the crowd. When three players became unresponsive, and another nine were left convulsing on the ground, someone in the crowd yelled 'SHOWSTOPPER!'

The stadium filled with screams. Black, white and teal blended with yellow and black as supporters rushed for the exits. Crazed opportunists jumped over the fence and ran towards their favourite players. Security guards who survived the stampede of fleeing spectators made it onto the oval and tried to help the players. Sirens and helicopter rotors were heard in the distance. The premier, pale and in a state of shock, was helped out of the box by his associates. He made eye contact with Martin on the way out. Martin showed no emotion as he stepped out of the box and merged with the evacuating Adelaide Oval staff.

By the time paramedics reached the scene, 14 players lay dead on the grass. The playing field was littered with blood, vomit and rubbish. Among the litter was a tray of drink bottles. Blue electrolytes leaked onto the grass and soaked into the dirt under the bright lights of the stadium.

CHAPTER 36

THEN - December 2008

Alex felt surreal waiting for the police when he wasn't in trouble. He sat next to Graham in a waiting area at SAPOL headquarters in Angas Street. Alex, now 18-years-old, was two heads taller than his adopted father. Graham whistled to himself as he looked around the room. His gaze fell on the officers behind the glass working at the desk. An anxious line of people queued outside the door. The sliding doors opened every couple of seconds as new people came in and realised the line trailed back outside.

'Know what you're gonna say, kiddo?' Graham asked quietly in Alex's ear.

Alex shrugged. 'Just gonna roll with it. Say everything was your idea.'

Graham chuckled. 'One piece of advice, kiddo. You're the only one that can get through this today. Just Alex. Also, I probably wouldn't mention all the, you know, detective work we've been doing. Hell, I would stay clear of discussing the driving practice before you had your Ls, just to be safe.'

'Is there anything else?' Alex mocked.

'Since you asked, I wouldn't disclose any further break-ins. I definitely did not teach you to pickpocket, pick a lock or pick your nose. And maybe don't mention Gaynor is your mother. Might be a bad start.'

'Mr Blakemore?' called out a tall police officer in his mid-fifties, clean shaven with heavy bags under his eyes.

Alex nodded and Graham followed close behind. The two men were led into a small interview room consisting of a desk and four chairs. Graham was the first to make himself comfortable. 'Can we get some tea going? Any chance of rustling up some biscuits as well?' Graham asked.

The officer stared blankly at Graham.

'Got any scotch fingers? Bloody love those,' Graham added.

The officer mumbled something and left the room. He came back a few minutes later with some disposable mugs on a cardboard tray along with a packet of yoyo biscuits. Graham thanked him and sipped his tea.

'Mr Blakemore, thank you for coming in today. Has it been explained to you why this interview was requested?' the officer asked.

'Yes,' Alex replied, 'I'm applying to be a licenced private investigator. Something was flagged in my probity check.'

The officer cleared his throat. 'Your application with consumer and business services is pending an approval from SAPOL. I've seen you have completed your Certificate III in investigative services.'

Lewis: *Bunch of fuckin' bullshit that was.*

'Yes.' Alex nodded.

'Then completed a Certificate IV in small business management.'

'Ah …' Alex hesitated.

Tony: *Took me four weeks in the evening, not very difficult assessment pieces. Nighty-night everyone went while I went to work. No break for poor Tony, not even his name on the paper. Doesn't seem fair.*

'Yes, that's right,' Alex clarified.

'Everything else appears to be in order,' the officer continued. 'With the exception of your arrest in 2005 after a break in at a Cash Converters store. This falls under 10 years ago, however you were a minor at the time. Given that you have since come under the care of Mr Graham Blakemore, who has a proven track record of rehabilitating disadvantaged youth, we have decided to initiate this interview so you can plead your case. Can you prove to me that you have good character?'

Graham opened the packet of yoyo biscuits and started dipping one in his tea. Alex looked back and forth between both men.

'I don't think I can. I've been nothing but trouble since I arrived at Graham's. I ran away, I nearly crashed his car, I've lashed out at him … But for some reason he didn't stop trying with me. I don't know why I deserved that. Then again, I've had to put up with his jokes. That's … ah … that's all I've got.'

The officer exhaled sharply. 'Can you describe a situation where you had to apply good character?'

Julie: *I wanted the last of the lamingtons last Sunday. But I didn't take it because Pa only had two and I had seven.*

Lewis: *Need to come up with something better than fucking lamingtons.*

Tony: *They were very nice. Tony likes lamingtons. Tony knows—*

Lewis: *Shut the fuck up, Tony.*

Julie: *Swear jar!*

Tony: *Tony knows the best judge of character. Good or bad, Tony knows. Tony's best friend, that's who.*

Alex thought back. *Yes, of course.*

Early afternoon at Tiddy Widdy Beach. Yolanda and Graham watched Rex, approximately 8-weeks-old, yapping at the seagulls. Alex threw a treat up in the air and Rex caught it.

'Come on, boy. A little closer,' Alex encouraged.

Rex slowly moved closer to Alex and took the treat out of his hands before he rushed back. Alex slowly made his way closer to the little puppy. He could still see the burn marks in the afternoon sun. Three treats later, he was able to give Rex a pat.

Tony: Rex already sleeps with Tony. Still making progress though. Progress is progress. Not as much progress as Tony though.

Alex tried a stick next. He threw it out to the shoreline. Rex bounded after it, still growing into his legs.

'Perhaps we could train him to be an emotional support dog?' Yoddi suggested.

Lewis: Just keep the fucker away from me. Bit me on the face the other night.

Julie: Swear jar!

Alex found another stick and threw it. Rex chased it.

'We can keep him, can't we?' Alex asked.

Graham shrugged. 'I think I would be outnumbered anyway. Let's go get him registered.'

'I risked my life to save a dog once.' Alex smiled. 'It was stupid, but one of the best things I've ever done. It took me several months to build trust with the dog. His name is Rex.'

'This also led you lot into finding that poor boy on Anzac Day, if you recall the story,' Graham added.

'Rex had been abused, and I was determined to show him not all humans are bad. I never thought dogs liked me, but after spending time with Rex, he reassured me I wasn't so bad either. As far as my character goes, I don't think you can find a better judge of character than a dog.'

Tony: *Don't mention who his favourite is. Probably not best to discuss dissociations. Very understanding man I'm sure, but not too many would understand dissociations.*

Julie: *It is a really big word.*

The officer sighed. 'Graham ...'

'Yes, young lad?' Graham snapped out of a doze.

'That's one of the best answers I've heard, I'll give him that. But he's young for an application like this. If he was applying for SAPOL we would get him to come back when he has some life experience.'

'Well, I certainly wouldn't want him working for you lot. I don't want him bloody miserable for the rest of his life.' Graham snorted. 'He's a good egg, David, you can trust me on that. We'll be working small cases close to home. My last few cases have been lost pets, a couple of adultery suspicions, and a domestic conflict.'

The officer stared at Alex. 'One more question for you, Alex. Why do you want to become a private investigator?'

Lewis: *Because we're fucking good at it.*

Julie: *We get to help other kids.*

Tony: *It keeps me busy. Brain needs to exercise, need to be put to work. Hi-ho!*

Alex: *Because without it I have nowhere to go.*

'It's a way I can help my community. It helped me when I was at my lowest. Now I can give back. And honestly … it's all I know. Hell, we live on Tiddy Widdy Beach. Graham's right, these aren't big cases. You will probably never hear of us again.'

CHAPTER 37

NOW

'And in breaking news, 14 AFL players have been pronounced dead during the semi-final clash at Adelaide Oval. Cause of death is still unknown, but poison is believed to be involved. This horrifying scene came just hours after a private inquiry took place between state and federal police forces on future action plans to manage these disasters. We are awaiting a statement from the police. Public events across the state could be forced to cancel due to the serial killer's MO.'

The radio switched off in the BMW and the driver cursed out loud. He pulled up out the front of his office. It was 8 pm and everyone had left. He was called in for an urgent meeting after receiving an email from the landlord of his office space. He couldn't understand the need for a face to face. But the Showstopper events were heating up and he couldn't afford any errors. His office was on the fifth floor of the building. The lights were on when he arrived.

Gaynor: *Alex, you will need to draw him into an environment he feels safe–or at least expects to be. Then find a reason to be alone with him. Get creative.*

'Hello? Is anybody here yet?' he asked.

His office was empty. It was a large space with floor-to-ceiling windows, large pieces of art that covered the walls, a small bar filled with different spirits, and a leather chaise at the centre of the room.

'Hello?'

Gaynor: *You'll need to buy yourself some time. I use propofol. I'll get you in touch with my supplier. Very fast acting. You can find out how much you need yourself when you have enough information on the subject.*

Cheng reached for his mobile phone just as Alex stepped out from behind the door and pressed a needle into his neck.

Cheng came to zip-tied to his office chair. A portable light shone in his direction, forcing him to squint. He called out for help in Chinese and English.

'Nobody can hear you.'

Gaynor: *Some people respond to fear well – it improves their attention to detail and decision-making. Others ...? Not so much. My victims were well chosen. You need to use fear, but make sure the subject understands there is no way out.*

Alex stepped out wearing a mask. It was clear plastic and covered his features. He wheeled out a small tray with knives, power drills, scalpels and matches.

Gaynor: *Now you could have some fun ... But something tells me that's not going to happen. So, you have to bluff. We know you can do that, don't we?*

'Oh, Jesus, oh, Jesus. Who are you?!' Cheng demanded.

Cheng heard a ceaseless beep come from his left and realised he was connected to a portable patient monitor. His heart rate jumped to 190 beats-per-minute as Alex picked up the power drill.

'Please, you don't want to do this. I'm connected to very powerful people.'

Alex leaned in close. Cheng could smell his breath.

'Tell me about it,' Alex whispered. 'Tell me about Martin.'

Cheng shook his head in anguish. 'If I tell you about the study, you're a dead man too. Is that what you want?'

'Yes,' Alex said quietly, placing the drill back on the table.

'Fine. What do you know already?'

'Rivett Shipping. I knew the business was involved with taking a boy. I found your name on a business registry. I knew you were directly involved. I know Martin is too.'

'A boy?' Cheng questioned incredulously. 'This is all about a boy? He is going to kill you. This isn't about a boy. It's about dozens of children every year. Rivett was back in what? The early nineties?'

'How could he possibly get away with that undetected?'

'Christ. Do you know how many children go missing every year in Australia? Tens of thousands. You do not want to get involved with this. If this is about the Showstopper attacks, you're wasting your time.'

'What's the connection?'

'Martin organised the purchase and capture of children. He ran experiments on them, bad stuff, alright? Then he kept tabs on them. Wanted to see what they would become.'

'What's this got to do with the Showstopper?' Alex asked.

'The Showstopper … It's just a study. The kids grew up to either become permanently institutionalised, locked up, or didn't get to grow up at all. But the remaining few reconnected with Martin. He nurtured them. He's given them projects. The show, Adelaide Oval, airport, etc. He's made them killers.'

'How are you involved?' Alex asked.

'I'm in data analysis. Martin has had everything logged and reported from day one.'

'What's the end goal?'

'Martin pays me to analyse the data, not to interpret it.'

'Show it to me.'

Cheng directed Alex to his computer and provided the necessary passwords and where to find the data. Alex watched closely.

'You see it, yes?' Cheng asked.

'What am I looking at?'

'There are three groups. Click on any one you like. You'll see names of subjects—34 children.'

Alex looked through all the data. He remembered taking psychopathy tests with Martin when he was 14. The results were all here. An inventory of what each child feared was listed and graphed. Juvenile crimes were included with a systematic analysis. There were plot graphs for every subject. Each living subject had a link to a project except one.

'What's this?' Alex asked, dragging Cheng closer to the computer.

'An outlier,' Cheng revealed. 'It's driving Martin mad. The subject is still alive; he's not institutionalised, but he hasn't killed anyone either. Martin was running a private test on him, but I don't know where it's at.'

Alex clicked on more information on the outlier. He found photos of him and Graham at Tiddy Widdy, their working cases throughout Ardrossan, and an image of him/Tony arriving at Greenwich.

Alex found another folder titled **PROJECTS.** He clicked on it and found numerous folders labelled with locations and dates.

- Adelaide Central Markets
- Adelaide Airport
- Festival Theatre
- Adelaide Show
- Harslett Prison
- Queen Elizabeth Hospital (Cancelled)
- Norton College
- Saint Francis Xavier's Cathedral

'Norton College …' Alex said to himself. 'That's tomorrow's date. Wait …'

Alex clicked on a link to live footage. It showed Martin working at a desk in a large classroom.

'Martin's there now? I need to call the police.'

'Police?' Cheng screwed his face. 'Who are you?'

Alex took off the mask. 'I'm the outlier.'

'Jesus…' Cheng breathed a sigh of relief. 'Untie me. Now!'

'No, you're staying here. Everyone needs to see this.'

Cheng shook his head. 'What is it you call yourself? A private investigator? Yes, Martin spoke of you. I know how fucked up you are, but you're not going to hurt me.'

Lewis: *Give me the drill, Alex.*

'You should have stuck to catching cheating husbands,' Cheng continued. 'If you give this information to the police, I die, my family dies, you die, everyone you love dies. And Martin? He probably has hundreds of exit plans.'

'Unless he's taken down.'

'Jesus Christ. You are delusional, a broken child. Martin Harslett is the brains behind the Showstopper. He owns the biggest penitentiary in this state and holds dozens of government contracts. He's been killing, manipulating and planning since before you were born, kid. What, who are you calling?'

'The police,' Alex answered, dialling 000.

CHAPTER 38

THEN - August 2019

It came to him then. Alex remembered watching Graham die.

Graham relaxed into the passenger side of his classic Toyota Crown Super Saloon. Alex was driving. It only took Graham four months before his GP approved him to get back behind the wheel after his stroke, but Alex was allowed to do the night driving.

'Do you think you would ever date, Alex? Find a nice girl?' Graham asked.

'I have never given it much thought. I doubt it. Why?'

'Well, if you do, don't tell her a 100-year-old man beat you at golf! She might wanna date me instead!' Graham laughed out loud.

'It was the second time I ever played!'

That only made Graham laugh louder. 'And I walk with a cane, and I still thumped you.'

Lewis: *Pass me his cane or a club, Alex, either will do the trick.*

'Lewis is not impressed with your sportsmanship,' Alex warned.

'Lewis can kiss my bum, loose sphincter and all.' Graham giggled. 'But thank you, kiddo, it was a lovely birthday.'

Graham had been talking about his 100th birthday for as long as Alex could remember. He knew the old man never had time to plan anything, not with all the medical appointments and keeping himself in line. He wanted to make it special for him.

'I'm sorry Yoddi couldn't make it,' Alex said solemnly.

'It's not your fault. It's her bloody daughter's for choosing this weekend to get married. Yoddi's too. It's her daughter's second marriage, so I don't see why Yoddi can't just wait a few years and go to her third marriage. It's not like I'm going to make another century. Never mind, she never really liked golf anyway.'

'We've just got one more stop to make.'

'If you've hired strippers, I'll know I've finally taught you right.' Graham's voice was hoarse from all the laughter.

Graham was told to close his eyes for the last 5 minutes. Alex pulled into the carpark at the Ardrossan RSL sub-branch clubrooms.

'I can hear a lot of people. Where the devil have you taken me?' Graham asked as he was guided out of the car.

They walked slowly towards the back entrance of the club.

'You can open your eyes in a moment. There's just one thing I need you to do for me. Have fun.'

'But there are people in there. Is this …? Is this a party? For me?'

'Have a look and see.'

Graham opened his eyes in wonder. They were outside the RSL club by the back door. Nobody had noticed them yet. The room was filled with over 60 people. There were '100' helium balloons at both ends of the bar. Alex knew Graham would be particularly elated with the age group of attendees. It was going to be a real party. There was a DJ in the back corner already entertaining the crowd. A projector screen at the front end of the clubrooms had a slideshow of pictures throughout Graham's years.

'But … how?' Graham choked. 'You don't bloody know anybody.'

Alex held out Graham's little black book. 'I made a few calls.'

Graham embraced Alex and kissed him on the cheek. 'Can I go in now and get myself a bloody beer? Or are we going to stand out in the cold all night?' Graham chirped.

'Just a moment.' Alex held him back. 'The man of the century needs a grand entrance after all.'

Everyone in and around the club heard the announcement from the DJ: LADIES AND GENTLEMEN. I'VE NEVER DONE THIS BEFORE, BUT TONIGHT WE ARE CELEBRATING A 100TH BIRTHDAY. AN INCREDIBLE ACHIEVEMENT. GIVE A BIG ROUND OF APPLAUSE TO OUR MAIN MAN AND CENETARIAN…GRAHAM!

Alex pushed Graham inside. Everybody cheered. *Stayin' Alive* by the Bee Gees started playing throughout the room. Graham laughed and looked back at Alex, who nodded with a smile.

Anyone seated, rose and applauded. Graham went over to every person who attended and gave them a high five while the song played. Someone put a police hat on him with *Bad Boy* written on it. Previous clients, medical staff, younger veterans … in fact, most of the people in Graham's little black book attended.

Graham beamed all night. Finally, a cake was wheeled in.

Happy Birthday to you,
Happy Birthday to you,
Happy Birthday, dear Grahaaaam!
Happy Birthday to you!
HIP HIP!
Hooray!

Alex sang in the background, away from too much attention. As the hip-hip-hoorays came to a conclusion, Graham took a moment to make a wish and blew out the 100 candles (after six attempts and a glass of water in between) on top of a two-tier chocolate cake. When the small fire was officially extinguished there was a round of applause.

Graham faced everyone and there was silence. 'Firstly, I just wanted to thank you all for coming. It's certainly not how I expected this day would go. Before I forget, I didn't grow up with much as a child and I spent most of my younger years hungry. Now I hate seeing food wasted. There's plenty left over so please get yourself a plate. I can rustle up some containers and you can take some home for your breakfast tomorrow. Please, eat up. I know as well as anybody I'm lucky to be here. I thought my time was going to be cut short in my first sea battle during World War II. If you can imagine 48 big deafening guns firing around you, as well as 15 guns firing at you, and seeing those shells above you while you're walking a tightrope … that was me at age 17, climbing a mast to attach a flag to the starboard outer halyards. I was sent to grab it because a bloody signalman let it slip from his fingers because of his bloody nerves. But here I am today. And I want to say two things: never take life for granted and just enjoy it. Don't spend it being bloody miserable. I've lived twice as long as most of you and it goes like that.' He clicked his fingers. 'Now I won't keep you, there's more eating, drinking and dancing to be done. But lastly, I want to thank this young man for organising such a special event.' He pointed at Alex. 'Please go up to him at some point tonight and ask him how he did against me at golf. Thank you all very much.'

The front doors opened and Yolanda stepped in, stifling a yawn. Her movements were sluggish but confident. Graham hobbled over in surprise and lifted her up in the air with newfound strength.

'What about the wedding?'

'My flight was delayed. I'm catching a red-eye flight. Alex and I figured that would give me more than enough time to have a drink with you. Happy birthday, you sweet man.'

They kissed. Another round of applause. Alex spent the evening ducking and weaving past the jubilant guests keen to ask him about his golf. He spoke with past clients and was surprised how different they were, how much they had changed since Blakemore Investigations came into their lives. But the initial chatter and the dancing started to die down after 10 pm. More and more people were glued to their smartphones. Alex unlocked his own phone and found a breaking news story. There was a fire at a school concert at Festival Theatre with fatalities.

Yoddi tapped Alex on the shoulder and gave him a hug. Alex thought she looked sad. She gave him a look he hadn't seen before.

'Did you see what happened at Festival Theatre?' Alex asked.

Yoddi nodded gravely. 'Awful. Absolutely awful. I better get going – I don't know what the city's going to be like after that. Closures galore most likely.'

'Are you okay?' he asked.

'Of course, I am. I have a grandson that I haven't seen in a long time, that's all. I'm hoping he's okay.'

'Will you see him at the wedding?'

'I'm not so sure. I have to get going, young man. You did an amazing job organising all of this. I'm very proud of you.'

'Thanks for your help, Yoddi. I hope you get to see your grandson soon.'

She gave Alex another kiss and Graham came over to wish her well. The centenarian was uncharacteristically quiet when Yoddi left. His skin looked grey.

'Graham?' Alex looked closely at him. 'Are you alright?'

'It's time we go home, lad.' Graham sighed. 'I've had enough partying for one night.'

Graham was tucked into his bed under flannelette sheets. Their dog, Rex, jumped up on the bed and curled up by Graham's feet. Rex was an old dog now. He had gained weight over the years and his hair had greyed. But he shared Graham's near-unnatural vigour for life. The regular runs on the beach and swims had kept him healthy over the years. Graham reached for him and Rex moved closer for a pat. Alex hovered.

'Just because I'm 100 doesn't mean I need to be tucked in.'

'Are you sure you're okay?'

'Never better.' Graham smiled. 'Thank you, my boy. You never stop making me proud.'

'Someone spoke to me about another case tonight. Want to hear about it tomorrow?' Alex asked.

'Sounds like a plan, kiddo.'

Alex frowned. 'Are you sure you're alright? You seemed funny when Yoddi left.'

'Yoddi's thinking about moving to Melbourne. She wants to spend her twilight years with her family. It's fair enough. I'm just … I'm glad I've got you, kiddo.'

'Me too. Goodnight.' Alex turned to leave.

'Alex!'

Alex stopped.

'For my 105th birthday party, don't forget the strippers.'

Alex shook his head, grinning. Rex started barking relentlessly. Alex tried to calm him down and let him outside. Alex heard a sound he couldn't recognise.

Stepping back inside, Alex froze in horror. A dark figure in a gas mask stood in their kitchen. Lewis took control and grabbed a knife. He lunged at the intruder, but his wrist was caught with frightening reflexes, and he found himself pulled in towards the intruder. Something covered his mouth. The smell was foul. His nostrils burned. He struggled. His vision went foggy, his body limp. He crashed to the ground. The dark figure moved to Graham's bedroom. Lewis heard a hissing sound, followed by a clatter. He fought off the need to close his eyes and crawled after him. He manoeuvred himself past Graham's wall of achievements; the photos of all the young men that attended respite care at the property. The final photo was of the two of them; Alex and Graham, hugging and laughing. Rex barked louder.

'Alex?' Graham called out.

Slow methodical footsteps. Contorted breathing. Lewis rolled to the side. He couldn't move his body, only watch as the man with winged ears took off the gas mask and sat on Graham's bed. Lewis was too close to unconsciousness to understand what it meant.

'What have you done with Alex?' Graham growled.

'He's unharmed. A mild anaesthetic. He will drift off soon. Stronger than I expected. Do you know who I am?' Martin asked.

'No. I think you've got the wrong house.'

Martin turned the small TV on in Graham's bedroom. The colour from the screen illuminated Graham's pale face.

TV reporter: 'We can confirm that this evening five audience members at the Festival Theatre have been rushed to hospital with severe burns. Early reports are suggesting multiple fatalities. Festival Theatre staff are currently under investigation for-'

Martin turned the TV off, darkening the room.

'You another loon? We got some odd calls after the Greenwich case. We're not interested in any more cases like that, so you can take—'

'Fire is far more unpredictable than poison …' Martin digressed, 'You have aged well. Remarkable really. Tell me, do you still have the taste for bread dipped in mutton fat?'

'You … the b-b-bus,' he stammered.

Martin stroked Graham's face. 'Yes. The bus. So long ago.'

'Please …' Graham whimpered. 'I don't know … anything. I—'

'I am not here for you,' Martin soothed. 'Alex is under my watch.'

'You … You're the missing piece to his past,' mumbled Graham.

'Yes, and you've managed to be an exceptional hindrance. I don't blame you. We are both foster parents in our own way. Guiding those who need it. But you have delayed this boy's potential. And I need to find a way to bring him back to me.' Martin took a look back at Lewis, who was trying to speak, but could barely focus on them. 'I saw the fondness he had for you. It's commendable, but inconvenient. I'm sorry, there is no other way.'

Graham chuckled. 'I've cracked the century. Thought my body would go long before my mind. Instead, it's going to be quick. I would have preferred you were a buxom young lady, but an old man can't have everything.'

Martin smiled. 'I admire your spirit.'

'Wait until you see his. Whatever you do to him … it won't change who he is. He's better than you. Better than me.'

'You don't know what I am,' Martin said as he reached for a pillow.

'I'm sorry. I should have done more for you. I should have kept going until I found you. I could have been someone to talk to. But you … that day … There was something inside you beyond my comprehension.'

Martin placed the pillow down on Graham's face. 'I understand.'

A border collie howled in the moonlight as a light breeze of salty air flowed through the Ardrossan home. Martin stepped away from Graham's body and pulled a mobile phone out of a plastic bag. He dialled three numbers.

'Police. 108 Tiddy Widdy Beach Road.' Martin pretended to hyperventilate. 'I-I was just out walking the dogs and I heard an a-a-argument. The house. Number 48. I think I've witnessed a murder. The young man. He's a local. Alex Blakemore. I think he killed Graham. Suffocated him. I … oh, God. Please hurry.'

Martin ended the call and carefully placed the phone back in the plastic bag. He drew up the blind before he stepped over Lewis's immobile body.

Tears spilled down Lewis's face before sleep overwhelmed him.

CHAPTER 39

NOW

Alex's hands trembled on the steering wheel of Graham's Toyota Crown Super Saloon. The memory made him feel numb. Violated. Weak.

Lewis: *We've just uncovered the crime of the fuckin' century. No time to mope. Let's watch the fucker burn.*

Alex: *I just laid there. I-I-I ... just laid there.*

Tony: *Nothing to be done, chemically impossible. Some form of anaesthetic gas administered. Possibly sevoflurane. Remarkable you saw as much as you did. Tony rather not see at all. Tony wanted to stay outside with Rex.*

Julie: *I didn't want Pa to go to sleep.*

Lewis: *Fucks sake, Alex. Focus. Remember what we've just done. We need to keep moving.*

Alex remembered. He had given Cheng another dose of propofol and left him tied up. He told the 000 operator everything before he left. It didn't matter if they thought he was crazy, the evidence was in his boot. He was told to stay where he was until police arrived, but Tony didn't feel safe waiting. Alex took Cheng's computer with them. He was going to hand it in at Martin's arrest. That same horrible thought occurred to Alex. If he only managed to get something from Cheng's laptop all those years ago ... *would all of this already be over?* He shuddered at the consequences of his fear. He took a deep breath and noticed Graham's little black book underneath the passenger seat. He must have collected it when Randall took control and discharged himself from prison. Sheets of tattered paper stuck out of the edges. *That's new.* Alex opened the book and found yellowed sheets with messy handwriting.

His heart began to race. Journal entries. Someone had left them for him to find and read.

3/2/1973

Dear Diary,

I never quite understood the need for diaries. Such intimate thoughts exposed out there to the big, wide world. But I have to try something.

I go by various names here at Norton College. Wingnut, Mr Bean, Dumbo, and even Freak-face by those less creative students in my class. It doesn't really bother me, sticks and stones and all that. My last school was worse. I would get spat on, peed on or hurt in ways adults wouldn't consider. Children are ruthless. Someone tried to cut one of my ears off once, which was the final straw for my parents. They pulled me out of Kadina High and sent me to Norton.

I have a love-hate relationship with Norton. The library is impressive and keeps me entertained every day. The science labs are fascinating. The religious classes, not so much. I was adamant on leaving because of the mind-numbing faith classes. But my dad convinced me to stay. In his own way he tried to explain how religion can provide community, values and relationships.

My dad had a habit of being incredibly useful without intending to. Not that any of this is his fault. He is an honest, hardworking man. He and my mum both work for council, they are directors in Corporate Services and Planning and Development. They both make good money, and they aren't stupid when they spend it.

Mum and dad taught me to be resilient. Twelve months after I was diagnosed with dyslexia, I became top of my English class and contributed in the school newsletter. I've come to respect spelling and grammar the same way I respect law – I may not be able to process it as quickly, but I can work my way around it.

I was always a shy kid. I suffered horrible anxiety whenever I had to speak at school assembly. Once I realised how it crippled me, I did what I could to overcome it. I faced my fears. Now I'm part of the drama and music club. I'm not sure what it is I love about drama. I spend all day at school trying to blend in, only to step on stage and perform in front of so many people. I think it's the fact that I can be someone else up there. That's a disguise in itself.

Nothing can beat the feeling when I step on stage,
I immerse myself in the characters and lose my rage,
Science keeps me learned and hungry for knowledge,
Religion opens doors to anyone with courage,
But it's my projects that truly keep my mind occupied,
Otherwise, the darkness cannot be denied,
It's comfortable enough dreaming ever so darkly,
But above all, I find that it is lonely.

5/2/1973

Dear Diary,

My mum was 43-years-old when she had me. I was a miracle child in her eyes. She took five years off from work when I was born and I became the love of her life. Her words. She said she could see stars amongst the inky sky in my eyes. I used to think Mum was emotional. When I started school, she used to say the other kids were jealous of my eyes. I couldn't understand envy.

A mother's love for her child is a love I will never be able to comprehend. It's why I could never let her down. The day I realised this was the day I decided to be a shadow.

Gerald Matheson was 87-years-old when he went walk-a-bouts. Everyone in town was looking for him until someone found his body in the river. His driver's licence is spinning above me, stuck to the top of my ceiling fan. So stupid. It will go. I will not allow life as I know it to be risked by the adhesive quality of sticky tape. I have a wind-up zombie figurine on my windowsill. I gifted my dad salt and pepper shakers shaped as snowmen. And I have a golden charm that I told Mum I found outside. All linked to a project. All must go. I have vivid dreams, to the point where I wake up and I can't remember what projects I've done, and which ones were fantasies. The trinkets help me remember, but they will go. I will find another way to remember.

It wasn't until my mother took me to see a play that it all came together for me. The play was Cyrano de Bergerac. Cyrano was deeply in love with his cousin but felt insecure due to his large nose. My ears once made me feel the same way. Cyrano provides romantic words to Christian, a handsome and less eloquent friend to woo his cousin. The cousin is touched by the words, and Cyrano gives Christian all the credit. Even on his death bed, Cyrano never tells his cousin the words came from him. The selflessness struck a chord with me. I respected it.

Credit wasn't needed. What if Christian was my trophy? As my parents always say, Christ is my saviour.

Gerald never struggled when I released his soul,
Angie's was an overdose, she always lacked control,
Allan got messy but clean-up was so fun,
Sandra only stumbled, she was in no shape to run,

23/2/1973

Dear Diary,

I am 14-years-old, and I have orchestrated the death of 19 students. I have gotten away with it. A driver, my Christian, has been arrested.

I didn't do this because I was bullied. I would never use something so trivial as an excuse. I don't have a traumatic past. I was never neglected. I don't have a family history of mental illness. What am I, diary? That's what I need to know. I can't be one in 4 billion. There has to be others like me. I just have to find them.

I've seen the news stories on serial killers. But I'm not the same. I don't have a need to do this, there's no desire to go on a rampage, and there's certainly nothing sexual. Can a chemical imbalance in the brain be all the difference between me, them and normality? I don't think anyone knows. If they did it would be rooted out, not televised. It makes me wonder if the average human is fascinated by murder. I am not fascinated by it. I am ambivalent to it. But if people are so fascinated by death, where will it lead us eventually? I foresee mainstream media dedicated to serial killers because it will sell. It's not exactly a deterrent, is it? No wonder some of them try to put on a show. Sounds like an easy way to get caught to me.

Incarceration certainly doesn't appeal to me. Everyone collected altogether.

They succumbed to the time of their metabolic rate,
It was a glory I had yet to behold,
And I found I still had to be part of the fold,
They give names, films and needles to those like me.
Unless I find my own special way to be free,
A light bulb illuminates in the darkest of places,
Prisoners could be trophies if I leave the right traces.

24/2/1973

Dear Diary,

My father assisted in a penitentiary contract last spring. He's a very generous man with information. I was surprised to learn Australia has the highest private incarceration in the world, with some private contracts extending out to decades.

My parents have had the talk with me about what I plan on doing after school. I'm not sure if university is the answer. Again, my father was helpful without intending to be. I was able to do my work experience week in his office, and I made some important connections. Connections that I'll reach out to when I'm older and people start taking me more seriously.

My age is helpful with my projects because I'm underestimated. I would always be considered a victim. But like with literally everything else my age is a hindrance. But that's only a matter of time, and I don't mean to wish it away. These years are filled with rich learning experiences.

One day I will have all my Christians stacked up neatly on display, and I will hold the keys. And then I will move on. Because I have to give this itch, this voice, something productive to do.

Otherwise, it will drive me mad.

It takes people and money to open big doors,
I'll start early and study the laws,

I will own the whole thing to maintain control,
It will lay foundations for my true role,
There will be other tasks and goals as I find my way,
It can't just be me who knows how to play,
A lifelong search may be required,
I will remain patient, for this I'm inspired.

Alex couldn't comprehend what he'd stumbled upon.

Alex: *How is this here?*

Tony: *Martin, he left it for us. An invitation, Tony thinks.*

Alex: *Martin's not just a ...*

Lewis: *Fucking serial killer?*

Tony: *Many more. He's split but not like us. He has other names but hides behind others. Showstopper, yes, but many more. Since he was a child. He was the boy on the bus. Met Graham before. Graham sniffed him out, just like Lewis. Didn't matter though. In over our heads. Is that what they say? I think that's what they say.*

Lewis: *What the fuck do we do then?*

Alex: *I can't just sit and wait. I need to see him arrested. Or I'll never rest again.*

Tony: *Tony doesn't want to be anywhere near him. But Tony is anxious. He doesn't want him in Tony's dreams.*

Julie: *I just want it to stop. All these bad things. I want life to go back to normal.*

Lewis: *What the fuck are we waiting for? I get control when we see him in cuffs. I'm going to give this fucker the finger.*

Alex: *Let's go to Norton.*

Alex started the car, determined to get to Norton College as fast as he could.

He thought he had been driving for half an hour, but he was still in central Adelaide. *Did I miss a turn?* He passed Queen Elizabeth Hospital and turned onto Port Road. Traffic started to thin out as he drove away from the hospital. With the onslaught of attacks across Adelaide, the city was quiet. He understood the fear. He accelerated, motivated by the opportunity to put an end to it all. He was instantly 300 metres up the road. *Not possible.*

Alex: *I'm losing time. Who?*

Randall: *Fucking cookie jar. Where's my sugar?*

Alex looked into the rear vision mirror; he didn't recognise the face staring back at him. The next moment he was off the road, hurtling towards a bus shelter.

Alex: *No!*

He lurched forward in his seat as the front bumper of the Super Saloon crumpled underneath the steel seats of the bus shelter. Glass shattered everywhere. A spark blew out from an electronic advertisement on the side of the shelter. The horn sounded. Whiplash. The seat belt cut into his collarbone. He smelt burning. He tasted blood.

'Randall.' Alex coughed. 'Stop this.'

Randall: *Honey, I'm just getting started.*

***

Alex stumbled across Hindley Street. Nightclub lights blurred his vision. It hurt to stand up straight. He staggered onto the footpath and tried to take a deep breath.

Randall: *Your car is trashed, sweetheart. Your face ...*

Alex was kissing a bearded man on the face when he regained consciousness. He staggered back in surprise. The sudden losses of time were nauseating. The man was nearly 7 foot tall, very well built, and dressed in his black and white motorbike club colours. A silent hush filled the room as the large man swung and hit Alex in the jaw. Alex tumbled onto the bar first then ricocheted onto the stained floor. A piercing sound echoed in his ears. He received two kicks into his gut, causing him to cough and splutter while he protected his wounded abdomen.

Randall: *You know nothing of pain.*

'Randall …' Alex choked. 'Please.'

Consciousness returned to Alex on the roof ledge of a building 20 storeys above the ground. He couldn't move as he took in the sights of the city. He could see the light reflecting across the dark waters of the River Torrens. Police lights could still be made out in the distance surrounding Adelaide Oval. Streetlights and cars filled his vision from every direction in a grid-like pattern. The Adelaide Town Hall and Adelaide Casino stood out with their illuminated facades rising up high into the dark night sky.

'Why?' Alex croaked.

Randall: *I needed the limelight, honey. You cast me out.*

'I-I don't have time for a new alter.'

Randall: *Honey, I am not new. Do you not remember me, little Alex? I was the first. Tony, Lewis, Julie … They know nothing of pain. I was the one that suffered. You know why you can't remember what happened to you? I happened! I took all the hurt for you.*

Flashes of knives, water, dogs …

Randall: *You discarded me while you played in a beach house with the others. You created a twisted family and excluded the one that gave you everything. I took all the hurt and none of the love. I needed it the most.*

'I'm sorry, I had no idea. Please—'

Randall: *You don't get to be sorry. Look at you.*

Alex realised he was naked. He hadn't felt the cold until now. His skin developed goosebumps against the wind.

Randall: *All those scars. I took every one of them. FOR YOU!*

'I didn't know. Please … Let me help you. We can include you. We can stop the man that did this to us.'

Randall: *Fool! You will send us back to him! Can't you see that's what he wants? I will not be hurt like that again. Could you imagine what would happen if I showed you every little thing that they did to me? There are things worse than dissociation. It would be the end of all of you. No, we jump!*

A surge of adrenalin and fear raced through Alex's body as he lost control and tipped forward …

… His head landed into a toilet and he vomited. He looked up and found himself in a clean bathroom stool. A poster of a drag queen event was hung above the cistern.

'Where am I?' Alex asked.

Randall: *I like it here. I'm having one last night before I hurl you off a building.*

Alex's posture became more erect. His pelvis tilted anteriorly, further accentuating his gluteal muscles. His wrists flexed forward as he flushed the toilet and left.

There was still some nightlife left in Adelaide. Randall danced and jived with a colourful group of men and women dressed to party, while a drag queen performed on a small stage. He had found concealer in a woman's bag and used it to help cover the bruising across his cheek. The music was loud and blocked out any voices as he laughed, drank and danced.

Alex: *Graham would have taken you to these places. If he had known.*

Randall: *Get out of my head! Think I'll chat up that young man by the bar.*

He ordered a craft beer and drank it slowly while whispering sweet nothings to the interested man.

Alex: *It doesn't have to be over for us.*

On the TV in the corner was another report on the Adelaide Oval tragedy. Randall left the bar holding hands with the young man, who was tall, with thick dark hair in a quiff. Randall started to caress his veiny forearms.

Alex: *Something's wrong. There should have been something on TV about Martin's arrest. About the school.*

Randall: *I'm busy here.*

He pushed the young man against the car, then ran his hands through his quiff. He gave him a long, deep kiss.

Lewis: *You fucking motherfucking—*

Alex: *You talk about pain but hide behind it. You're looking for vices to take your mind away from your memories. We need to face them, Randall. You have hidden from me all this time. Why spend more time hiding when you finally have control?*

'Enough! Go away!' Randall hollered.

The young man pulled away from his embrace and ran off deeper into the car park, muttering insults under his breath.

'No, not you. Just … never mind.' Randall sighed.

His alters were repelled into the dark abyss that he called home. Never seeing, never hearing, never feeling. Just lost time. At least for now, he wouldn't have to deal with their voices. He was alone. *Too alone.* Randall slowly made his way back to the pub, his shoulders slumped, his movements lethargic. He kept his head down, avoiding what was on the TV screen as he made his way to a payphone at the back of the hotel. He hesitated, his fingers hovering over the buttons on the phone before he dialled a number.

'Hey … It's me. I know it's been a while, but I'm back now. Truly. I remembered your number, didn't I? Do you wanna catch up? Look I know I've probably messed things up for you. But I'm ready, I know it. Can you please just …'

Randall tried to absorb the response, but his gaze kept shifting back to the scenes at Adelaide Oval on the TV in the bar.

'I just ...' Randall continued. 'I miss you. I can be what you want. I know I can.'

Randall heard the reply, but he didn't want to accept it. A tear ran down his face.

'But I ... just got back. I ... just wanted to see you.'

Randall felt numb when he hung up the phone. He felt control wasn't all it was cracked up to be.

Alex woke back in Graham's moving car. He quickly took control of the steering wheel before he veered off the road. The engine made a funny sound, and smoke was rising from the bonnet. A single headlight lit up the road. It was badly damaged, far from roadworthy, but it still ran. Alex got his bearings and worked out he was an hour north of Adelaide.

Lewis: *She'll make it.*

Alex: *Is it over? How?*

Randall: *You have bought yourself a little time, sweetie. You're lucky it was a dull night. Just don't think you can dispose of me, I'm here to stay.*

Alex pulled over. He was almost unrecognisable in the rear vision mirror. Randall's make-up couldn't hide the bruises and fat lip. He wiped off the concealer, his face tender to touch. He pulled up his shirt and groaned. There was bruising all across his chest but the stitches along his abdomen were intact. He had a raging headache, one of the worst he had ever experienced.

Lewis: *Anything to say for yourself, you fuck?!*

Randall: *I should have got his number before I scared him off. He definitely thought I was sexy in a rugged, beaten-up sort of way.*

Alex checked the time. Several hours had passed since he left Cheng's office. Something was wrong. *If there was an attack planned at Norton College, police should have found something by now*, he thought. *It should have made breaking news.* He knew he had to go there while he still had some control. *But if Martin was there, what could one broken man do?*

Alex: *Randall ... What did you just say?*

CHAPTER 40

It was midnight when Alex arrived out the front of Norton College, expecting to see a parade of police cars and Martin in handcuffs. The gates were closed and it was deathly quiet. He wanted to see red and blue lights surrounding the school but instead could only see a few dim lights on at the other side of the campus. He heard sirens in the distance. He parked far enough away to not get in the way, but close enough to see when the police arrived. A moment later, he saw the police in his rear vision mirror. His mind eased. But only one police patrol car arrived.

Lewis: *Not exactly prepared for the bust of the fuckin' century.*

Tony: *Not right, not right. Police never came. This one is far too late. Makes Tony's stomach sad and queasy.*

The police patrol parked directly behind Alex's inherited Super Saloon. He wound down his window as the police officer got out and approached him.

'Are you the one that called this in?' the officer asked. Alex assumed he was in his early thirties.

'Y-yes,' Alex stammered. 'Did they get Cheng? When are the rest coming?'

The officer looked across the road before he got his gun out.

'Get out of the car, Alex, now. You make any sudden movements, you die. There's no help coming. Cheng's been seen to.'

Alex's blood turned cold. He went into autopilot and did as he was told. The officer gave him a set of handcuffs and forced him to restrain himself behind his back before he was pushed into the back seat of the police car. The officer didn't say another word as he drove off to a quieter part of town.

Alex shifted uncomfortably in his seat. They drove for 10 minutes before the officer pulled over under a bridge. He shot Alex a glance in the rear vision mirror. He lit himself a cigarette and opened the window. 'Do you remember much?'

'About what?' Alex asked.

The officer turned around in his seat. There was something in his eyes that made Lewis' inner voice hiss.

'When you were caged,' the officer said simply.

'How do you know?'

The embers of the cigarette lit up bright orange, reminding Alex of a crueller time. He scratched at his childhood burn marks. The officer stared at him, as if that was some sort of reply. Then he reached back and put out the cigarette on Alex's forearm, who flinched. The officer flicked what was left of the butt out the window and unbuttoned his police uniform. His chest was covered with faint burn marks from a lifetime ago.

'You're one of them,' murmured Alex.

'What do you remember?'

'I remember being in the cage, sometimes with another. I remember we were on a ship, but to be honest, I can't recall how I got my scars.'

Randall: *No shit, Shirley.*

The officer nodded. 'I am the same. Martin came to me again when I was 14-years-old. He found me in a juvenile detention centre.'

The coincidence wasn't unnoticed by Alex. Someone else found him in the same place.

'He approached me in a psychiatric clinic. I thought he was a psychologist. He must have broken in,' Alex said.

'Martin doesn't need to break in. People like him are given keys. He would be a benefactor of the practice, no doubt. They wouldn't have known what he was doing … but he would have found his way in easily enough.'

Alex assumed that much was true. 'What does he hold over you?' Alex asked.

'The feelings I have for Martin are conflicting. Something between adoration and fear. He listened to me. Allowed me to find myself. My darkness made him proud,' the officer recalled.

Alex's throat went dry. 'You know he organised everything, right? This is all just some sick study for him.'

'He told me there were others,' the officer explained. 'You are the first I have met.'

Lewis: *We're not going to get through to the fucker. Martin's got his hooks in too deep.*

'He knew I was coming?' Alex asked.

The officer nodded again. 'He is everywhere. Prison, the police, schools … he has his claws in every network he requires.'

'And you're a cop? A real cop?' Alex pushed.

The officer pulled out his wallet and showed Alex his identification. Officer Jonathon Spader.

'What do you want with me, Jonathon?' Alex asked, dreading the answer.

'He wants me to kill you. Is it true you have never killed before?' Jonathon asked.

'Yes.'

'You are too weak to kill, but strong enough to stay out of the psych hospitals. I want to know why.' Jonathon looked deep into Alex's eyes, searching for some understanding.

'I don't consider killing people to be a strength, just the opposite.'

'I never felt *strength* when I pulled the feathers off birds, or skinned cats. But people … that's different. The act separates

248

you from people. You become more. I became powerful when I heard the screams at the Show.'

'The Showstopper murders, it's all been you?'

Jonathon shook his head. 'The Royal Show was mine; the rest were done by others. You don't know what you're missing. You could have been a part of something great.'

Jonathon pulled out his gun and inspected it. Alex's heart continued to pound. His body broke into a cold sweat.

'Can you tell me something?' Alex asked. 'Why the public displays? Why not do it discreetly?'

The officer turned on the radio: 'The latest Showstopper massacre at the Adelaide Oval has seen the—'

He flicked to another station: 'With a rising death toll of unrelated victims, the Showstopper is—'

He tried another: 'Police are now no further in their investigation in the Showstopper case—'

'Yes, publicity, I get that. But why?' Alex asked.

'Strength. Power.'

'How so?'

'Martin manages the biggest government prison contract in South Australia. People feel unsafe, budgets rise.'

'This is all about money?'

'Maybe. Maybe not. I don't care. Martin has shown me my purpose. I would die for him.'

Lewis: *He doesn't have a fucking clue.*

Jonathon pointed the gun at Alex's head.

'We can stop him together. He compromises himself by involving himself in his work. You could call for back up and arrest him,' Alex blurted.

Jonathon shook his head. 'Will I find the computer in your car?'

Alex nodded and closed his eyes.

Alex: 'Thank you. All of you, for protecting me. Sorry I took so long to hear you.'

He heard the cocking of the trigger. Jonathon watched as Alex started to rock back and forth. Alex had changed in an instant. His posture, his gaze, his voice …

Tony: *I'll do it. I'll do it.*

Tony called out, 'I'll be the one to take the last hit. Out and down for the count. Yes, I can do it. I never look. I should be the one. But maybe once, maybe just this once, I will look …'

Tony raised his eyes and stared at Jonathon.

'What is this?' Jonathan asked.

'My name is Tony. Tony Blakemore. Son of Graham Blakemore. May he rest in peace. And me, peace for me now, too. Just please don't shoot my dog. Rex is a good boy, old man now they say he is. But he's my mate, please don't shoot him, he's a good man.'

'Why does Martin care what happens to you?'

Tony started to whine, forcing himself to keep looking up at Jonathon. Tears started streaming from his eyes.

Jonathon got out of the car and paced back and forth. Tony tried to keep staring but it was too much. Too exhausting. He stared down at his feet and Tony tried to count all of his favourite things. Then his door opened and he was ripped out of the car. Tony staggered, then tripped over Jonathon. His fingers brushed across Jonathon's belt on the way down. Jonathon pushed him away and Tony landed shoulders first onto the ground.

Lewis: *Tony, you little fucking ripper.*

'You are as broken as the rest of the rejects,' Jonathon verbalised, 'Multiple personalities?'

Tony didn't respond, he just rocked back and forth on the ground. Jonathon couldn't see Tony's fingers working behind his back.

'What happened to us made us what we are today. I am strong. But it has broken you. He would want me to put you out of your misery. But how have you stayed out of the hospitals for so long?' Jonathon asked again.

Tony unlocked the primary lock to his handcuff.

'We had Graham.' Tony mumbled.

Tony unlocked the secondary lock.

'Who is Graham?' Jonathon noticed a urine stain spread across Alex's crotch. Jonathon shook his head in disgust. It was at that moment that he lowered his weapon for half a second.

Lewis: *That'll do it. He's mine!*

Lewis pounced. His head rammed into Jonathon's gut, winding him. A gunshot echoed below the bridge as the officer squeezed the trigger in response. It deafened Lewis, but he didn't feel a bullet. He didn't feel anything. With both of them on the ground now, Lewis punched Jonathon in the throat.

Lewis: *Thanks, Tony.*

Tony: *Mmm hmm.*

Lewis: *Look away, Julie.*

With a burst of ferocity, Lewis landed another blow to Jonathon's solar plexus and kneed him in the balls before he pushed himself off and lunged for the gun.

Lewis, puffing and damp, took the gun and aimed the weapon at Martin's protégé.

'What are you?' Jonathon cursed.

Lewis tossed Jonathon's keys and the unlocked handcuffs by his feet. He forced Jonathon to cuff himself. When he heard the click behind Jonathon's back, he made sure the cuffs were extra tight and searched him thoroughly. He pocketed the officer's mobile phone.

'You should kill me now,' Jonathon said, no emotion in his voice.

'Move the fuck back, away from the car.'

'Even now you show weakness.' Jonathon shook his head but stepped further back anyway.

'You're a trained police officer who lost his gun to a handcuffed man that wets his fucking pants. I think somebody else showed their weakness tonight.' Lewis smiled and fired the gun, the bullet missing Jonathon by a metre. He flinched anyway.

Alex: *Now what do we do?*

Randall: *I say we get him out of those pants.*

A moment later, Jonathon, in only his briefs, watched his police car speed away, leaving him to choke on a gust of dirt that carried over from underneath the tyres.

Alex searched the street signs as he drove to get his bearings.

Lewis: *That won't buy us much time. The cop will find a way to get a message to Martin. We need to fucking get there first. Go back to the school. You're not alone, Alex. You can do this.*

CHAPTER 41

Alex thought Norton College looked haunted. A dense fog blanketed the school grounds, giving the front entrance an eerie, dreamlike landscape. He parked the police car behind Graham's car, right where he'd left it. Alex wondered if the ghosts of school children would haunt the yards on nights like this if he stayed in the car and did nothing. He imagined them tucked away in their beds, blissfully unaware of the hidden danger. He checked the boot in the Super Saloon and felt a wave of relief when Cheng's computer was still there. Dressed in Jonathon's dry pants, he took the gun and left Jonathon's phone in the car. He stayed away from the streetlights as he approached the schoolgrounds. He would try the police again. But he wanted eyes on Martin first. He wasn't going to let him out of his sight until then. He would stay in the shadows and find the man that had psychologically taunted him all this time. The man he thought was nothing more than his own madness. A ghost.

He moved quietly and reached a path to the recreation centre. Tony: *NO. NO. NO.*

Alex stopped, looked up. A security camera had been installed on the corner of the next building. Alex remembered Martin had access to the cameras. Alex closed his eyes. Tony took control and opened them. He manoeuvred himself around the campus until he reached a water fountain near the canteen with a good view of the recreation centre entrance while staying away from the security systems.

Alex regained control and waited in the cold until he saw Martin outside the recreation centre. His abdomen began to ache when he saw the winged ears. He heard the protective hiss from

Lewis when he saw Martin's curved smile and dark blue eyes. Alex grabbed his phone and texted: *We are a go.*

Now he could sit and wait. Alex felt exhilarated. This wouldn't end quickly, he understood that. But he knew he would remember this moment forever. After following the breadcrumbs, he tracked down a man the world would never understand. When the cavalry arrived, he wanted to be the first person that Martin saw. He scratched his ribs. Some of the stitches had opened from the brawl, and blood soaked into his shirt. *But that doesn't matter, nothing matters any—*

Alex's thoughts stopped. Martin held out his hand. A young boy, in his early teens, shook Martin's hand. Alex watched Martin put a hand over the boy's back and lead him inside. They walked past a room with large letters above the door that he could make out: **Harslett House.**

Alex had a flashback of Martin leading him into the psychiatric office so many years ago.

He is doing it again!

Alex couldn't help himself. He ran into the building, ignoring the warnings of his alters, just as he had 10 years ago when he waited in that office for Martin. *Martin the psychiatrist. Martin the fraud. Martin the killer. Martin and his psychopath study.* He could hear a familiar song playing on a piano.

The automatic doors opened for Alex as he made it to the entrance. He knew Martin and the boy had turned right. The music was getting louder. The reception area was dark, as was the gymnasium. He could see lights on in the basketball court and cautiously approached. Martin was playing Beethoven's *Für Elise* on the piano with little effort.

Randall: *R-A-N*

Alex's heart began to race. He held the gun in his hands. *Now or never.*

Lewis: *Alex, no!*

Alex ignored him and ran into the court, gun held high.

'MARTIN! STOP!' Alex yelled. 'It's over!'

The music stopped. Martin turned to see Alex dressed in Jonathon's pants, his gun held high. Martin started clapping. 'Fantastic, my boy, fantastic!'

The teenager, dressed in Norton's school uniform, appeared nonplussed as Martin walked towards Alex. The teenager had sweaty dark hair that stuck to his face. *Just an average kid*, Alex thought.

'Stop moving!' Alex warned. 'I swear to God I'll put a bullet in you.'

Martin stopped, his hands behind his back. 'I knew there was promise in you, Alex. You have control over your dissociations, control of your urges. That's how you beat Jonathon, I'm sure. Did you kill him? No? Of course not. Well, I haven't given up on you. You can still be part of a project.'

'Send the boy over to me,' Alex ordered.

Martin beckoned the boy over to him and placed his hands on the boy's shoulders. The boy's head reached Martin's chest.

'Always the hero. What is your plan here, exactly?' Martin enquired.

Alex cocked the gun. 'I was raised by a detective. I know how this works.'

'Samuel, please walk over to the man pointing the gun,' Martin said.

Samuel, now looking a little pale, walked slowly towards Alex. Alex whispered to stay behind him.

'It's over, Martin,' Alex declared.

'How so?'

'I have evidence on the study.'

'So will everyone when I publish it.'

Alex started sweating again. 'Publish? What were you doing here?'

'I volunteer here. I run a student behavioural program. I'm setting up for a presentation at assembly tomorrow.'

With a sudden shock, Alex cringed in pain and dropped the gun. He turned to Samuel and saw a pocketknife in his hands, slick with blood. Samuel kicked the gun over to Martin and concealed the knife back in his pocket. Effortlessly, Martin picked up the gun and balanced it in his hands. Samuel walked back to him, looking proud of himself.

'It's Samuel you have to watch out for. This is his project.'

Randall: *D-A-L-L*

Alex, holding onto his bleeding arm, dropped to the floor. 'Just tell me why you killed Graham.'

'Surely you know this by now? You were the flaw of my study. I manipulated you into thinking you were a killer. I believed that would end your inhibitions. Didn't work. Then I was curious. Would you, or one of those in you, attempt to kill me out of revenge? That's why I let you out of my prison. But no. Cheng told me I needed to accept outliers. Samuel, my boy, Alex here wanted to destroy everything we've worked for. Take the next step. Give the voices something productive to do. Feed them. Kill him.'

Martin gave the boy the gun. Alex's phone beeped. Alex picked himself off the floor. 'You're not going to shoot me, Samuel.'

Martin cocked his head in interest.

'Why's that?' Samuel sneered.

'Because I have something for you. Something he could never give you.'

Samuel took a quick glance at Martin. 'What's that?'

'Trust. I know you don't truly trust him—he's psychotic. I bet there's always been a warning in the back of your mind about him. But you deserve the opportunity to trust someone. Really trust. It breaks my heart that nobody's ever given you that. I want to try. You can have my full attention. You can have my home. I'll never ask for anything back. I just want to give you a chance. What have you got to lose?'

'What is this shit?' Samuel asked.

'Nothing good will come of what you're about to do,' Alex continued. 'You will be hunted for the rest of your life. I'm offering you another life. You can live with me, learn how to manage those negative voices. I bet part of you has always wanted to be normal. Well, normal comes at a price. You need to know what love is. Whatever happens tonight, mate, my offer will always stand.'

'Kill him now, Samuel!'

The sound of automatic doors made Samuel hesitate.

'What is that?' Martin asked. 'Who else did you bring?'

'Graham.' Alex smiled.

'Graham is dead!' Martin snapped.

'No, he's not. He's a community. And we're putting you under citizen's arrest.'

'Shoot, Samuel!'

Twin sisters with mousy-brown hair and freckled button noses stepped forward holding cameras. 'Don't shoot if you don't want it all over social media, kid.'

'Just kill them all, we'll call tonight a rehearsal,' Martin demanded.

With a bang, double doors opened behind them and four men stepped inside. Alex recognised them from the Remembrance Day when Graham had presented the ode.

'Where are all these people coming from?' Samuel asked.

Alex threw a small black phone book onto the ground. Graham was old-fashioned. He included names, phone numbers and addresses for all of his clients. Alex called every client that lived near Norton. Dozens of people started filling the room. The underprivileged. The victims without a voice. The local cases nobody cared about.

Samuel and Martin watched in alarm as they were surrounded by 36 people eager to pay back Graham. They stood together as one. Martin swiped the gun off Samuel and pushed him to the ground.

'I see … Alex … you truly are a monster. You've sentenced all of these people to death. I have guns hidden everywhere around this school. The men by the exit I'll shoot first. Whoever comes at me, I'll shoot. These people might be willing to help you, Alex, but die? Is anybody here ready to die tonight?'

Alex stepped forward.

'Just one then?' Martin asked.

'No,' Alex grunted, 'many, many more …'

Thoughts came together in unison.

Tony: *Tony is ready, time for action, time to go.*

Lewis: *I warned you for so long about him … I'm not afraid anymore either. I'm going to make him fuckin' scream.*

Julie: *Screw the swear jar. Let's fuck him up.*

Randall: *It's time, snookums. I'll help, just this once. Let's all get cosy together.*

Alex: *For Graham.*

Alex and his alters lunged at Martin together. Martin aimed and lost his balance with a shooting pain in his ankle. Samuel had kicked him. Alex/Lewis/Tony/Julie/Randall tackled Martin to the ground. A gunshot went off. A ringing in his ears. Everyone swarmed them.

A frenzy of struggling limbs. Sharp pain. Grunts and cries. Alex couldn't catch the voices - everyone yelled at once. *Martin … Where's Martin?* Alex searched in a panic when he hit the ground. He could hear dozens of people flooding the emergency lines with 000 calls. His eyes landed on Martin, winded and subdued on the ground. Alex had been shot in the shoulder.

People fussed over him, trying to stop the bleeding. More sirens could be heard. Alex rested on the floor while others watched over him.

'Why?' Alex panted. 'What was all this for?'

Martin had relaxed against the seven men pinning him down, resigned to his fate.

'One day … you will see,' Martin answered.

'No, I proved you wrong. You broke me, tried to groom me. But I still didn't become what you wanted. Your project failed. All for nothing.'

Martin tried to shrug. 'I had no traumatic past. I was raised well. My parents were normal people. And look at me. There is so much we don't understand. One day we will.'

Alex started feeling faint. He looked up and waited for help to arrive. *Somewhere up there, he's watching.* Alex closed his eyes and smiled.

Lewis forced Alex to make eye contact with Martin once more. He grinned broadly and gave Martin the finger.

Randall: *Smell him.*

Alex: *What?*

Randall: *His cologne. He was wearing it then. Remember, Alex? Remember what he did to us. You're ready.*

Alex was 5-years-old when they broke him. The tall man with the bald head and vulgar words carried him into the common room on the ship. Alex's limbs were too weak to resist. He could hear the girl sobbing behind him. The room was eerily bright and clinical and reminded him of the dentist. The man pulled him up onto a dentist's chair and strapped in his arms and legs. The straps were so tight it cut through his skin. He cried. Something else tightened around his arm. He recognised the man with the irregular speech and the glasses pumping a cuff up around his bicep and taking notes. Lights blinded him, burning his eyes. He blinked the tears away and saw his own reflection. Four mirrors were fixed to the roof directly above him, reflecting his bare pale skin, covered in goosebumps.

Robotic voice: 'Breathing rate and blood pressure have already reached threshold. Mirrors will not be necessary to—'

A man with winged ears stepped forward. 'We do not change protocols. You above all others understand the importance of reliability in these tests. The mirrors stay so he can see what we do to him. They all receive the same dose of fear.'

Alex could smell the man's cologne. Sour at first, but it made him think of oranges and forests. He heard squeaky wheels next. Alex strained to see. He spied the tall man, with shoulders broader than his foster father, wheel a tray of what looked like shiny cutlery. 'Yeah, this fucker has been a pain in the ass, just give him everything.'

The man with the winged ears raised a finger and the big man shrunk back. 'Name?'

Robotic voice: 'Alex.'

'Hello, Alex. You see the mirrors above you? I want you to watch. The more you watch, the sooner it will stop.'

Robotic voice: 'Subject 16 of the Foster Study, 7.30 pm. Initiating intervention now.'

'Sweetie... it's OK.'

Alex looked around for his mother. He thought he heard her voice.

'Sweet boy...'

For a moment he felt pain. He looked up and found the source of the voice. His own reflection staring back at him. Talking to him. He could see blood and knives down below.

'Look up you brave little man, look at my face.'

Alex felt tugging and pulling, but he focused on the soothing voice of his own reflection. The face appeared brighter than his own. He began to feel dazed. His body tensed and relaxed without any coercion.

'You don't need to worry about a thing.' The boy that looked like him smiled. 'Everything is going to be OK.'

He heard the girl wailing for something to stop. He caught her reflection in the mirror on the right-hand side.

'Don't worry about her. She's going to be OK. She will stick with you forever.' The melodic voice continued.

Robotic voice: 'That's enough, no need to continue, he's already—'

The tall man stepped forward, now visible in the other centre mirror.

The sweet voice continued: 'You're a strong boy, Alex, just like him. You don't have to worry about him, Alex. You can be just as strong.'

The man with the robotic voice reached for something near Alex's stomach, his swaying frame was reflected in the last mirror.

'He is just a friend, Alex.' His doppelganger soothed. 'They are all special friends. I heard a brave little boy started school this week, is that true?'

Alex tried to nod. His reflection flinched, as though hiding his discomfort. Alex's vision began to blur.

'Focus on me Alex. Tell me, who's the strongest in your class?'

'L-L-Lewis.' Alex slurred.

'A strong name. Who's the smartest?'

'T-T-Tony.'

'And the youngest?'

'Jul-Julie.'

'Lovely.'

His own reflection started to mix with the girl, the tall vulgar man, and the one with the robotic voice. Four different versions of Alex looked down on him. Then one of them screamed.

Randall: *Enough now*.

CHAPTER 42

Alex: *What is it, Tony? Your anxiety is making me queasy.*

Tony: *Tony can't control the anxiety. Anonymity we have lost. Tony doesn't like all the bright lights; makes the eyes very sore.*

Lewis: *Fuck anonymity. I've been catching small fish for so long. It was only a matter of time before I caught a shark.*

Tony: *Martin is not a shark. Definitely not a shark. He is one of those deep-sea monsters that hasn't been discovered yet. So much left to learn. He nibbled on our hook out of curiosity. Tony knows this isn't over. Not much of a private investigator if you're not very private.'*

Julie: *'Can we go home now? Pleeeeeeeeeeease.*

Alex: *Yes, I think we can.*

Alex was released from the Adelaide Federal Police headquarters 48 hours after police and paramedics arrived at Norton College. Graham's Toyota Crown Super Saloon had been picked up and delivered to the carpark.

Yolanda stood by the car with her arms crossed. 'You should have called.'

'Yoddi!' Alex grinned and walked over to her. They held each other's gaze for a moment before they both broke down and embraced.

'He's gone.' Alex nuzzled against her neck. 'He's really gone.'

'Never. He will be with you forever,' Yoddi snorted, wiping back her tears on her sleeve. 'I could have helped you, you silly boy.'

'You would have been damn handy in prison.'

Yoddi laughed and sniffed at the same time. 'Is Lewis still pissed off I kicked him in the balls? Tell him I'm sorry.'

'What you taught us kept us alive, Yoddi.'

Lewis: *Does she want another round? I don't care if she's over fucking 80-years-old.*

'Good.' Yoddi exhaled. 'Because I'm really not. That was the highlight of my week. I told all the girls at the CWA about it. Are you alright, Alex? Truly?'

He nodded. She took him in. His hair was shorter than she had ever seen it. His face was black and blue with bruises, he wore clothes supplied by the AFP that didn't quite fit, and his left arm was in a sling.

'I brought you something.' Yoddi smiled and opened the car door.

Rex bounded out of the car, barking happily. Alex bent down and embraced the old border collie. Rex almost knocked him down when he nuzzled his nose into the wound on the side of Alex's abdomen. Rex settled for licking his master's face instead.

'Rexy! Hey, boy!'

Tony: *Good boy. Best boy. Nice shiny coat. Good boy.*

Lewis: *Get him to cut out the licking or I'll throw him into a stew.*

Julie: *Ewww ... No you wouldn't! I've seen him sit on your lap at night.*

Lewis: *That was one fucking time! And he was feeling poorly, goddammit.*

'Hey boy! Thank God you're okay. Thank you, Yoddi. Thank you so much!' Alex grinned.

'No need to thank me. I've been worrying myself sick and he's the only thing that's kept me sane. These last few weeks just don't feel real. Come on, listen to this.'

Yoddi got into the driver's seat of Graham's car. When Alex got in the passenger seat, Rex jumped up and sat on his lap, still insisting on licking him. Yoddi started the car and switched on the radio. They heard snippets of news:

'Martin Harslett, director of Harslett Prison on a 10-year government contract, most known for driving the recidivism rates to the lowest in Australian history, has been connected to the Showstop—'

'Norton College has been identified as the next intended location to the Showstopper's string of brutal attacks, with a school shoot-out planned by Mr Harslett.'

'Harslett Prison is now in the process of government closure, with a high percentage of prisoners being transported to Sydney to serve out their sentences.'

'Evidence of a bizarre research project has identified five accomplices to the Showstopper murders including a police officer and doctor. All five suspects are in police custody.'

'A small private investigation company, Blakemore Investigations, has received recognition from the Australian Federal Police for its assistance in this case.'

'Martin Harslett has been denied bail, and his lawyers are yet to comment at this time.'

She turned the radio off. 'He would be so proud of you. All of you. What happens now?'

Alex looked pensive. 'I need to see someone.'

Alex, Yoddi and Rex entered the foyer of Sunnydale Community Assistance Village. They were greeted by the receptionist.

'You're looking quite the sight, Mr Blakemore. Are you okay?' the receptionist asked.

'Better now. How is she?'

The receptionist's face became stern. 'She's having a bad day. You will make all the difference.'

'Go.' Yoddi smiled.

Alex clicked his fingers and Rex followed his master down the hallway, tail wagging all the way to Room 48. Alex knocked first. Rex didn't wait for a response, as he pushed open the door and jumped onto the chair in the corner of the room.

'Come in,' a hoarse voice croaked.

Alex entered. She didn't look well. Despite their similar age, Alex thought the girl in the bed looked much older today. Her pigtails had been dyed red. There were dark rings under her eyes. Her face was pale and vacant … until she saw Alex.

Rochelle's smile lit up the room.

'Alex!' she cried. 'You came back to visit me!'

Alex sat on the bed next to her and held her fragile hand. 'I'm sorry I didn't visit you more often, I should have.'

'Who cares! Today you make me happy! I saw the news. That shit's crazy. Are you OK?' Rochelle yawned.

'I'm fine. Enough about me, how are you?'

'I had a terrible dream. You and I … we were in a cage, on a boat somewhere. Weird huh?'

Alex squeezed her hand tightly as his mind went back.

The two children held onto each other in the cage. They shivered from the cold wind. The ship rocked back and forth as it crashed into unseen waves. They heard more voices in a language they did not understand. They no longer shared words with each other. Their touch was the only part left of their childhood. A shadow stepped out and inspected them. Alex made out winged ears but nothing else; he nestled back into the girl's shoulder in fright.

'They have become non-verbal?' the shadow asked.

'Correct. Traumatic experience to this extent affects the pre-frontal cortex and language centres in the left hemisphere. Amygdala becomes hyperactive. High risk of dissociation for these two,' the man with the thick glasses relayed as he rocked back and forth with the current.

'The non-verbals rarely show much promise. Cease the intervention and send them out,' the shadow said.

Unclear voices.

'No, we have enough for the city of churches. This boy has been alert, taking things in. The girl, Rochelle, I anticipate she has seen the last of me ...'

Alex held tightly onto Rochelle's hand. The hand he wished he had never let go of. But he was just a child then. He had always suspected they had a connection, but he never knew for sure until he saw Rochelle's name on Cheng's computer.

'It's just a nightmare,' Alex said calmly. 'It's not real.'

She nodded, which took effort. 'Alex. There's a dog in the room.'

'Yeah, his name's Rex. I thought he might keep you company for a little while.'

Rochelle smiled at that. 'I'm so tired. But I don't want you to go.'

Alex smiled back. 'I don't need to go anywhere. In fact, I'm not leaving until you've had a rest and something to eat.'

That satisfied her. She rolled over towards him and closed her eyes. 'Alex? Will you still be a private investigator? Without Graham?'

Alex held onto her cold hands. 'I'm not too sure anymore,' he answered quietly.

'I thought of a name,' she whispered back. 'For you. The bad guys are always the ones that get the trippy names. You showed people that sometimes the broken can be good. You deserve a trippy name too.'

'Shh, rest now Rochelle. I'm done with all that.'

'Maybe. Maybe not. Things happen for a reason sometimes.'

Tony: *Blakemore Investigations is over. Can't do that without Graham. No. No. No. Pity he didn't see the papers. He would've bought a bunch and spread them round town.*

Lewis: *Wasn't making any fuckin' money anyway. What do we get for catching fuckface? Nothing!*

Julie: *I liked helping people.*

'Rochelle?'

'Mmmm?' She started to doze.

'What was the name?'

Rochelle smiled in her sleep. 'The Dissociative Detective.'

CHAPTER 43

Yoddi gave Alex's hand a squeeze. 'Graham had fears too, you know.'

'I didn't think anything in the world scared that man.'

'Oh, yes, he certainly did have fears. You and I just saved him from ever having to face it. Can you guess?'

Tony: *Loneliness.*

'Loneliness,' Yoddi revealed. 'You helped give that man a rich life, Alex.'

The fifth-generation family law firm was situated in the heart of Goodwood in an old church building. Alex and Yoddi sat in the waiting area below a gold-trimmed ceiling fan that helped keep them cool on the 40-degree day. His phone vibrated. He ignored it. A short man in a well-fitting suit greeted them. They had seen his picture in the hallway – Steven Fogey, a fourth-generation lawyer that ran the business with his daughter, Elaine. His handshake was warm and firm, and he spoke quietly as he introduced himself.

'Thank you for seeing me, Alex. I am terribly sorry for your loss. Graham was a great man.'

'Thank you,' Alex said. 'This is Yolanda. She practically lived with Graham.'

'It's lovely to meet you, Yolanda – Graham spoke very warmly of you. I know how much your companionship meant to him. He told me all too often.'

'Just know that he might have exaggerated parts. He was known for that,' chuckled Yoddi.

Steven smiled. 'Graham? Never!' He ushered him them into his office and they sat around a large oval desk. Alex's phone went off again.

'Can you turn that thing off?' Yoddi whispered.

'Thank you for meeting me on such a horrid day. I hope you found a park, okay? Good. Well, Graham assigned me as executor of his will to ensure his wishes were met.'

Steven picked up a large cardboard box with **GRAHAM BLAKEMORE** printed on the side and placed it on the desk. He retrieved a small wooden box from within it, which was shaped like a wedding ring box, and handed it to Alex.

'A confidential message from Graham to you, Alex. He asked me to play this privately for you before we continue. I will give you some time. Yoddi, would like to join me next door? Graham had some matters that require your private attention as well.'

Steven had set up a projector screen at the end of the room and connected the USB to a laptop. He asked if Alex would like a tea or coffee before he pressed 'play' and left the room with Yoddi.

Graham's beaming face filled the screen.

'Hello, my boy!' Graham began. 'Well, let's be honest, it had to happen eventually! I'm sure my passing was quite standard, probably too much sex with a bunch of fitness models. Ha-ha, let me tell you, kiddo, it would've taken me all night to do what I used to do all night long, if you get my drift! That's probably not overly appropriate. I wonder if I can restart this thing? Do I push this button? Oh, bugger it! On with my final message!

'I have seen so much in my life, but I *never* expected my biggest challenge and delight to arrive in my 85th year. You. You have achieved so much and made me so proud. But my biggest concern was what happens to you when I'm gone? I was forever in fear of you being in a social vacuum. Spending your life alone. Whatever happens, whatever you choose to do, just live, kiddo.

'You asked me once if I thought you could be a psychopath. I did some research. Various people debate whether psychotic traits come from genetics, or from our environment and experiences. My boy, you are the son of evil. You have also come from a traumatic, abusive and neglected childhood. In other words, you're fucked.' Graham laughed. 'You should be the very worst of us. *But* how have you spent your years with me? By helping others, even when it meant putting yourself at risk. You could have ignored me and lived your life as a typical teenager. But what did you do? You presented me with adoption papers and asked to become a Blakemore. It was one of the happiest moments of my life. And I … well, I love you to death, kid. You are not a psychopath. For a little boy to come from so much chaos and to become the man that you are … You are the best of us.

'I wasn't a good father, not to my poor boy. I was always busy. I can't remember what with to tell you the truth. And I hadn't properly dealt with what happened in the navy. I never helped my son with his homework, or showed him how to shave, or taught him how to drive. And we fought all the time. I didn't understand his choices. If I had only supported him, he would never have been drunk in that car. Those boys' deaths are on me. When they died, the guilt tore at me. I've been trying to make amends ever since by helping other young boys. You see, it never came from nobleness or even a place of selflessness. I did it to try and make myself feel better. Selfish, I know, but everything that happened led me to you.

'I have to admit my intention early on was to try and fix you. Beat this condition of yours. But it's a part of you, kid. You could be rid of it all if you wanted to, the dissociations. But I don't think you will ever try, not when you can still help people with them. I should never have worried about you being alone, because you never really are, are you? Lewis, you made me bloody nervous. But you saved my life, and you make the best bloody fish and chips I've ever tasted. Tony, your intelligence and your kindness, especially to animals, humbles me. I'm forever in your debt for what you have done for this family. Julie … never grow up, kid. You've seen what adults are like, they're boring as hell. Thank you all for giving a poor old man a family. I know we're all probably batshit crazy. But what family isn't? The things that we've done for our community … it's … special. I love you all. Goodbye. Now where is the goddamn button? Ah!'

The tape ended. The screen went bright blue. After a while Steven and Yoddi came back with refreshments. He offered Alex a tissue. Alex didn't realise there were tears running down his face. He thanked Steven and blew his nose. Yoddi looked like she had been laughing and crying at the same time; her face was red and puffy but the creases around her eyes and mouth showed the remaining traces of joy.

'Now, Mr Blakemore, we have two items to discuss today. Graham's funeral and his will. Are you still happy to go through this now?'

Alex nodded.

'In regard to the funeral, we have a rather unique pre-paid event. Graham had requested a party at a rather large church. I have a long list of items here for you to approve or not.'

Alex looked over the list. It included the following notes:

    - Lots of good food, I hate people going hungry.

    - Not too many old people, they will keep thinking they're next.

    - A jumping castle for the kids because funerals can be bloody boring.

'Sounds perfect.' Alex smiled.

Steven couldn't hide the small smile on his lips. 'Then on to the will. As the primary benefactor of Mr Blakemore's trust, you become owner of his small business, Blakemore Investigations.'

'I'll close it. We never really made money from it.'

'Hmmm … I'll let you go over those finer details with an accountant. Naturally you are receiving his other assets as well. He owned his home without a mortgage. And when you remove legal and funeral fees, he has a personal sum just shy of 4 million dollars.'

Lewis: *He was a millionaire?*

Tony: *Multi-millionaire.*

Julie: *Is it enough to buy me a dolls' house?*

'I didn't realise there was so much.'

Steven nodded again. 'A large portion of this was in the stock market. Compound interest had many years to work its magic. He has provided professional contacts to help you manage this, Mr Blakemore, if you choose to use their services.'

Alex's phone vibrated again. He apologised and checked it in the empty office next door. He had 50 text messages, 37 voice messages and 60 missed calls. He called his voicemail bank:

Voicemail 1: 'Is this Blakemore Investigations? My son has been missing for three days, I think he's involved in something.'

Voicemail 2: 'My name is Andrea. Can you please call me back. I've got a very discreet case and I'm happy to pay a deposit.'

Voicemail 3: 'Blakemore Investigations, I think my brother has been wrongly convicted, can you please call me.'

The rest were much of the same. Requests for Blakemore Investigations.

Lewis: *Fuck 'em. We don't need their money anymore.*

Alex: *We never did. It was never about that.*

Julie: *So, what do we do all day then?*

Alex: I keep my promise.

Randall: *The time for ignoring me is past, handsome.*

Alex: *I'm not ignoring you. You are a part of me, but I can't lose control if I'm going to do this.*

Randall: *Honey, you're talking about making promises. What about making one to me? I helped you when it mattered most. Twice now. I'm not going to fade into the background again.*

Alex: *I understand. I wouldn't be here if it wasn't for you. I'm listening.*

Randall: *A man that listens— my, my. Your heart's in the right place, sweets, but we don't need any more cases. You will have enough on your plate with little old me! All this time searching for answers ... You could have just asked me. And I know so many more delicious secrets. The things you have yet to uncover.*

Alex: *What things?*

Randall: *You gotta buy me dinner first. You have a way to go before you earn my trust too.*

Alex: *So, what do you want?*

Randall: *Can't you guess? I want to be included. I missed all that time with Graham. Now you need to find a way to make it up to me.*

***

There was a banging on Gaynor's cell door. She placed her hands in the hole in the door and let the guard cuff the cold steel around her wrists. The main lights were out in the middle of the night. Other women were sleeping in their cells, or pretending to, when she was led down a hallway. Her olfactory senses had adapted to the smell of disinfectant and decay after her time in captivity. She knew every crack in the walls, every exposed patch of concrete behind the peeling paint, every dud light that flickered in its worn-out globe.

She was directed to one of the small visitation rooms. It was empty and dimly lit with a black landline in the centre of the only table. The guard asked her to sit on the plastic chair before he cuffed her to the table. The phone started ringing when he left. She noticed the tiny red light on the camera in the corner of the room. She reached for the handset.

'Swanson Residence,' she answered.

'It's done,' Alex said over the phone.

Gaynor smiled. 'Did you get your answers, little Alex?'

'Yes.'

'Hmmm … The one with the ears?'

A pause. 'You know about Martin?'

'They let me watch the news in here, it was hard to miss. It made a bigger story than mine, did it not?'

'It's over.'

'What was he to you?'

'A ghost. Something I don't think I understand yet.'

'Then it isn't over.'

'A part of me wanted to thank you for your help. But I won't be needing it again.'

'Which part, I wonder? So many parts. You have the curse of the fostered minds. Too many guardians, too many environments. Your values are fractured. Split. Your journey into this dark world is still in its infancy. I have a question about your multiple personalities.'

'What?'

'Are you an alter, Alex?'

A longer pause. 'No.'

'Tsk. It's an interesting question though, no? The paperwork the old man found; the name Alex only came about after your adoption to this Maninga family. There would have been other names before that. You can't help but wonder if there's someone else in there.'

274

Gaynor licked her lips and broke into song:

Hush little baby don't say a word,
Mumma knows your identity is blurred.
But if you worked up the courage to sting,
Oh, what horrors you would bring.
Your alters put you at an impasse,
You never had a mother who could show you class.
I shoulda been there from the moment you woke
I was busy burning dad in a cloud of smoke.
You faced terrors when you shoulda been in school
Now your many faces struggle to rule.
You'll need a mother when you face the dark
'Cause evil forms from the tiniest spark.

The line was dead. Gaynor wasn't sure when Alex hung up.

CHAPTER 44

Graham's funeral had one of the largest turn outs in the cathedral's history. A polished coffin was set up at the end of the pulpit next to Graham's picture; a recent head and shoulders shot in his dress uniform. His medals were pinned on the left side above his heart. A Royal Australian Navy sash lay across the hinge in the closed coffin. The church pews had been shifted and stacked to the side of the nave of the church. It was filled with people mingling around small circular tables reminiscent of his birthday party. Veterans, previous clients, neighbours, various policemen, in and out of uniform, several social workers, everyone from the RSL, and most of the Ardrossan community filled Saint Francis Xavier's Cathedral.

The front doors of the church were left open, allowing the children to be heard as they played on the inflatable jumping castle out the front. At the far end wall, a slideshow of Graham beamed from a ceiling projector. The photo presentation began with the few rare images of his childhood. He was very thin but always had the same roguish smile on his face.

The funeral celebrant, a humble old man with years of experience, spoke to the congregation of mourners. 'He lived from 1919 to 2019. That date is printed on the memorial program you have all received. But there is a dash between those numbers. We are here today to celebrate everything in Graham's dash. I can tell by how this church is set up today, that Graham was quite the character, and fulfilled his dash in many ways. A survivor in his youth. A war hero as a teenager. A hard-working police officer. A mentor to the disadvantaged. And an investigator in his twilight years, where he not only found ways to service his community, but recently made national news, which I believe wouldn't have fazed him one bit.'

Some light laughter.

'Graham has left requests for this day, most of which we have delivered, however, we beg his forgiveness in not organising a magician for the kids. Another request was for me to keep this short. There are many here today who hold Graham close to their heart and have offered to present a eulogy. First, I would like to present his son, Alex.'

All eyes diverted to the young man standing out the front. His sparkling gold eyeshadow made him stand out. He wore a bright flamboyant jacket and green shoes. A light rose-coloured lip balm had been applied earlier, and he rubbed his lips together as he looked around at all the faces. All the unknown. He took a deep breath and climbed the steps of the pulpit. Alex's slightly rounded posture had gone. This moment had been given to Randall. He tapped the microphone and looked out to everyone.

'I want to thank all you lovely ladies and gentlemen for comin' down.' Randall cleared his throat. 'It would have meant a lot to the old timer, and it means a lot to me that so many of you are here. First things first, in true Graham tradition … plenty of food has been organised so make sure you eat up, the last thing he would want today is anyone going hungry.

A few laughs from the procession.

'Graham never pretended to be anyone but himself. He was proud of his identity. And he never got shunned for it. He experienced loss and had some challenging years, but it didn't make him miserable. And as he would say, he lived for a bloody long time. Maybe there's something in that? I have a song to play before the next speaker. I hope it resonates with you in some way.'

Randall bowed and stepped off the pulpit as *The Last Day on Earth* by Kate Miller-Heidke played throughout the church. It could be heard outside and the tunes faded out into the healing city of Adelaide.

Randall became aware of his heart rate as he weaved through the crowd receiving various pats on the back and respectful nods. He entered a room off to the side where various trestle tables were getting set up for the wake. There were two agency caterers bringing out hors d'oeuvres and large trays of lasagne and salad.

Randall smiled at them. 'Looks great. Thank you,'

The caterers acknowledged Randall and headed back outside to their truck to continue bringing in food and drink. A fridge had been set up in the corner. Randall opened it and found a small hidden recess at the bottom of the fridge. Inside was a velvet-lined tray with a dozen small spray bottles. He could still hear the smooth melodies of the song. It brought him back to his rare moments of freedom.

***

At 14 years of age Randall woke under hypnosis at Greenwich Hospital. Martin sat before him with a curious expression.

Randall: *Sleep now, little Alex.*

Alex: *Who …? Okay …*

Randall looked around and broke into a series of chuckles. 'Usually this gets disorienting as hell. But this? This is hilarious! What's with this room, Mickey Mouse? Are you redecorating?'

'Something like that.' Martin replied.

'What time is it? I didn't know quacks like you did after hours. It is very late though.' Randall got up and stretched. 'Don't get me wrong, I would be happy to stare into those dreamy eyes of yours, but this isn't going to work. Is that what this is about? Are you some pedo?'

'Remarkable,' Martin said in admiration.

'Me? I've been called many things, remarkable is one I could get used to. How about I just get the fuck outta whatever this is and we call it a day?'

Randall walked out with a sway of the hips. When he opened the door, he noticed a cleaner leaving. The main lights were out and the hallway was dead quiet.

'Ah … This place ain't even open. Are we even supposed to be in here? Is this actually some sex thing?'

'I got in here through a favour. I have made several donations to this establishment,' Martin explained.

'Ah-huh. And Alex, he just …'

'I made the appointment with Alex. I had opened up before he arrived. He had no reason not to think I was a therapist. It would also mean there is no record of my encounter.'

'Okay, sugar, so what is this about?'

'I wanted to meet Alex, but perhaps you as well?'

'Why?'

'You're dissociative. I assume you know that. I have met several like you before. But you are different.'

'How so?'

'You're not institutionalised, or dead. But you're close to one or the other. The psychiatric hospital is three doors down from this very room.'

'Look, this is getting all too creepy for me. And I don't trust you at all, so I'm out.' Randall flapped his hand dismissively and moved back to the door.

'I am your father.'

'Pah-lease. I am definitely out of here.'

'Oh, I am. Dissociative identity disorder stems from trauma. I was responsible for that trauma. I created you. Your 'identity' or however you refer to it would not exist without my actions. I can prove it to you, if you would like.'

Something in Martin's expression removed any doubt about what was being said. It made Randall shiver. 'What do you want?'

'To help you. If you're the first identity to come out of from this hypnotic trance, then you are important. You are the one I want to deal with.'

'And Alex?'

'Alex controls you all. He may not know how to yet, but he will. I'll need to get through to him too, with your blessing. You're in a hurry to get out of here. I take it you don't get out as much as you would like. I can help you with that. When Alex blacks out next, wouldn't you like to be the one that rises?'

Two days later at Elizabeth Shopping Centre, Randall is hyperventilating. He coughs and splutters. 'I need to get out of these horrible clothes.'

'Randall?' Martin ran over to check on him.

'It worked. You got me out again. How?'

'Alex will be prone to black outs when he faces his fears. If I can encourage him to engage in tasks that will cause him to dissociate from fear, you have the highest chance of release. Mirrors didn't do it but somehow knife collections did.' Martin explained.

'What if he gets stronger?'

'Stronger than you? I think not.'

'And the others?'

'They are connected tightly to him. Not you. I first saw you break into yourself when you were very young. The others came later. I do not know how much time we have. I have much to show you.'

They walked out of the store together and into the food court. Randall surveyed the crowd closely. It had been a long time since he had been around large groups of people. He preferred it over isolation immensely.

'Watch closely,' Martin said softly.

Randall never saw Martin run, but his movements were sudden and fast. Randall struggled to keep up as Martin rapidly weaved through masses of people while still managing to blend in. He eventually bumped into a heavy-set man with a suit and apologised. Nobody but Randall saw Martin spray something onto the man's food tray. It only lasted half a second before Martin pocketed a small bottle no larger than Randall's preferred hydrating mist toner. Martin told Randall to sit. They watched as the man made himself comfortable at a two-seater table on the other side of the food court and tucked into the contaminated food.

By the time the man finished his meal he started vomiting and convulsing. Shoppers and cleaning staff near him shouted out. Security came running. The food court quickly cleared out. Martin watched him closely. Randall was in control and couldn't help feeling excited; his pulse quickened, his eyes took everything in.

'It doesn't bother you?' Martin asked.

Eight weeks later, Randall danced in the mosh pit at the Black Dragon. Through a combination of hitchhiking and public transport, he made it to the nightclub two hours after breaking into physical consciousness. Then he danced and drank. Then danced and drank some more. He had found some cash in the beach house while he was still in a state of delirium. That paid for the first round. The rest of the alcohol was purchased by prospective young males. Randall could tell he didn't have long. He could feel the autistic nuisance fighting back for control. He couldn't afford to waste time on proper clothing and makeup. Security was already keeping a close eye on him. He looked too young in their eyes. He found a payphone hidden behind a queue for the bathrooms. He had memorised the number he was supposed to call. He punched in the numbers via the 1-800 reverse line and heard the click of the call being answered after the second ring without any words spoken.

'It's me. Randall. I don't think I've got long.'

'Randall ...' Martin's raspy voice on the other end sounded distant. 'You have taken some time to get back to me. Have the others beaten you into submission?'

'I'm here now, aren't I? I can look after myself.'

'You're a broken piece of a mentally unstable teenager living with a geriatric in the middle of nowhere. There is little you can do for yourself. I'll need more assurances from you before I invest more of my time.'

'What can I do?'

'Your specialty is pain. Prove to me that you can bring pain to Alex and the others. That's how you break free. Until then, don't call this number.'

Randall: *Can you see my memories, Alex? You all thought you were so strong. So righteous. You thought you could discard me like a bad dream. You thought you had won. But Martin wanted it this way. Then you gave me permission, Alex. That was the final ounce of strength I needed to take control. That's how I can silence you. At least for the next few minutes. After that I don't care what happens. You can do nothing else to hurt me. No matter what good you did with Graham, Alex, this one act I'm about to do will forever define you.*

Like a zombie, Randall withdrew the case of spray bottles and looked over at the trays of food. He took one last look at the service. The slideshow of the old man's life continued. The song was up to its final verse. It would all end soon. His eyes fixed momentarily on Graham's photo next to the coffin. He took a small canister out of the drawer and aimed it at a tray of food.

'Randall?'

'Walk away, Yolanda.'

Yoddi noticed the canister. Her eyes began to moisten, fists clenched. 'It makes sense now. This is why that madman let you go. It's why you went through so much in that horrible prison. He was trying to get you out, Randall. This was his plan. Oh, you silly boy.'

'Just get out of here, Yolanda.'

'Why, Randall? Why let that monster win?'

'I'm sorry, Randall. That's why I tried getting these tickets for you. Just on the off-chance you could enjoy them.'

'I couldn't. I own nothing. No clothes. I couldn't.'

'Come with me.' Yoddi winked.

Randall followed her into the bedroom. 'I'll have to remind you, I don't swing—'

She opened the double doors to her walk-in wardrobe.

'Goodness me. Yolanda, you little firecracker.'

Her wardrobe was 5 metres long with rows and rows of colourful apparel. In the middle was a dresser with a complete makeup station.

'I get a lot of free clothes from my modelling shows with the CWA. They let me keep them and they're too good to throw out.'

Yoddi sat at the dresser. 'Come on, let's figure out what blush suits that skin tone of yours.'

Yolanda stood in front of Randall by the fridge. 'I can't let you do this, Randall.'

'It's done. It's all here. You can't stop me. I've always said you are one fit, saucy, tail. But look at you. You're too old to overpower me.'

'I can scream.'

Randall aimed the small bottle at Yoddi's face. 'I don't want to do this to you.'

'You won't do it to me. Or anyone else.'

'Wrong.'

'There's too much love in you to cause so much death,' Yoddi stammered.

'Love? I don't love anyone.'

'But you love him.'

'Alex? Fuck Alex, he is—'

'This isn't about the Alex that you know. Or Tony, or Lewis, or Julie. This is about that little boy who was taken. The little boy that couldn't face the despicable ordeal he was put in. So, you, the protector, came to be. You loved that little boy so much you took all the hurt for him. Oh, you have so much love, Randall. That boy deserves a life, so don't let the pain you took take that away from him. You're the reason he has a life.'

Randall's finger was on the button. His hand trembled. Emotion overwhelmed him. He placed the dispenser on the table and pulled Yoddi in tight.

'I'm sorry,' he cried. 'I'm sorry. I'm sorry.'

He repeated those words as he took big heaving cries. Yoddi didn't let go. Their embrace was held for over a minute before he finally withdrew and looked into her eyes.

'This really is a nice jacket. I can't believe you made it.' He took a moment to control himself. 'What happens now?'

'We let Graham save the day one more time,' she said with a smirk.

Randall took one last look at Graham's picture. He thought the old man had an all-knowing smile.

***

The coffin was carried towards the grave by six pallbearers. Five veterans who spent time at Tiddy Widdy during their troubled youth had a strong grip on the chrome handles. Leading them was Alex. The pallbearers placed the coffin in position. They watched it descend into Graham's final resting place.

'Thank you. For everything. I won't let you down,' Alex whispered.

Tony: *Farewell Graham, I don't know where you go next, but I hope it's somewhere with dogs and ladies.*

Lewis: *I'll keep up the fishing, old man. Fuck it. I miss him.*

Julie: *[Inaudible crying]*

Randall: *I'll give it a try, Mr Graham.*

They all stayed and watched the burial while others made their way back in for the wake. There was no tombstone yet. Just a mound of dirt to represent all that he was and had been. Graham was now at rest. A case of war medals had gone down with him, but Alex had replaced the medals with the poison canisters. He didn't think Graham would mind helping him out one last time.

EPILOGUE

Alters have secrets. It was five past midnight when Tony unlocked the city office to Blakemore Investigations. He had waited until the last media truck pulled away before he crossed the road, his body swaying with the wind. He locked the door behind him and left the lights off as he shuffled to the consulting office. He switched on the single light and surveyed the room.

Alex: *What are we doing here Tony?*

Tony: *Tony wants to show you something.*

Tony retrieved a stepladder from the corner of the room and climbed up to the ceiling. He shifted a loose panel and pulled out a briefcase. He placed it on the table and turned the combination locks to 739. It snapped open.

Alex: *Jesus, Tony, you had this the whole time?*

Tony: *Everyone has secrets. Not much of a secret if everybody knows. Everyone sleeps when Tony works. Have to start getting some longer candles. Tony always burns the candle at both ends. Is that what they say? I think that's what they say. They say a lot of silly things, don't they?*

Tony placed Cheng's broken laptop on the table.

Alex: *Wait. I dropped this. It was ... I thought this was gone.*

After 15 years the computer was crudely connected together to more modern PC components.

Tony: *Tony replaced the screen, cooling system and the battery. Hard drive and motherboard appeared intact, but Tony couldn't get access. Tony needed the password if he wanted to keep the data.*

He turned it on. There was a slow hum before the screen flicked alive, requesting a password.

Tony: *Tony was watching closely when Cheng showed us his computer. Tony wonders if the password is the same. Tony doesn't recommend keeping the same password, but not everyone is as cautious as Tony. Habits, habits. Everyone has habits.*

Tony closed his eyes and typed in the same password Cheng had entered on his more recent computer. The machine Alex dropped as a teenager became accessible. Password accepted. The screen looked the same, just with less folders than the modern computer now in police custody.

Alex: *We should take this to the police.*

Tony: *No. We shouldn't.*

All of the alters were now aware. They watched Tony touch-type rapidly until he brought up a file with various names. He clicked on the top name. Notes and footage of a child. He clicked on the second and reviewed more information.

Alex: *More children? They would be ...*

Tony: *Teenagers now.*

Alex: *What are you thinking, Tony?*

Tony: *Tony thought that was obvious. What's more important than investigations? More important than us? You know exactly what Tony wants to do. Continue the legacy.*

ACKNOWLEDGEMENTS

I am deeply grateful to my early readers that gave me the feedback I needed to develop this craft. This includes the team at SA Writers Centre for their invaluable programs and support. If you have a story you want to take to the next level, I highly recommend you start with a manuscript assessment at your local writer's centre.

A heartfelt thank you to my agent, Fiona Smith, at Beyond Words Literary, and to the CYA writers and illustrators conference for the introduction. To the team at Contempo Publishing, thank you for taking a chance on me and turning this Microsoft Word document into a real book!

A special nod to my favourite authors (Stephen King, Thomas Harris, Graeme Simsion, JRR Tolkien – to name but a few!) for making the art of storytelling an endless source of inspiration and joy.

To my wife—thank you for your love, patience, and for letting me write deep into the night when there was no other time to make this dream real. This book exists because of you.

And to you, the reader; thank you for letting me take up some of your valuable time. If you feel like reaching out, I would love to connect. You can reach me on my website (www.ryangaryjoel.com). I'm keen to hear if you enjoyed the book. Or not.

I'll be back with a better one.

www.ingramcontent.com/pod-product-compliance
Lightning Source LLC
Chambersburg PA
CBHW011553190726
48287CB00010B/2880